BUCK
Wild

OTHER TITLES BY LAUREN LANDISH

Irresistible Bachelors Series

Anaconda

Mr. Fiancé

Heartstopper

Stud Muffin

Mr. Fixit

Matchmaker

Motorhead

Baby Daddy

BUCK *Wild*

BENNETT BOYS RANCH, BOOK ONE

LAUREN LANDISH

Published by Montlake Romance, Seattle

www.apub.com

Amazon, the Amazon logo, and Montlake Romance are trademarks of Amazon.com, Inc., or its affiliates.

ISBN-13: 9781503902886
ISBN-10: 1503902889

Cover design by Eileen Carey

Cover photography by Wander Aguiar

Printed in the United States of America

To my sister, who truly is a shining star. I love you, forever and always.

CHAPTER 1

JAMES

With a squeeze of the snips and a twist of my pliers, I finish one more section of fence. Gazing left, then right, I can see just how much I've done and just how far I have left to go. The answer is the same as the last time I checked: not enough and too much.

We need this pasture secure before we move the herd over, and that's happening one way or another by the end of the week. Unfortunately, this fence was totally wrecked last winter, and with everything that's happened to the family, it's been put off until the last minute. And it seems that *last minute* is my new middle name.

I know I need to hurry, but my back needs a break more. This isn't a sprint, the eight seconds of exhilaration and adrenaline that I'm used to. There are still hours of work left, and if I'm not careful, I'll end up useless with miles of fence to go. I stand tall to stretch, raising my arms high above me and lifting my face to the bright sun of the June day.

Taking a deep breath, I can feel the sweat rolling down my face, so I pull off my hat and mop a rag across my brow. It's strange, but in the barely blowing breeze, I can feel my dad's presence, proud that I'm back here, home on the ranch, doing what he always wanted me to do. In the rush of the creek just on the other side of this rise I'm working on fencing, it almost sounds like he's chuckling in that way he used to when he knew something would happen even if my brothers and I swore it never would.

His passing is still so new that it sometimes doesn't feel real. Turning to the refreshing wind at my back, I tuck my rag in my pocket and adjust the Stetson on my head. "So, you're watching, are you? I know exactly what you're gonna say, Pops. *Fence ain't gonna fix itself, boy. Back to work. Only way to get done what needs to be done.* I know, and I'm gonna get it done."

Taking one last deep breath, I let the air current guide me back to the next section, ready to roll for another few hours. It's been hours already, or maybe minutes. Shit, it's hard to tell when the work is this repetitive. All I know is that I'm in that eternity between my quickly eaten lunch and sunset when I hear hoofbeats coming.

I don't even have to look to know it's my older brother. Especially since both of my brothers are older than me and have never let me forget that I'm the baby. But right now, I know it's my oldest brother, coming to check on me like he always does.

Turning to face Mark, I tug the brim of my hat down to shield my eyes from the sun, which is hanging pretty low in the sky. Ah, hours then, not the minutes I'd feared. I've kept up a good pace; the end must be in sight.

"Hey, Mark." I greet him with a single lift of my chin.

He reins in his horse, Sugarpea, his favorite gelding that he's had since he was a teenager. "Have you been napping out here or something, James? This as far as you've made it? Gonna be some early mornings and late nights to get this pasture prepped in time. Guess it's a good thing you brought the ATV; it'll let you work after dark with those flood lamps."

He makes a tsking sound that both irritates me and makes me laugh. I take a closer look around. I've got less than a half mile to go before I reach the corner and today's goal. "Fuck you, man. I'm working my ass off out here while you've been pushing papers around in the barn office. I bet I've earned more sweat in the past half hour than your big ass has sitting in that old swivel chair all day. But don't you worry—I'll be in for dinner."

He leans on the horn of his saddle to look down at me with a knowing grin. "Of course you will. I might be a scary fella, but none of us want Mama chasing after us. She's the scariest son of a gun I know."

I twist my face into a fictitious mask of fear, staring behind him with wide eyes. "Oh, you done bought it now!"

Mark spins to look behind him, just as I'd planned, but there's nothing there besides the wide-open acres of golden-green land. "Shit, you had me thinking Mama was right behind me. You been taking acting lessons or something on that rodeo tour?"

I laugh, and the gentle shake of my body and lightness in my head feel good. Laughter has been foreign lately and may be just what I need. Mark, never one to laugh, merely smiles, but for him, that's basically the same as laughter, so I'm calling it a win. "You've always been easy to fool. Remember when we were kids, and I jumped from the hayloft and faked breaking my leg? You were so scared you damn near pissed your Levi's. It don't take being Daniel Day-Lewis to get you."

Mark's mouth thins, but he nods and gives me an evil grin. "Well, I planned to help you with a length of fence, but after that stunt, I'm thinking maybe I'll go on in and have a shower before dinner. Might even prop my feet up and watch some of Mama's shows with her while she gets dinner ready."

My jaw drops; he's so serious that when he plays it straight, it's hard to tell if he's joking or not. "The fuck you will! Get your ass off your high horse and help. Just because the corner's just up ahead don't mean the whole damn fence is done! We've got miles to go and not enough time to do it."

Mark shakes his head, looking a lot older than he really is. Sure, I'm the baby of the group, but Mark isn't that much older. But in the afternoon light, the weight of responsibility hangs on his face so much that he looks like he's pushing forty instead of still two-stepping with thirty. "There's never enough time. Hasn't been for a while now."

The silence stretches for a moment, both of us lost in thoughts of missing Pops. He loved this land, the land he bought on faith back in the time when everyone was saying old-fashioned family farming and ranching were going the way of bell-bottoms and the Marlboro Man. He'd been the one who saw what this land could be: a harsh mistress that still loved us back and provided for a man who was willing to use his brains as well as his body and heart to tend it.

He loved us boys, all three of us. He'd spent every day teaching us how to be men and how to be ranchers. He'd taught me to ride almost as soon as I could walk, to respect the value of a man's hard work, and that sweat was sometimes more valuable than gold. And he taught us to love.

The best example of that was how Pops loved Mama. He would often tell us about how once he saw his Louise, he knew right then and there that he was going to marry that girl. He'd been eighteen at the time.

His passing had hit us hard, especially Mark. He'd been the one to find Pops lying just beyond the big elm tree we've got in the front yard, a peaceful look on his face and his hat somehow placed respectfully over his eyes like he was taking a nap.

By everyone's guess, Pops had realized what was coming, the years of hard work and workman's breakfasts catching up to him, and had lain down and sent his horse back to the barn. As soon as Duster had nickered at the back door riderless, Mark had known something was wrong. It took him a while to find Pops, but it didn't matter. He could have been faster than the Flash and he would've been too late. When the Reaper comes for you, there's never enough time.

Mark found our father lying next to the same tree that he'd proposed to Mama under thirty-two years earlier. We didn't have the years with him we'd thought we would. I'm back home for now, but only for the long summer. When the fall circuit starts up again, my ass needs to be on the back of a fifteen hundred–pound pissed-off bull if I want to get my sponsorship checks. I'm not sure how Pops managed to time his unexpected passing with the rodeo schedule he always hated, but since he did, I've got a long stretch of months to stay here, to settle in with Mama and my brothers, and to make the ranch work somehow without Pops's fiercely loving hand guiding us all.

My eyes meet Mark's, and he growls, swinging off Sugarpea and tying him off on the back gate of my ATV trailer before bumping my shoulder as he passes by me in a sign of brotherly love that also means *Shut the fuck up*. Saying nothing, he roots around in the back of the trailer and comes out with another pair of snips. "Okay, James, let's see if we can get all the sections from here to the corner and a few beyond done before dinner. Deal?"

I eye the length of fence, not seeing too much that needs repair. This part of the pasture is in the lee of the rise, and because of that, it doesn't catch the driving winds that some of the other areas do. "Hell, if it's mostly just inspection, I bet we can do five or six. Let's hit it."

We get to work, side by side, the same way we did for years, words not even needed as we dance around each other, checking each level of wire and all the barbs, careful to scan and fix any weak spots.

We complete our goal, loading up our tools in the back of the ATV just as we hear the ringing of the bell out across the flat land. Mark grins and unties Sugarpea's lead before swinging up into the saddle easily. "Nice job."

I smile, hopping behind the handlebars of the ATV. "Told you we'd make it. How about I race you to the house. If I win, I get your roll. If you win, you get—"

He interrupts me, already wheeling Sugarpea around. "I get your whole plate."

Before I can even register what he's said, he's off and running, Sugarpea tearing up great hunks of turf with every step like Mark's racing him in the Kentucky Derby. I twist the throttle on my ATV, but I'm held back some as I can't just floor it, or else I'll flip the small trailer and send my tools flying everywhere.

Still, it's a race of one horsepower versus twenty-eight, and I'm close on Mark's heels as we get to the barn. He unsaddles and stalls Sugarpea while I unload my tools before we both wash our hands and splash our faces with the cool water from the old-fashioned pump, then go bursting in the back door, still jockeying for position. The race is more about bragging rights than dinner, but make no mistake, Mark will totally take my plate if he wins, and I'll damn sure enjoy that extra roll if I win, moaning about how delicious it is, just to stir the shit.

Our roughhousing catches Mama's attention, though, and she turns from the stove, a big wooden spoon in her hand, the same kind that she's threatened to break over my ass if I don't behave myself. "What the hell are you two doing? Behave yourselves in my house, or you'll be eating on the back porch with the dogs. And they don't get dessert."

We sober up, knowing that she's dead serious, but the competitive spirit we've always had doesn't just stop, so we discreetly rib each other, daring the other to make a sound and be the loser. Neither of us will ever give in, though, and ultimately, we sit at our respective spots at the table. Pops's spot is empty. Mark's is at his left as the eldest son, while Mama will sit at the other end of the table, nearest me. Luke used to sit on Pops's right, but he's adjusted; he'll sit next to Mama.

Mark glances over, removing his hat and hanging it off the back of his chair. "I'm getting your plate tomorrow." He swings two fingers between his eyes and mine, indicating that he's watching me. I grin and give him the finger. Like hell he will.

Mama turns around in a huff, thankfully slow enough that I can hide my hand. "Mark Thompson Bennett, did you just say you were gonna eat your brother's dinner? You know how hard he works, how hard you all work, and he needs his dinner. You'll do no such thing."

Being the baby in the family is sometimes the most annoying thing in my life, but other times, like this, it's a blessing.

Deciding to needle Mark just a little bit, I rub my stomach, moaning a little. "I'm so fucking hungry. I worked damn hard—I'm almost halfway around the back pasture and didn't have enough lunch because it was too far to come back to the house for a nibble. Is that my favorite pot roast?"

Yeah, I'm laying it on thick, but the hard expression on Mark's face is worth it. He's spent most of my life eating the grisly end of pot roasts while I've been getting the nice, juicy cuts. No wonder he prefers steak or hamburgers over roast.

Apparently, I overplayed, though, as Mama turns around, pointing her spoon at me. "Boy, do I look like a fool? I packed your lunch, and you had two big sandwiches in there, so quit needling your brother and just eat. And don't you dare cuss at my dinner table. You might be a grown man, but you're not too big for me to bend you over my knee and remind you of those proper manners I taught you growing up."

Mark smirks at me, finding the image of our petite mother, who's barely five foot two and maybe a buck fifteen soaking wet after Thanksgiving dinner, bending my six-foot-three-inch, two-hundred-pound frame over her knee to deliver a whuppin' quite comical.

I duck my head, putting my hands in my lap. "Sorry, ma'am."

Thinking to do what she said and "just eat," I reach for a serving dish of potatoes before feeling eyes on me. Looking up, I realize Mama's eyes are boring into me, and I snatch my hand back so fast my knuckles rap on the edge of the table.

"I think those rodeo folks aren't doing you any favors, James. Bunch of wild heathens. You don't start until everyone's at the table."

I sigh, knowing that Mama's right. There are advantages to being a professional rodeo rider, and not waiting on big brothers is one of them. "Where is Luke, anyways? He's late."

Mama swats me in the back of the head before I can reach for the potatoes again, clucking her tongue. "He'll be just a minute. He's checking on Briarbelle."

Suitably chastised, I glance up as the back door swings open and slams against the frame.

I lean back as Luke, all lanky six feet two of him, comes in, his face still streaked with dirt from the barn. "Well, speak of the devil, and he shall appear."

He doesn't respond, just turns to the big industrial sink by the back door to wash up, but I see him sneak me a middle finger, so I know he heard me. Once he sits, Mama brings the roast over and prays quickly so we can dig in, passing dishes back and forth and filling up our plates.

Dinner is a rowdy affair, full of fast eating, belly pats, and moans of delight when Mama brings out chocolate pudding for dessert. "Now, boys, I appreciate all the hard work you're doing . . . so there's a little bit extra in here tonight for all three of you."

I don't know how she does it, never really thought about it, I guess, but she's been feeding the three of us and Pops for decades, and every meal is delicious and filling and worth all the hard work to earn a place at her table.

It's odd to have the head of the table empty now, but for the most part, our conversations about the ranch take up enough space to make it feel like Pops is still ghosting about in his vacated chair.

"Make some headway on the fence today, James?" Luke asks.

"If you can imagine it, Mark actually helped a little," I admit. "We got around the far corner and six sections back the other way. It'll be ready."

As we take our empty plates to the sink and rinse them off for the dishwasher just like we were taught, Luke fills us in on Briarbelle, his favorite mare. She's old for a first-time mother, and it's been tough on her.

"Briarbelle is ready to foal, but she's not handling it too well. She's been pacing and sweating all day, and she's already leaking milk. I'll watch her tonight, but I went ahead and told Doc to be on alert. He plans to come out bright and early in the morning. I just don't have a good feeling."

Luke is the best of any of us with the horses. There's something about his manner, his mellow presence, that sets them at ease, so his having a bad feeling is not a good sign.

Mark dries off his hands and leans against the big counter in the kitchen, his eyes dark with concern. "Shi—sorry to hear that," he says, still aware of Mama's presence as she scrubs at the roasting pan. Just because dinner is done is no reason to curse in Louise Bennett's kitchen. Clearing his throat, Mark continues, "Need a hand tonight? I can take a shift to watch over her."

Never one to be outshined by my brothers, I speak up. "Me too. Whatever you need."

Luke shakes his head, smiling a little. He's always been the one of us to be sort of solo, not really antisocial but just . . . private. "Naw, I've got it. She's comfortable with me, and I already got my cot set up so I can rest when I can. But come on out in the morning, nice and easy. Hopefully, we'll have a new foal and both mama and baby will be healthy."

CHAPTER 2

SOPHIE

I can't help it, bouncing side to side as excitement courses through my body. It's either bounce or fidget, and I know if I fidget I'm going to end up looking like I need to pee. Actually, I probably look like I need to pee now, but I can't stop.

Who'd have thought a few years ago that a summer internship with a crusty old seen-it-all vet way out in the country would turn into a job that causes this degree of joy in my heart, especially when the sun's not even up yet?

Definitely not me. I grew up a city slicker, the sort of girl who was wealthy and never had to worry much because my brother, Jake, always took care of me . . . and everything. He was a little overbearing at times, but I didn't fault him for it too much.

After all, he didn't ask to be both brother and caretaker. When our parents died, I was barely out of elementary school, and he didn't have much choice. But he stepped up and was the best fill-in parent an orphan could have, and I know he worked his ass off to make sure I had a happy life, even when I went through a rough patch in my teen years and gave him more than his fair share of hell.

But Jake never wavered, never questioned taking me in. It was just the two of us against the world for a lot of years, but he'd met and married the love of his life, Roxy, several years ago, and in her, I'd found a friend and sister before going off to college.

My original plan had been to follow in Jake's footsteps, attending the same private university he had and getting my business degree before staying on track for my MBA. I'd figured I could join Jake in business and make oodles of money just like him. And that plan worked through my freshman year, when I took the same old boring English and math classes as everyone else. But a mess-up in my schedule my sophomore year changed everything for me.

I'd filled out my course request for basic biology, an easy-A class that would let me check the box before moving on to my business courses. But one typo in the computer, and I found myself in Animal Studies, and no matter what I tried with the counselor, it was just too late to switch.

So, I resigned myself to studying dogs and cats and rabbits for a semester. Considering I'd never even had a pet, the experience was eye-opening and . . . amazing. Somehow, in the sixteen weeks of that intro class, my whole life changed. Getting to see the wonderful tapestry that is life on this planet up close touched me in a way that all the money Jake had in the bank just . . . didn't.

I changed my major from business to pre–veterinary studies and never looked back, spending the next three years learning all about animals, big and small. My semester with large farm animals was my absolute favorite, following our John Wayne–esque mentor around on his ranch, checking on his cattle, administering vaccines, and doing wellness checks before the cattle went to market.

I did a summer internship with him to prolong my learning, and that was when he taught me to ride horses. I loved the freedom of riding, feeling the wind in my face and a powerful beast beneath me, willing to cede control and go where I led.

It was exhilarating, and I felt honored to experience it. It was then that I knew my specialty as a vet would be large ranch animals. The more time I can spend on wide-open land, keeping the herds and horses healthy, the happier I'll be. Not that I mind deworming a dog or spaying a cat, but there's something about the large animals that calls to me.

Jake and Roxy have been supportive, if a little confused by the drastic change I've gone through in the last few years. I think Jake is wondering if I've had a brain transplant. For the most part, they're still living a jet-setter, urban trendsetter life, and as happy as I am for them, I want something different.

Which is why I'm bouncing around on my toes now, looking more like I'm getting ready to fight Ronda Rousey than go to work. I officially graduated two weeks ago, so my bachelor's degree is in hand and my invitation to vet school is pinned to the refrigerator in the small house I rented for the summer.

Sure, I could sit on my ass and take a couple of breather months before jumping into my vet courses, but I'm too much like Jake. I want to *do*. So I found a summer job in an area where I can be close-ish to my support people, but far enough away that I can stand on my own two feet.

I was lucky enough, and damn well qualified enough, to snag a summer internship working with a local vet called Doc Jones. It's a perfect fit, really. He's well versed in everything animal related, having likely seen it all and done it all at least once, while I bring what he calls "fresh air" to the office. Better than that, he's actually a really great teacher, willing to share his knowledge and help me get ready for a career with big animals.

Like today, the reason I'm bouncing. Doc got a call last night, and this morning we're doing a wellness check on a foaling horse at a ranch way outside of town. It's a lot better than what I'd expected, which was preparing two thousand doses of vaccine for a local sheep rancher. I'm sure I'll be sticking sheep in the ass at some point this week, but seeing a live birth? That'll get me standing here on the curb outside my tiny house in town, two insulated cups of coffee in hand and a thermos of caffeine nectar in my bag at my feet.

It's nice and crisp right now, but it's supposed to be hot as balls today. Even so, I need my morning coffee fix, and Doc Jones *definitely* does. I hear him coming long before I actually see him, the squeals of his old-as-hell GMC pickup audible before he even turns the corner. As he cranks to a stop in front of me, he looks like he always does, sort of a cross between Sam Elliott and DeForest Kelley, which I guess is appropriate. "Hop in," he says, reaching over and pulling up the old-fashioned lock on his passenger door. "I just talked to the boy at the ranch, and Briarbelle's foal still isn't here. If we hustle, we'll get to see her deliver. You seen that yet?"

I nod, sliding in and handing Doc his coffee. "Oh yeah. Actually, I've seen four deliveries. But they were pretty by the book; only one needed a minor assist."

"Well, I'm thinking this might not be as textbook. Hope you don't mind some funk."

I shake my head, sipping at my coffee. "I don't mind. It's always amazing to see, it's such a miracle every time."

I know my eyes are sparkling with anticipation. I'm not just blowing smoke—I really do love to see the miracle and make sure mom and baby are okay.

Doc looks over at me, studying me. "Eager, aren't ya?"

"Come on, Doc," I complain a little. "Aren't you just as excited?"

He laughs and pushes the gas on his old truck a little harder. He could afford a new one, but I think he's determined to run this thing to the half million–mile mark before he'll feel like he's gotten his money's worth. "Well, I've done this a few more than four times, but I reckon it's always a sight to see."

As we drive out, Doc quizzes me on what I'm likely to see, what I need to be concerned about, procedures if this happens, what about if that happens, and more. I nail every single one of them, and as he turns down the last road, he gives me a satisfied grunt. "That'll do, Miss Sophie. That'll do just fine."

I can feel the blush on my cheeks at his praise, pleased to have answered his questions correctly. This might be just a summer job, but I want to be the best at it.

Doc gives me a half smile and makes another little grunt, patting the dashboard.

CHAPTER 3

SOPHIE

The air is still and cool as we get out of Doc's truck, and I spare a moment to look around. The setting is idyllic, a huge ranch-style house that looks surprisingly balanced—old-fashioned and modern blended together—with two big barns dominating the space behind me before the fields start, rolling in the hills with the mountains that Great Falls is famous for off to my right in the north. "Wow."

Doc quietly grabs his bag. "Sort of looks like a little slice of paradise, don't it? Come on."

We enter the barn soft and slow, not wanting to disturb the laboring mare, who I can hear panting, obviously uncomfortable in her stall. There's not much light, just what filters in from the sun rising behind me and a single fluorescent track near the stall. As my eyes adjust, I can see a man sitting still as a statue, leaned back and almost disappearing into his surroundings.

Doc said he talked to the "boy at the ranch," but who I see is definitely no boy. The man is tall, judging by his legs. He's lean, his waist much trimmer than his shoulders, and his T-shirt is tight across his back but loose where it disappears into the waistband of his jeans.

I can't see his face; his hat is tipped down too low, and the angle of his head makes me think he's side-eyeing the moaning mare in the stall. He notices us, though, and brings a hand up slowly as we approach, touching the rim of his baseball cap in a sort of salute. "Good morning, Doc."

Doc returns the salute with a nod before he kneels down, spry even though he's constantly making jokes about being an old man. "Hey, Luke, how's Briarbelle doing?"

Doc's voice is quiet and calm, and Luke responds in kind, sounding almost country-Zen in his softly drawling reply. "She's been up and down, pacing and lying, but no real progress. She might need some assistance, Doc."

"That's what we're here for; don't worry. We'll help her."

Luke looks up, a little bit of pride flaring in his eyes. "I'm happy to help. Just tell me where you need me."

Doc smiles and points back at me. It's one of those things I've not quite gotten used to, not being introduced to people until it feels about five seconds too late. "Thanks, Luke, and I'm gonna need your help, too, but I meant me and Sophie. She's working with me this summer."

He nods at Doc, then meets my eyes and gives me a chin lift of greeting. "Assistant, huh?"

I give him a smile and nod. "I got my degree a few weeks back, and I'm going to vet school next year. I work hard and will do Briarbelle right."

Luke nods, and I think I see him crack a smile. Guess I handled that right—confident without coming off as some book-learning city girl. Doc gestures me toward the door of the stall, keeping his voice soft but unmistakably commanding. "Okay, slow and steady, let's get in here, give soon-to-be Mama Briarbelle an exam, and see what seems to be the problem."

Luke doesn't move out of our way, so we gingerly step over him and into the stall, moving slowly so as not to startle the mare. I can see that she's in pain; her eyes are wide but not glassy yet. Still, we bend down carefully to stay out of range of her potential kicks, knowing that an animal in pain can sometimes strike out. And a horse, even one that's pregnant and weakened with birthing pains, could do serious damage if I'm not careful.

Doc starts to ask me questions. "What do you see, Sophie?"

I scan the mare from nose to tail, taking in everything as I slowly circle, still aware of her hind legs. "She's struggling, you can see the foam on her where she's been sweating, and her breathing is ragged. I'd say she's getting close to exhaustion, but she's still got fight in her."

He asks a few more questions, some of me and some of Luke. I kneel down, gently rubbing her flank and trying to comfort her through the pain she's feeling, when I hear another voice. "Luke, how's she doing?"

I look up, and my eyes lock on another man, again definitely not a "boy," although this one appears a little younger and has a wildness in his mysterious, dark eyes. He's dressed for work in jeans and a faded denim shirt, although he's not wearing a hat, so I can see he's got dirty-blond hair.

He appears a little more muscular than his brother, wiry muscles corded along his forearms where his shirtsleeves are rolled up. He's looking at Luke, running his fingers through his hair as he waits for an answer.

Luke, who's still sitting in his chair with infinite patience, looks up. "They're checking on her now. James, this is Doc's assistant, Sophie. Sophie, this is my brother James."

I nod at him, never stopping my gentle soothing of Briarbelle, but my attention is lock, stock, and barrel on James.

Holy fuck, he's hot.

I could lose myself in those eyes, so dark blue they're nearly navy, mysterious like a summer's night where magic and mayhem run hand in hand with warm breezes and explorations of things that you don't tell your overprotective older brother about. I want to run my fingers through his hair just like he's doing, and I'd give my left pinkie toe for him to turn around so I can see his ass in those tight jeans that look to be sculpted over his muscular thighs. The faded, ripped look was popular on campus this past year, but James's jeans got theirs the old-fashioned way . . . he *earned* them.

Hmm, maybe my summer gig just got even better.

James seems to be smiling back at me, but his mouth never moves; it's all in a slight crinkling around his eyes, and I swear he knows what I'm thinking.

He goes to open his mouth to say something, but before he can, Doc swears, and it draws my attention back to him and Briarbelle. "Sophie, it's a red-bag delivery. Tell me what that means."

I don't even have to think, the textbook answers rolling off my tongue like I've engraved them on my brain during multiple study sessions, which I did. I'm not the kind to just cram facts in for a test and then forget them an hour later. "The placenta is coming first due to premature separation from the womb wall. It's urgent to deliver the foal immediately before hypoxia sets in. This type of delivery is rare and associated with placental infection. Commonly, both mare and foal need antibiotics postdelivery."

Doc grunts. "Good enough. C'mere. Ain't got time to glove up."

I move to where he indicates, surprised when he hands me a pair of scissors. "Quick and easy; watch the foal. Just let off the pressure, and we'll get it out quickly afterward."

I look at him, shocked. This is something I've studied but not actu-ally done. Technically, you're not supposed to even try this until you have your DVM. "You want *me* to do it?"

Doc nods, no humor at all in his voice. "Clock's ticking. Can you do this?"

There's no judgment in his question; he just genuinely wants to know if I can or not. If I say no, he'll take care of it. But he's giving me a chance to excel, to show that I'm ready. I take a big breath and calm myself.

"Let's do this." I lean down, bringing the sharp edge of the scissors to the sac, releasing a gush of amniotic fluid that covers the hay and dirt of the stall, with a good amount getting on my jeans too. No time to worry about that right now.

Behind me, I can hear James talking to Luke. "What the hell? Why isn't Doc doing that? Is she even qualified?"

Luke seems to be shushing James, but it's not enough, and it distracts me. Looking over my shoulder, I glare at James, my voice steely without raising the volume and startling Briarbelle. "Shut up or get out. Your choice."

James sputters, obviously not used to being talked to like that, and I decide that my earlier thoughts of him were off base. Screw him and his doubt that I can handle this. Still, I see Luke grin a little, glad to see his brother get scolded.

Fuck it, I've got this.

I reach deep inside myself, seizing hold of my guts and my knowledge, and with an ease I'm surprised to demonstrate, I deliver the foal successfully.

She lies in the hay, breathing and alive, and Briarbelle lets out an exhausted whinny, calling to her baby. The foal whinnies back, and I finally feel like I can breathe again. Doc takes care of injections for both of them while I put the tools away.

After a moment, Briarbelle moves, nosing and nudging her foal, and we step back and out to let them bond without interruption.

Doc smiles at me, nodding his pleasure at the good job I did. It makes me feel warm inside, but really all the reward I need is lying in the hay in the stall.

My buzz is thwarted when James interrupts the moment, his voice near outrage. "Doc, what was that? Why'd you let her do the delivery? That could've cost us a good foal."

Doc clears his throat, but before he can answer, I jump in, pointing a finger toward the middle of James's muscular chest. "He let me do it because he knew I could. Briarbelle is fine, the foal is fine, and I'm fine. The only person not fine is . . . you. You were the one out of control, raising your voice and scaring her while I was trying to save the foal's life."

His eyes flash fire, and I wonder what's about to come out of his mouth. I'm sure it'll be a doozy. But I'm almost disappointed by what he comes up with. "You've got a real bitch streak in you, you know that?"

I laugh, dismissing him from my mind even as he stands in front of me. "As if I haven't been called that before. Try for some originality next time, why don't ya?"

Doc tries to break the tension, yanking back on an invisible halter. "Okay, let's rein it in. Get it . . . rein? It's a horse joke."

Not getting the laughs he was hoping for, he gives up and focuses his attention on Luke. "I was keeping watch the whole time. Briarbelle and her babe are fine. I want them to have antibiotics for a little bit just in case. They'll both need daily checks for the next week, and maybe even some follow-up after that. You don't mind, do you?"

Luke nods like a bobblehead, seemingly on board. I feel Doc's eyes on me and glance back at him as he looks over to James.

Doc nods and continues, "I think checking in will be part of your daily duties, Sophie. You can leave the office early and head out here to check on them as your last duty of the day before heading home."

My stomach churns and my heart stops. Is he serious, having me come back out here every day for the next week?

Shit.

Well, I guess if I have to deal with Luke, it'll be fine. I'll just cross my fingers and toes that I don't have another run-in with James. Besides, I think Doc's teaching me a lesson here too: you don't have to like your customers; you just have to treat your patients with care and your customers with a bit of respect.

"Sure thing, Doc. Guess I'll be here tomorrow afternoon then."

I nod at Luke, pointedly ignoring James, and turn to blow a kiss to Briarbelle before heading to the sink to wash up as best I can. Man, am I glad that I wore old jeans.

CHAPTER 4

JAMES

Luke's quietly laughing his ass off at me as Sophie struts out to Doc's truck. I can't help but watch her go, her dark hair swishing back and forth right above the heart shape of her ass in tight jeans. Total bitch . . . but she's hotter than the noontime sun; there's no doubt about that.

I'm for sure gonna hate seeing her every day for the next week, but I can handle it as long as I get to watch her leave like that.

Luke leans against one of the barn's support beams as Doc and Sophie pull away, giving them a wave while he talks to me out of the side of his mouth. "Damn, James, you show off those skills with all the ladies when you're on the circuit? Why, I bet you must take home a woman once a year with game like that."

I jab him on his shoulder, laughing. "Fuck you, my game is just fine. I could take a different woman back to my hotel in every city if I wanted. I wasn't trying to put the moves on that one, just trying to save the foal. Which is supposed to be your job, I might add."

He doesn't take the admonishment like I intended, laughing instead of getting pissed off. "Oh, I was doing my job just fine. Doc wouldn't have allowed her to do that if he weren't confident. You've been away from the farm too long, James. Besides, Doc's getting old. This ain't the pro tour, where organizers have nothing but top-flight docs on call all the time. That pretty girl needed to learn. Also, I was rather enjoying watching my famous little brother go down in flames of his own making."

My face screws up, slightly pissed. I've been hearing it from Mark for years now; I don't need this shit from Luke too. "Goddammit, Luke, I ain't famous. What the hell are you talking about? I just ride bulls. Not like I'm a movie star or some shit."

Luke brushes off his hands on his jeans and heads back into the barn to fetch his hat. Jamming it on his head, he turns and points toward the house. "You keep saying that. We've watched every ride you've made that's televised. I saw the signs in the audience in Vegas, what those women were holding up. 'Ride me, James.' 'Bennett's Bitch.' Oh, and just a little FYI—Mom was pissed as a hornet about that one especially. You wanna say you're not famous, that's fine. You can lie to yourself; you can lie to me about it. Next time you really start thinking it, though, I'll make sure to bring up those signs and remind Mom. You can see what she has to say about the matter. Spoiler alert: it ain't gonna be pleasant."

He flashes a wide, toothy grin at me, and I know he'll damn well do it just to rile Mama up and aim her my direction.

"Kiss my ass, Luke," I growl, knowing I can't win this argument. "I guess I'll head out to the back pasture and see how many more sections of fence I can get done before dinner again. I'll leave you here with your horses."

I give him a middle-finger salute after surreptitiously making sure Mama isn't on the porch and head out, his laughter ringing behind me.

While I drive the ATV with its cart of supplies out, I fume about Luke and his bullshit. Yeah, I make more money than most farm boys, and a few people might know of me. But it's only for a few years. Bull riding isn't an old man's game, and I'm by no means getting rich. So fuck them. I'm riding bulls because of me.

After getting out to the fence, I work my ass off all day again, my thoughts mainly focused on the fence, the ranch, and how we're gonna keep it running. I'm not totally selfish; I'll do what I can, even if it means missing some of the smaller events on the circuit. But I have to be my own man, too, not third fiddle in some fucked-up version of *King Lear* or something.

Unbidden, Sophie keeps slashing into the pictures moving across my brain, feisty and sassy, self-assured and not taking any shit, especially from me. I thought she was going to slap me when she got in my face, her eyes fiery and her lips wet and juicy . . . yeah, she's got a face as pretty as the rest of her.

In the moment, it pissed me off. But in hindsight, it makes me smile a bit. That touch of wild fire is intriguing, and so similar to the one in my core. That spark is what ignites inside me every time I climb on the back of a bull. I've been riding bulls since I was a boy; I grew up in the ranks of small-time amateur rodeos, even when travel was difficult. Pops had always gone to bat for me, telling Mama that I just had a little more of a wild side to me than most folks, and riding bulls was a damn fine way to let it out. "Better than a lot of kids, Louise," Pops said the one time Mama protested really hard. "Too many of them going out, gettin' drunk, and starting fights in bars. At least James has a chance to *buy* a big house instead of *go* to the big house."

I smile at the memory, still hearing his voice in my mind as he called me his "wild child" and told Mama that's why I was last—because if they'd had me first, I'd have been an only child.

But I haven't been on a bull in months, not since Pops passed and I told Mark I'd spend the whole summer on the ranch instead of blowing in and out like usual. Nope, I've been too busy busting my ass getting things straightened out before finals in November.

Of course, busting my ass means a lot of doing the same thing, day in and day out . . . fence, cattle check, eat, sleep, repeat. I hate to sound bitter, even to my own ears, because I know Pops worked so hard to buy and keep this land. And he raised us right on this ranch too. But Mark was always Pops's right-hand man, the firstborn golden child to carry on the family legacy. I don't fault Pops for that, or even Mark for being a bit bossy.

I'd have never been right for running this whole place anyway. There's a piece of me already on the lookout for an escape back to the rodeo, a new town every weekend, the adrenaline rush of strapping myself to a bucking bull and hanging on for dear life and eight seconds.

Riding a bull is like nothing else. You can prep, you can rosin up your glove and cinch that rope in tight, but when the bull just decides to say, "Fuck you," and do something you never could have prepared for, nothing matters.

The argument with Sophie this morning was kinda like that, an unexpected ride of excitement in what I thought would be the same old day. My mind sweeps back to her sneering at my "unoriginality" as though she was disappointed I didn't insult her better.

After watching how she handled the situation with Briarbelle, and honestly, the situation with me, I realize I don't really want to insult her again.

Hell, maybe I owe her an apology when she comes out here tomorrow.

Maybe.

The dinner bell rings across the pasture, and I finish the last tie on this section, realizing that my fingers have been damn productive while my mind wandered. One more solid day of work and I think we'll be able to move the cattle over.

That thought makes me feel good as I bring in the ATV and put it away after topping off the tank with the gas can just like Pops taught us. Mark and Luke come in around the same time, and after washing up, we all stumble in and sit down at the table to pass around a casserole dish of noodles and veggies.

I lift my fork to take my first bite, but Mama can't wait any longer. "So, how's Briarbelle doing?"

Luke grins around a big spoonful of casserole, nodding. "She's doing just fine. Her foal too. Little mare with paint spots like her mama. Doc came out with his new assistant, Sophie. She did the delivery, even with the complications."

"Oh, I didn't know he had someone working with him now," Mama says, very interested. "It's about time. That man runs all over the county, and when you get to be our age, that kind of life can be too much."

Mark gruffly corrects her while I keep my mouth shut, not wanting to step anywhere near this conversation. "'Our age'? He's near seventy years old and should be retired, Mama. You're in your fifties and still move like a woman ten years younger. That's nowhere near the same thing."

Mama just nods, patting Mark's hand comfortingly like his grumpy ass is normal. I guess it mostly is, especially these days.

"You're too sweet, honey. I think I'll have to go out to the barn and see her tonight after dinner. By the way, Luke, what kind of complications? Anything we need to be worried about?"

Luke shakes his head, sipping at his glass of iced tea. "Nope. Just needed some help delivering, but all is well now. Doc said that Sophie would come by and make daily checks for about a week just to make sure, though. Isn't that right, James?"

I look up, feigning ignorance. "Huh? Oh yeah, right . . . she's coming out tomorrow to check on them and bring the antibiotic dose."

Mama eyeballs me, and I can feel her piercing gaze delving into the deepest parts of my brain like the lie detector she's always been. "What are you not telling me?"

I shrug, seriously wishing we could move on. I smell lemon pie, and while it's not my favorite, it's a damn sight better than talking about this. "Nothing, really. I might not have been gracious about her doing the delivery instead of Doc."

Luke's mouth drops open, and I know what he's going to say even before he says it. "That's what you call it? *Not gracious?* She had to tell you to shut up or get out so she could do the delivery, and then you called her a bitch."

Mama screeches, slamming her fork down on the table. "You did *what?*"

"Mama, I—"

That's all I'm able to get out before she continues her scolding. "I didn't raise a son of mine to call a lady a name like that, especially when she was just helping. What were you thinking?"

I'm silent, knowing that I not only crossed a line but hopped way over into no-man's-land when I said that, as far as Mama is concerned.

Luke helps me out, and I consider just yelling at him later instead of taking a pitchfork to his ass. "The best part was after he called her . . . that . . ." he waffles, "she tells him to try for some originality next time! She swatted him away like a mosquito in the spring."

He laughs, unable to control it until Mark gives him an evil eye. Never mind; the pitchfork's too good for Luke . . . I think the chainsaw sounds about right.

Mark sees nothing humorous in any of it, though for him, that's just normal. "That's enough, guys. So, she's gonna be out here again tomorrow? Sounds like you owe her an apology, James."

I know he's right. Hell, I'd already come to the same conclusion myself, but it chafes to have your bossy big brother tell you what to do, even if that's what he's always done. Maybe more so *because* that's what he's always done. Bossy Big Brother. "Yeah, thanks, genius. Like I didn't come up with that before lunch."

Mama heads off the argument at the pass, sounding pleased for some reason. I guess she has been pretty devoid of female company recently. "She's coming in the afternoon? Sounds like you should apologize and invite her to dinner too. If she's new in town, she probably needs some friends, not some grumpy old boys too stupid to do the right thing when it smacks them in the face."

I grimace but say nothing. I'll apologize, but I'm not asking her to dinner.

It must show on my face, because Mama turns hard eyes on me, picking up her fork again in that way that says she's about to lay down the law, and the Lord above won't change what she's about to say. "Apology *and* dinner. You won't eat at my table until she gets both."

I sigh, knowing her threat is real. One time Pops was being stubborn about something the pastor said, and Pops went off on him. Pops ate outside on the porch steps for a week until he became the better man and apologized. "Yes, ma'am."

"That's my boy," Mama says sweetly. "Now, who'd like some lemon pie?"

CHAPTER 5

SOPHIE

The miniature pig snuggles into my chest, nibbling the Cheerio snacks from my fingers rather delicately considering she's a pig. "Who's a good girl? That's right, you are, little Miss Bacon."

I pull my hand back, rubbing behind her ears and marveling at how delicate her eyelashes are. Seriously, I'm jealous; I'd kill for those. She snorts, and I laugh as she wrinkles up her snout. Honestly, who names their pet pig Bacon? Definitely someone with a twisted sense of humor.

After finishing her checkup, I place Bacon back into a large kennel along the wall to wait for her owner. She promptly curls up in her fuzzy blanket and starts snoring in seconds, utterly content and secure in the knowledge that the whole world loves her. Pampered little princess pet pig.

Doc, who's been checking on a schnauzer that got a nail in its paw, comes over with a small bag. "Good job today, Sophie. You still okay heading out to the Bennett place?"

Internally, I groan. It's a bit of a drive out to their ranch, and while I'll get to see the new foal and mama when I get there, I'm hoping I don't have to see that asshat James. I don't know if I can handle any shit after a long day.

I wasn't exactly professional yesterday, and I had been nervous Doc would be disappointed in my lack of customer-service skills, but he told me that James deserved it given the circumstance. "That boy's alright at his core, but sometimes his mouth writes checks that it shouldn't," he told me. "You handled him just right, and if I know that family, he'll get a hidin' from Louise over it as soon as she finds out."

It'd been a big relief, but I promised myself to behave better from here on out. That should be easy, if I don't have to cross paths with James again.

Maybe the nice brother will be in the barn instead. *Although he wasn't as gorgeous,* a traitorous voice says in my head. But I shut that thought train down with more rational thinking because I don't need to stare at gorgeous eyes and cheekbones; I just need to get my work done.

I nod and take the bag from Doc. "Yes, sir. I'll take the truck like you said and then drive it home. You want me to pick you up in the morning?"

He shakes his head, pointing down at the casual sneakers he's wearing today. "Nope. My granddaughter keeps saying I need to get more 'meditative exercise,' whatever that is supposed to mean. So I'll stroll on home tonight, and I'll walk back in the morning. Maybe I'll even stop and get us some doughnuts on the way in."

I hum in appreciation. "Sounds delicious. Actually, I haven't had a doughnut since my freshman fifteen!"

Doc snickers. "In that case, I'll bring you more than one, and you can indulge. Gotta keep fueled to handle these big animals—their owners too."

He gives a little wink, and I wonder if he's thinking about yesterday too. I hide my blush with a little pose, flexing my right bicep and grinning. "There you go, Doc. More power than any man can handle!"

He laughs, shaking his head. "Okay, okay. Go on and head out. It's after four, and the only thing left today is for Bacon to get picked up. When you get out to the Bennett ranch, make sure you give Briarbelle and her foal their injections, and note if you think I need to head out there. Oh, and see if they named the baby yet for me, 'kay? Need it for my records."

"Sure thing. See you in the morning." I head out to Doc's truck, slide behind the wheel on the old, blanket-covered bench seat, and start it up.

The drive out to the Bennett ranch is stunning in a way I never thought would appeal to me. As soon as I clear the city limits, things start to open up, and I can see for miles to the horizon line, just an occasional tree or fence line breaking the expanse.

I make the last turn onto the road that leads out to the Bennetts', almost overwhelmed by the vibrant green of the grass and cloudless blue of the sky that stretches unendingly in front of me, a cloud of dust rising behind me as I bump and jostle down the dirt road.

Turning the country song on the radio down, I mentally go over my checklist for the horses, preparing myself to be efficient, professional, and most of all, to look like I know what the hell I'm doing. I actually do, regardless of what that jerk thought.

Seeing the metal arch that proclaims the BB Ranch is just ahead, I slow down to turn into the long drive. The gate is closed today, and I don't see a call box to phone up to the house.

Grinning, I problem solve and give the truck's horn a few short blasts. *Beep-beep-beep, beep-beep-beep, beep-beep-beep-beep-beep* . . .

It's just a couple of minutes of honking out "Jingle Bells" before I see a small cloud of dust stirring up behind a horse and rider, silhouetted with the sun at their backs. I cross my fingers, holding out hope that it's the *nice* brother, or maybe a ranch hand. But even though his face is in a dark shadow as he touches the front of his hat and dips his chin in greeting, I can tell it's James.

It's in the width of his shoulders, the dark blond hair that's just a little long and peeking out from under his hat, and if there was any doubt, it's in his smirk as his eyes meet mine.

He bends down, one muscled forearm leaning against the saddle horn. "Good afternoon, Miss Sophie. You're lucky, I was just giving Cooper here an afternoon stroll. Here to check on Briarbelle?"

Deciding a combination of crisp professionalism and kindness is my best course of action, I stick my head out the truck's window and nod. "Yes, and please, just call me Sophie. No need for the *Miss*. Did she do well last night?"

He climbs down off the horse gracefully, unlocks the gate, and gives it a forceful shove so that it swings wide open. "Yep, she did just fine, I think . . . Sophie."

It looks like it actually pained him to call me by my name and not add the modifier to it, which makes me smile a bit. It's cute in a country-boy-charm way. "Well then, that's good."

"Come on through. Drive up to the house to park, and I'll walk you over to the barn," James says. "If you don't mind, take the lead? Cooper doesn't like being followed by vehicles too much."

I do as instructed, driving slowly so I don't kick up too much of a cloud behind me as he follows me on horseback. Once I've ambled to the front of the house, I shut off the truck, and I'm reaching to the passenger-side floorboard to grab my bag when the door opens behind me.

Turning, I see that James is offering his hand to help me climb out of the truck, but I've leaned pretty far over, and his eyes are decidedly fastened to my ass.

Giving him the stink eye, I ignore his hand and hop down on my own, my boots making a little thud as I land. The truck's not that high, but I'm on the shorter side, so it's a bit of a drop for my little legs. "I'm fine. I've been getting out of cars and trucks on my own for at least a few years now."

He shrugs, obviously not embarrassed at all about getting caught looking, and leads Cooper off toward the barn without looking back to see if I follow.

But who am I kidding? Of course I'm gonna follow. I'm here to see the horses, after all. And the view from back here is quite nice—I'm enjoying the sweet cowboy ass as James walks, his jeans stretched tight over his muscled butt, making me want to squeeze his cheeks like melons.

As he crosses the threshold of the barn, he stops suddenly, turning back before I can look up, and a dazzling-white smile breaks across his face. "See something you like, darlin'?"

Darlin'. It rolls off his tongue without hesitation, and there's a hint of sexiness to his voice mixed with a cocky bit of arrogance, like he's used to women checking out his butt.

It makes me feel bratty and thorny inside, and I automatically shoot back. Maybe he's used to little wilting wildflowers, but he doesn't know me. "Just seemed like a fair turn considering you were checking out my ass back there. Or were you checking to see if I'm a Levi's or Wrangler girl?"

I expect him to deny it, or at most maybe apologize for being improper, but I'm surprised when he admits to peeking.

"Oh, I checked out those Levi's," he says with a smirk. "Couldn't help myself when you leaned over and presented your ass up for my eyes. You should just be glad I had enough restraint to keep from giving you a good smack."

He mimes smacking my ass in the empty air in front of him, and it's so outrageous a laugh bursts out of my mouth before I can stop it.

"I guess we'll call it even then." *Although a good smack on the ass can be fun,* I think to myself but dare not say.

I'm still smiling and surprised that, with his antics, he's settled the ire I was already prepping, and we head into the barn.

I check on Briarbelle, noting for Doc that she seems well, with no obvious signs of infection, and administer her medication dosage.

I do the same for the little foal, watching her nurse for a moment and gently petting along her mane. "She's beautiful. I'd say you've got yourself a very good little filly here. You decided on a name for her yet?"

"Nope, not yet."

"When you do, let me know? I need it for Doc's paperwork," I explain, rubbing the little foal's ears and looking into her eyes. They're so big already, and it's obvious she's gonna be sweet-tempered.

James leans against the doorframe, watching me but not interfering this time. He clears his throat, the grumble breaking the silence, and I glance up, never stopping the soft rubs along the foal's side. He scrapes his thumbnail across his lower lip, and he looks shy, although I already know he's anything but timid.

"Something on your mind?" I ask.

James clears his throat again, and when he speaks, his voice is a little softer, less cocky than I've heard him before. "Hey, Sophie? About yesterday, I'm real sorry for being a jerk about you taking care of Briarbelle. And I wanted to apologize for calling you . . . you know. It was uncalled-for and rude. Won't happen again."

I stare at him, looking for any tell of insincerity but finding none. He seems truly apologetic. I'm so surprised that my hand stops rubbing the foal, and I turn to face him, just to be sure. Finally, I sigh. It's hard to be mad at him when he's looking at me with those damn sexy puppy-dog eyes he's got going right now, begging forgiveness.

"Apology accepted. Admittedly, tensions were running high, and you don't know me. I understand that it could've felt like it was risky for me to do the delivery when I'm not a vet yet. As for calling me . . ." I look left and right like I don't want to get caught before continuing in a stage whisper, ". . . a bitch? Like I said, not the first time, and definitely won't be the last. I'm sorry for being a bit combative back; it didn't help the situation either. Truce?"

I offer my hand, and he takes it, pulling me a bit closer before shaking it. "Truce."

There's a ringing sound outside, and he winces. "Um, there's just one more thing. Do you want to eat dinner with us? Mama insisted that I ask."

He looks nervous, like he expects me to say no. He couldn't be more wrong. I haven't had a good home-cooked meal since I moved out on my own, and dinner sounds like heaven to me. Besides, maybe I can find out a little more about James and why he goes from cocky to sweet seemingly at the drop of a hat. Still, just to tease a little, I give him a doubtful look. "Well, can your Mama cook?"

He looks offended at first, then smiles. "Of course she can."

I rub my hands together, grinning. "Well, alright then, show me the way, Cowboy."

James nods, smirking. "Don't worry, we'll do you right."

He walks away, and a little voice in my head notes something. He didn't say *Mama* . . . he said *we*.

CHAPTER 6

JAMES

I feel like this is a bad idea as I lead Sophie up to the back door. If she opens her mouth about my flirting about smacking her ass, I'm a dead man. Even if she does have an ass worth taking a few risks for.

Before I can even hold the door open properly to lead Sophie in to wash up, Mama is yelling for me. "James, you'd better have that girl with you for dinner, or I'm splitting your serving between your brothers!"

Sophie looks at me, her eyes questioning. I look skyward, knowing I look like a damn whipped mama's boy and wishing my mother didn't have to embarrass me like this.

"We're getting washed up!" I yell before I sigh. Lowering my voice, I explain, "Luke *had* to tell her about yesterday. She said that until I apologized and got you to come to dinner, I wasn't invited back to her dinner table."

Sophie laughs but thankfully keeps it low. "I think I'm gonna like her."

I grin, relaxing a little at Sophie's smile. It's even cuter than how she looked pissed-off and poking me in the chest. "Just make sure you get under your fingernails, or else you'll find yourself in the doghouse right beside me."

We finish washing and head inside, where Mama makes a huge fuss over Sophie, leaving her pots and pans behind to come over and greet her with that double handshake that seems to be the specialty of farmers' wives. "Hello, dear. I'm Louise Bennett, but don't you dare call me that. Everyone calls me Mama or Mama Lou; best you do the same."

I see the genuine smile on Sophie's face. Mama's got a big heart and can be a bit intense for some people at first, but Sophie takes it in stride, like she's dealt with overly forward women before. "Nice to meet you, Mama Lou. I'm Sophie Stone."

Mama lets go of her hands, and she gathers Sophie in a hug, patting her back. "Bless your bones for helping Doc out. Goodness knows that man can use an extra pair of hands."

Releasing Sophie, Mama holds her at arm's length, locking her in place physically and with her eyes. "Now you tell me the truth. Did this boy of mine apologize properly for his unseemly behavior? I want you to know that I raised him better than that."

Sophie smirks, and for a moment I think that she might say no, just to see what happens. But she relents, nodding. "Yes, ma'am, he did. We both did, actually. I didn't exactly try to defuse the situation. James was a gentleman, though. We called it even: a truce."

It clicks a split second after the words are out of her mouth that she's teasing me. We called our ass ogling "even" and our apologies a "truce." She's teasing me about looking at her ass in front of my own mother.

Laughing inside, I realize I underestimated her. She's more than a pretty face and sweet ass in jeans. Shit, this girl might be trouble. And if there's anything I like more than riding bulls, it's *trouble*.

Mama clicks her tongue, eyeing me like maybe I did something wrong even as Sophie tells her otherwise. "Fine then, c'mon in, you two.

If you don't mind, Sophie, dinner's going to be a bit more casual than normal; it's just too warm for the dining room."

"Not a problem, Mama Lou," Sophie says.

Mama leads us to the far side of the kitchen, where we've got a space that some people call a screened porch, but to Mama, it's the "casual eating room." It's got a big, classic picnic table that we'd have to wrestle out into the yard whenever Pops would throw a thank-you barbecue for any seasonal help, but instead of benches, we've got chairs.

I see Mark and Luke already sitting down, obviously eavesdropping on every word we've said. Luke is grinning like a madman, and Mark just raises an eyebrow at me, which is basically the same thing considering his stoic nature.

I realize that Mark isn't sitting in his usual spot. Instead, he's moved over next to Luke, leaving the chairs on the other side for me and Sophie. I give him a nod in appreciation and pull the chair out for Sophie.

She sits, and after scooting her in, I lower down to sit beside her. Mama nods proudly, as if I don't know how to be a fucking gentleman when the situation calls for it. Granted, I rarely find myself in those types of situations since I spend most of the year surrounded by rodeo guys. We're more rough and tumble than proper, but I have learned to be charming on occasion.

"So, Sophie, did you find the ranch easily?" Mama asks after she says grace and dishes start getting passed around. Tonight's roast beef with potato salad, along with my personal favorite, asparagus that Mama roasted with the beef.

"It was easy. And Briarbelle seems to be doing well—her foal too. By the way, I asked James. He said you guys didn't have a name for her yet. Any ideas?"

Luke answers, always happy to talk horses with anyone who'll listen. "She's doing well, thanks to you. And no name ideas yet. That's Mama's honor, and she's still thinking about it."

Mama nods, suddenly looking a little sad. "I've named every animal we've ever had on the ranch. If they had a name, I chose it. This will be the first time I've picked alone, though . . ."

An awkward silence settles over the table as us boys all realize something we hadn't even considered: Briarbelle's foal will be the first birth since Pops's passing.

It wasn't a milestone that even registered with me, and given the looks on Mark's and Luke's faces, they hadn't considered it either.

Sophie seems oblivious to the weight of the moment and charges in. "Alone? I'm sure one of these strapping sons of yours can help if you need a little inspiration. Oh, what about Lunares? It means *polka dots* in Spanish, and the foal does have the cutest little paint spots along her hindquarters."

Mark clears his throat, and Sophie's eyes dart around the table as she realizes the minefield she's stepped into. "Oh, I'm so sorry. I didn't mean to overstep."

Mama pats Sophie's hand but keeps her voice sweet. "No worries, dear. I just meant that this is the first name I'll pick since John passed away. It's bittersweet, but a reminder that life goes on, is begun again and again, long after we're gone."

From the side, I see Sophie's jaw drop a split second before she covers her mouth, the gasp still audible. "I . . . I'm so sorry. Truly, I'm sorry for your loss. I had no idea."

Mama smiles back at her, shaking her head. "It's alright, dear. You had no reason to know, and I like talking about my John. He was a good man, and I miss him every day. I still expect him to walk in the house every night and give me a kiss as he proclaims that 'something smells good in here.'" Mama smiles, but I can see her eyes are wet as she dabs at them.

Sophie smiles at Mama, somehow understanding the most important part of what she said. "Can you tell me about him?"

Mama takes a big breath, and I swear I take just as big of one in a futile attempt to swallow the lump in my throat. It's been the one good thing about being so busy with monotonous work around the ranch—I don't have too much time to think about what's changed.

Mama smiles, sets down her spoon, and folds her hands under her chin, looking off into the evening's purple light. "He was a ranch hand who came to work in my hometown back when we first met. I was just a townie, working at the local diner, and I'd seen plenty of men like him before. They'd come in with the drives, leave in winter, and generally you saw them for a year, maybe two, before they went somewhere else. But as soon as I saw him that first time, something told me John was different. When he came in, I always made sure to get his table. I knew his order by heart, but I always went over so he'd tell me, just so I'd have a chance to talk to him. And that November, when most of the other hands moved on . . . he got a job working nights at a gas station until he could get on permanently with one of the ranches.

"Anyway, we dated a few years until I was old enough to marry, and by then, he'd saved up enough of his wages to make his move. My parents thought he was crazy at first; it was halfway across the country and on unincorporated property, just a patch way out in the middle of nowhere. But I believed in him, and I believed in our love. So we did it. We both worked long hours, seven days a week. Over the years, we bought the land around us, raised more cattle, and along the way, did our best work . . . raising these three ragamuffin boys."

She pauses to look around the table, meeting eyes with each of us before settling her gaze on the empty chair opposite her at the table. "It was really around the time James was born that I realized we'd 'made it,' at least by rancher standards. We could tend our own, we made our payments to the bank on time even in bad years, and we were putting a little aside every month for the boys. John was so proud, and he vowed to me that they would have better lives than we had."

We all kind of look around at each other, taking in what she's saying before she continues.

"And John was right, they've all grown up to have their own lives . . . Mark here with me running the ranch, Luke working the horses and traveling for his breeding and training programs, and of course James, the wild child who risks life and limb to ride bulls in the rodeo."

Sophie gives me a sharp look, staring at me like I'm nuts. "Rodeo?" she mouths, but I just smile back, not willing to interrupt this stroll down memory lane.

"I thought it was paradise . . . but life has a way of throwing you curveballs from time to time. John passed away, and it hasn't been the same since. But we're family, and we've pulled together the way he would've wanted us to. We're doing as well as can be expected, I believe."

Mama shakes her head, seeming to let the moment pass. I'm glad; her last words have me damn near on the edge of tears, and I think Luke feels the same. Mama moves on, looking at Sophie. "So, tell me about you. How'd you end up with Doc?"

I'm actually interested to hear this story myself, something about her gorgeous looks and sassy spirit not really seeming to translate to being a girl who grew up in a barn.

Sophie smiles, even though her eyes are glistening a little too. "If you'd have told me five years ago that I'd be out here, I'd have called you crazy. I was a city girl who got stuck in an agricultural-science class on accident. Or maybe it was fate, who knows? But I fell in love with the animals and changed majors, much to my brother's chagrin, and here I am. I wanted to keep busy this summer before starting vet school, so I talked with my adviser, and in a network of connections, I got the job working for Doc."

"All on your lonesome?" Mama asks, and I'm surprised too. Takes guts to do what Sophie's done so far.

"My brother and sister-in-law are nearby, plus some friends and extended family, but pretty much I'm running solo. It's good, though;

I feel lucky to work with Doc. He sees such a variety of animals, and it's great to be out in the field, really working and being of service. Jake, my brother, hoped I'd spend some time back home this summer before buckling down for vet school, but the timing worked out for both of us; since I wasn't coming home, he could go on tour with his wife."

I look over, intrigued. "Tour? What kind of tour?"

Sophie smiles at me, but it's a bit shy, like this is a part of her life that she's not exactly parading around. "Um, an album-release tour. Sorry, I don't usually throw it out there in my first conversations with folks, but my sister-in-law is Roxy, the pop star? She married my brother when I was a teenager, so it's just normal to us, but folks kinda flip sometimes when they find out."

She looks around the table, eyebrows raised as if appraising whether we're those type of folks, but we're all straight-faced; pop music isn't really our music of choice. Still, everyone knows who Roxy is. I guess I can understand why Sophie would want to keep that quiet; she's trying to get respect on her own. Admirable.

Mama smiles. I know she sometimes listens to a little pop when she thinks us boys aren't around. "That was a lot about your brother, but your parents must be quite proud since it sounds like both of you are successful?"

Sophie's smile falters, but her voice never quavers. "Yeah, my folks were great, but they passed a long time ago. Car accident when I was ten."

She shrugs like she's explained this repeatedly over the course of her life. "I had ten great years with them, and Jake took over raising me without ever once moaning or complaining about it. He finished college while taking care of me, used the inheritance to start up his own business, and has been very successful.

"They would've been proud. I'm probably most proud that he didn't give up on me during my teen years when I was going through that self-absorbed, know-it-all, bad-boy phase I think every girl goes through.

He could've ditched me on a street corner and bailed, and honestly, I would've deserved it. But we got through it, and we're closer for it. Even if he doesn't 'understand the appeal of working on a dirty, smelly, animal-infested ranch.'"

Her voice pitches deep as she says the last part, obviously mimicking her brother's.

Luke laughs loudest, lightening the mood as he waggles his eyebrows at Sophie. "Bad boys, huh?" he says, giving me a pointed look.

We finish dinner and a dessert of Mama's peach cobbler in companionable conversation, the weight of Pops passing and Sophie's life summed up in one ramble left behind as we debate names for the foal.

By the time we've washed up the dishes, a decision still hasn't been made, though I think Mama is leaning toward Polka Dottie. But we call a pause on the discussion either way. I offer to walk Sophie to her truck, popping my elbow out. She hooks her small hand through, resting it on my forearm.

It feels formal, like we're walking out on the field at homecoming, but right now, I just want her hands on me any way I can get them. This seemed the most gentlemanly, especially considering I'm already contemplating some very ungentlemanly ways I'd like to touch her as I scan her sexy curves and bright eyes.

"Thanks, by the way," I say as we come around the curve of the house. "For making it easy and not asking anything embarrassing. Luke and Mark would've had a field day with it."

Sophie nods. "Sometime I'll have to tell you my *Little Mermaid* story," Sophie says, smiling. "What I mean is, I understand. Trust me, Jake was a good surrogate parent, but he's still my big brother."

We reach the truck all too soon, and I open the door for her as I extend a hand to help her inside the cab.

She takes my hand but turns to face me. "James, this was great. Thank you so much for inviting me to dinner." She winks. "Or should I say, tell your *Mama* thanks again for forcing you to invite me to dinner. Really. I haven't had a family moment like that in a while, so I appreciate you letting me into yours for a few minutes. I hope it wasn't too heavy there for a bit."

I smile. "No, I think it was just right. It seemed like Mama enjoyed it and it was good for her. It's still a bit hard to hear for us, but we needed it, too, I think. Thank you."

We look at each other for a moment, and I can see the moon reflecting back in her eyes, lighting her cheekbones and leaving the contours of her face in shadow. It's magnetic, and I want to lean in to see if her lips are as soft as they look.

Sophie notices and clears her throat, although she sounds a little reluctant to leave still. "Well, guess I'd better be going. Maybe I'll see you tomorrow when I come to check on Briarbelle?"

I can hear the hope in her voice, and it makes butterflies storm in my gut, but I try to play it cool, not letting on just how much she's affected me today.

"Absolutely. I'll meet you at the gate. And Soph . . . truce stands."

She smirks, apparently my coolness not played all that well after all. "Truce stands, but I'm about to get in this truck, and something tells me you're gonna check out my ass when I do."

I grin, enjoying the flirty tone to her voice and knowing she's damn sure right. I lean in close, Sophie not seeming to mind at all. "You know what? I sure am."

She nods, her smirk widening into a little grin. "Good. But make sure when you walk inside, you do it right. Because I'll be checking out your ass too . . . you know, so we're even and all."

With that, she turns and climbs up in the truck, and for a split second, I get a full visual of the round globes of her ass, swaying as she swivels into the driver's seat. Blood instantly rushes to my cock as an image comes to mind of her bent over the seat as I fuck her, jeans around her ankles as we stand in the open truck door.

Without thinking, I adjust myself for some relief, but she catches me, I think, because I see her smirk.

She grins through the open window, her eyes still twinkling. "Okay, Cowboy. Show me what you got. Fair's fair, and even's even."

I grin, turning to show her my backside, and give a little wiggle before walking inside.

Her giggle at my antics is like a balm for my soul, lighting up my playful side that's been dormant for too long.

And suddenly, life on the ranch doesn't seem quite so boring after all.

CHAPTER 7

SOPHIE

The next day flies by as I shadow Doc and check on his patients along with him. He's a good teacher, constantly quizzing me and humming in approval every time I answer correctly.

He's showing me the difference between "book smarts" and "street smarts," and that's vital to my future. One of the most important lessons he's taught me so far is that nothing is routine. Even the most common of appointments, like vaccine administrations, have to be treated with the utmost care.

These animals are their owners' livelihood and their pets, sometimes as much a part of their family as their children. He's already letting me have more autonomy, and I've been successful with every opportunity he's given me so far. Including Briarbelle.

After finishing the last appointment of the day, an eye infection for a dog that got its head in the toilet at the wrong time, Doc comes in. "Hey, Sophie, take the truck out to the Bennett place again today, but can you drop me off at home first? It's been a long day, and walking home might do me good, but doesn't sound that appealing with how exhausted I am."

I smile, looking forward to the drive. "Of course—it's your truck, after all! And it's too warm to walk anyway. Weatherman said it's been over ninety degrees all day, and with the humidity, it's ugly out. Load up, and I'll be right there."

Doc heads out to the truck, and I take a quick minute to run to the bathroom and check myself over. If I'm seeing James again, I don't want to smell like I've been working in the barn and look like the mess I feel. After all, fair's fair . . . and maybe I'll get another eyeful.

A quick pull of my hair back into its ponytail makes my overall look a bit more perky, and a sweep of pink gloss on my lips lights up my face. Or maybe that's the sparkle in my eyes at the prospect of seeing James?

Whatever, it's as good as it's getting right now, and Doc's waiting. I pretend not to see Doc's knowing smirk as I climb into the truck and roar down the main drag toward his little house in the residential section of town.

"So, which one is it?" he asks as we wait at a light.

I glance at him, not taking my eyes off the road for more than a split second. If anything, my parents' accident taught me to be a cautious and conscientious driver. Maybe I can use it as an excuse for not answering him too.

"Hmm?" Doc intones slowly like I didn't understand him. "Which one? Which brother?"

I blush instantly at the awkwardness of my boss, someone I want to impress by the good job I'm doing, seeing through me so readily and knowing that I'm obviously interested in a client. "Huh? Just wanted to look pulled together. You know, make it apparent that I know what I'm doing."

Doc nods wisely, tapping his hand on the dash in front of him. "Ah, James, then. He didn't give you any hassle yesterday, did he?"

I sputter a bit but decide that protesting too much might be even more obvious. "No, he was fine. We both apologized, and I even had dinner with them."

"Mm-hmm. Did Louise make you any of her pie?"

"Cobbler," I admit. "It was delicious."

"That woman can cook," Doc says. "As for James, he's a good man. A little wild, but nothing illegal, mind you. Just a bit of a troublemaker in his younger days." He laughs a little. "Well, a bit of a wild child still, I guess, if you keep up with the rodeo news."

"Mama Lou said something about that," I say, exposing my ignorance of some of the country life. I've never actually seen a rodeo. "James is a bull rider?"

Doc raises one eyebrow at me, a knowing look in his eye as the light switches to green and I pull forward. "He is, but you should probably ask him about it—I only know what I read. Google *James Bennett* and see what you get. You do know how to use the internet, right?"

It strikes me as funny that Doc, a decidedly elderly man, is advising *me* to use Google, but in this case, he's right. Maybe I should make it a point to do that tonight.

"Well, here we are, Doc," I say, pulling up in front of his house. "What time do you want me to swing by tomorrow?"

"Make it seven thirty," Doc says. "But keep your phone on tonight. It's unlikely, but if I get an emergency call, I'll need you to come get me."

He hops out, closes his door, and shakes it to make sure it's secure. "Sophie?"

"Yeah?" I ask, looking over.

"This isn't advice from your boss, but an old man to a nice young woman. Be careful, okay? The heat can make people do crazy things, and this summer, it's been really hot."

I nod, giving him a smile. "I'm always careful. Thank you for looking out for me."

～～

Just like he promised, James is already waiting by the gate when I pull up, this time on an ATV instead of a horse.

"No horse today?" I ask.

"Had some work that needed me to carry more stuff than I like putting on a horse," James says, swinging the gate open wide. "Did Doc sell you his truck or something?"

"Yep, paid fifty cents and a bowl of soup for it," I joke as I pull through. James closes the gate and pulls up next to me in the ATV. "Is it me?" I ask sarcastically, posing with a hand on the steering wheel and my other hand running along the window frame.

"You paid too much," he says, twisting his throttle. Today he leads the way up to the barn, swinging to the left as we get near to go over to the other building, where I guess they keep the mechanical equipment. He's back in a minute, though, finding me just as I close the door to the truck.

"How's your day been?" I ask.

"Just fine. Another day, another fence. Oh, and Mama insists on you joining us for dinner . . . if you're willing. Her exact words were 'the house needs some youthful exuberance.' And besides, you look like you're starving," he says with a smirk.

He's so cocky. I can tell by his expression that he thinks I look hungry for more than whatever delicious thing Mama Lou is serving tonight. Bad thing is, he's right. I spent too many minutes last night and today thinking about him, but I'll be damned if I'm going to let him know that. "Sounds great . . . dinner, that is," I sass right back at him. "How's Briarbelle and the baby doing?" I ask as we head into the barn.

"They're good. Luke keeps a good watch on them."

Briarbelle's checkup goes well; she's recovering quickly, and her foal whinnies softly, nuzzling my arm when I give her an ear scratch. "Well, I like you too," I tell her, looking in her eyes. "You're a good girl, aren't you?"

"That she is," James agrees. He's standing next to Briarbelle, feeding her some oat cookies slowly to ease her disquiet about someone messing with her baby. "I'm guessing you'll be the one to teach her how to be bad."

I grin, rubbing my forehead against the foal and pretending to ignore James. "You listen here, baby. You be as bad as you want to be; nothing wrong with that at all."

~~~

Dinner is delicious—crunchy, battered fried chicken that Mama proclaims to be her specialty and a recipe she can only share as a wedding gift to her future daughters-in-law. She gives each of her sons a serious side-eye as she says it, but other than Luke smirking a little, they seem to shrug it off as normal.

"Makes me want to throw up my hands in despair," Mama Lou says to me as we clean up. I insist on at least helping her rinse off the plates before putting them in the dishwasher, a very modern appliance that looks out of place in the old-fashioned kitchen, but apparently it was a gift from James. "Them boys just don't quite get that once a woman reaches a certain age, money doesn't matter as much as other things."

"Like grandbabies?" I ask, thinking of some of the older women in my family. The grandbaby syndrome seems to be contagious.

"Not just that," Mama Lou admits. "They're good boys . . . good men. I want to see them happy, that's all."

Her words cause me to glance over my shoulder, where the three brothers are sitting at the table still, sipping drinks. Mark's got a coffee, Luke's got a beer, and James sips an iced tea. The three of them are talking about their days and planning out what needs to be done tomorrow to keep the ranch on track.

It's pretty easy to recognize that all three of the Bennett brothers are virtual checklists of cowboy hot . . . dirty-blond, blue-eyed, muscled men with ruggedly handsome faces, and each has his own unique character. Mark's sort of taciturn, the type who looks gruff on the outside, but he's obviously intensely loyal and loves his family. Luke seems to be the jokester, using humor to counter Mark's seriousness, but otherwise a bit quiet. They don't quite do it for me, but surely they're some lucky lady's cup of tea.

James, though . . . that's my flavor for sure, all wrapped up in straining cotton and denim and topped with a dose of flirty wiseass, a bad boy who's turned the corner and making good. It's too bad I'm only in town for the summer. I don't want to get tangled up in something complicated or messy. Still, he might not be looking for anything complicated either. Maybe he's up for something fun and casual?

After the dishes are done, we head out the door. He pops his elbow out at me, and it's kind of feeling like a habit. I slip my arm through his. This time, though, instead of leading me around the house, he strikes out the other way, in the direction of the barn that I haven't been inside yet.

"Uh, you get lost suddenly?" I ask. "Truck's over there." I point with my free hand back toward the brown beast sitting in the dirt parking area, but James grins cheekily.

"Nope, got something to show you . . . if you think you can handle it."

I hear the challenge and nod my agreement. I remember my earlier thoughts about messy complications, but maybe he and I are thinking along the same lines. Either way, I want to see where this is going.

We slip farther from the house, passing the barn so that the quiet of the night surrounds us, the inky sky stretching above and the dark ground below. The only light comes from a slice of crescent moon beaming down on us, and I'll admit that I feel a quiver of primal fear. I never experience this type of dark quiet in the city; it's unique to being in the country, far from the flashing lights and noise of people coming and going at all hours.

Once upon a time, I thrived in that action. The sun going down meant it was time to get the day going, and more than once I saw the sunrise before going to bed. But now, even though I still feel that tremor of fear that my caveman ancestors did as they sat around the fire ready to fend off predators, I am starting to appreciate this still calmness. It feels . . . good.

Like James. It feels good to be close to his warmth, while at the same time he makes butterflies dance in my belly. There's a tension, an attraction brewing between us, an anticipation of something. As the lights from the house disappear behind a small rise, we get deeper into the night, and I know it's building.

I can feel it in his arm where my hand gently rests, sense it in the way his body crowds against mine as we walk. Still, the night and the enormity of what I'm sensing are beyond words. We're silent as James leads me to a small clump of bushes, and I hear . . . water?

"Where are we?"

James is quiet, his voice barely above a warm whisper. "This is my favorite place in the world. Pops paid more for this one acre of land than for half the damn ranch because it has a natural pond, fed by an underwater spring. It's rare around here; the runoff from the mountains mostly goes the other way. But this keeps the cattle well watered when we use this pasture. I learned to swim right here when I was a boy—did cannonballs off the little dock on the other side."

It feels special that he'd bring me somewhere this meaningful to him, but what do I know? Maybe he's brought every girl he's ever known here, and they have weekend barbecues on the bank.

We go quiet again, and I try not to let that harsh the buzzy feeling in my heart that he's sharing this with me. James pulls on my hand a bit, and as I sit down, I discover a blanket already spread on the ground along the shoreline.

It's too dark for him to see my smirk, but I know it's in my voice. "Well, aren't you the prepared Boy Scout?"

He laughs, teasing, but there's a new huskiness to his voice . . . I don't think this is something he does often. "No, just hoped you'd come out here with me and figured if you shot me down, a quiet night of just me and the stars wouldn't be too bad."

I hear him shuffling, and then he offers me a cold bottle. "Beer?" he asks.

I laugh, understanding why he was drinking iced tea while Luke had a beer. "You lugged down a cooler too?"

He chuckles a bit. "Woman, you're just lucky I'm sharing. I could've had the whole six-pack to myself. Besides, I told you I had some work that needed the ATV today. I just didn't say what exactly that work was."

I feel him scoot closer to me, our shoulders leaning against one another, and I lean into him slightly. I feel him trace his fingertips along my arm, my breath catching slightly until he finds my hand clutching the beer bottle and he clinks his bottle against mine. "To truces and being even."

"To truces," I echo. We sip, letting the cold pilsner cool off the heat that's burning from my core and has nothing to do with the residual heat of the day in the air. It's good beer—nothing fancy, but just honest-to-goodness beer. "Nice. What brand?"

"Negra Modelo," James replies. "A little rare around this area, but I was introduced to it during a tour stop in Tucson. So, when I decided to stay here for a while, I ordered two cases through a shop in town."

"I'm honored," I say, sipping at the beer. I take a deep breath, looking at the glimmer of the moon on the water and speaking my mind again. "I like this. Being out here like this. On the surface, it's dark and quiet. Almost like sensory deprivation. But if you use all your senses, there's more."

"What do you sense?" James asks, and I feel his warmth shift closer to me again. I smile and sip at my beer before answering.

"It's not really quiet. I can hear the cattle mooing quietly far away. There's the moon, and every once in a while I can see a flash of fire-fly light if I watch closely." I laugh, then continue, "I can even smell Mama's cinnamon crumble and beer on both our breaths. There's more going on than you think at first."

I close my eyes, tuning in to every nuance, and hear James swallow, maybe a gulp of air, maybe beer, I can't tell. "And what about your sense of touch?" he asks. "What do you feel?"

Before I can say a word, I feel his fingertips tracing up my arm, this time to find my jaw and cup it in his hand. He turns my head toward his, guided almost blindly before pressing his lips to mine. It's sweet, not tentative, but it's like he's testing me out, exploring without pressuring me too much. Forward, but respectful . . . and exciting.

I move my lips to adjust slightly, tasting him. He must feel my agreement because he takes our kiss deeper, hotter, more forceful. Setting my beer down, I wrap my arms around his neck, our tongues starting to tangle as he threads his fingers through my belt loops and pulls me into his lap to straddle him. Dimly in my mind I hear a clink as one of our beers tips over, but I really don't care.

Feeling his already thickening cock underneath me gives me another jolt, and I roll my hips against him, grinding myself against the ridge in his jeans.

"My touch is telling me a lot of things . . . all of them good and hot," I rasp as he kisses my neck. "Very fucking good."

He gently grabs my ponytail, pulling my head back to give him access as he moves down my neck, licking and kissing. He reaches for the hem of my shirt, slipping it over my head before cupping my bra in his hands.

I can feel the coarse, rough calluses on his fingertips and palms as he traces over the swells at the tops of my breasts, humming in appreciation. "You're soft as silk."

"I'll admit I like pampering some," I murmur as I tug on the back of his shirt, finding his skin and tracing his muscles. James growls, running his palm across my bra-covered nipple in a velvet, soft caress that is my total undoing.

He could be rough and fast, fuck me brutally with nothing but his strength and his animal passion. I'd take it, love every minute, and go home totally satisfied and with a smile on my face. I'd even feel respected the next time I came out here, because here in the dark, I'm not ashamed to admit that's what we both desperately want. But him being gentle with me, worshipful as he dips his mouth to suck me through the plain cotton of my bra, feels even better.

I moan at the onslaught, my scalp prickling as he holds my ponytail tight, the warmth of his kisses on my skin, the fire at my core. I grind my hips harder against his rock-hard cock, finding a rhythm that makes us both pant. Two sets of denim are between us, but I'm still soaking my panties, rolling and riding the bulge as the heat builds inside me. His hands lock onto my hips, guiding me at the pace he wants, but I want it too.

"Fuck, Soph," he rasps. "You're gonna make me come in my jeans like a damn teenager. I can feel your heat even through our clothes. Rub that pussy on me, use me to get yourself off."

I do; I buck against him, finding his mouth in the dark and stifling my cries in our kiss. I don't know if he even planned for things to go this far . . . but right now I don't care.

I throw my head back again, lifting my chest to the night sky and offering myself to James's ravenous mouth. "I'm gonna come . . . God, I'm gonna come just feeling your thick cock against my pussy."

"Then come, darlin'," he growls, kissing my exposed skin in between words. "Show me how fucking hot you are for me."

I squeeze my eyes closed, but the dark view doesn't change until I see white sparks across my eyelids, the orgasm taking me over the edge, and I cry out.

I can feel my body shudder, the rhythm turning into spasms, but he takes over, pushing and pulling my hips as he works his cock against me, prolonging my orgasm and chasing his own. He's grunting, gasping in need for release, and I give him all I have left, satisfaction sweeping through me a moment later as his breathing catches, and he growls. "Soph . . . fuuuuckkkk . . ."

His words disappear into a groan, and I feel him lift me off the ground as his hips buck once, twice, three times before he falls back on the blanket, unable to control himself. I ride him through his orgasm, prolonging his the way he did for me. As he begins to pant, he wraps his arms around my hips, stilling my movements and pulling me tight against him to meet my mouth in a heated kiss.

We stay there for a short eternity, both of us catching our breaths. James touches his forehead against mine, a little chuckle making him shake beneath me. "Fuck, Sophie, I don't think I've dry humped a girl since high school. But damn, I don't think it was that good, even back then."

I smile, knowing he still can't see me, but the humor is obvious in my tone as I tease him back. "I'm betting this was your plan all along, Cowboy. Take the new girl to your special spot by the pond, get her buzzed, and hump the fuck outta her."

He laughs, stroking my back with work-roughened but still gentle hands. "That would've been a great plan. Wish I'd thought of it, but it seems to have worked out okay in the end."

It's surprisingly not awkward as we clean up, both of us knowing that if we stay out much longer, someone's going to start asking questions. Even as we walk back toward the house, it's a comfortable quiet, although judging by the way we're both walking, our jeans aren't quite as comfortable as they usually are.

James helps me into the truck, and I smirk at him, knowing he's going to check out my ass again. I'm expecting that, but I'm not expecting it when he gives my right cheek a nice smack as I get in.

"Oh, is that how you like it?" I ask, glaring at him. Still, I can see the playful grin on his lips, and I know I'm smiling too; it's obvious that everything's in good humor. "You want to smack my ass a bit, watch it jiggle back and pink up from your handprint?"

James's chest rumbles as he moves fast as a flash into the truck's doorframe, pressing his hips against my ass as he pulls me close again. "I could definitely be talked into it if that's what you want. I just wanted to show your curves a little love and appreciation, but right now, you just expanded my fantasy from last night to involve a little light spanking action."

He looks up, as if he's lost in a daydream, and I can't help but ask. "You were fantasizing about me? Tell me more."

James steps back a little, enough for me to turn around, before he answers, "Last night, as you were leaving, I pictured ripping your jeans down to your boots—enough to let me in but keep your legs locked together so you could grip me tight. Then I'd bend you over this old truck seat and fuck your pussy from behind until you screamed my name."

My breath rushes out of me in a whoosh, and I'm glad the porch light is on and it's still early enough someone might be awake inside. "Damn. I'm glad you didn't say that last night, because I just might've let you."

He moves in close, cupping my neck and looking in my eyes. "Well, I told you now. How about tonight? Trust me, I've still got enough in me to make you scream my name."

Before I can answer, there's a loud bang as the screen door on the house closes. Our gazes snap to the door, and Luke sheepishly waves. "Hey, you two. Just heading home."

He ducks his head, striding quickly out of sight.

"Where's home?" I ask, almost surprised. "I sorta imagined you all lived here in the big house."

Realizing the moment has passed, James lets go of my neck and steps back, gesturing off to his left, toward the road. "We've got bedrooms here . . . but Luke and I live out in the ranch-hand bunks right now. We don't have any this time of the year, so it gives us a sense of privacy that living with Mama doesn't. Mark's got a little trailer out on a back pasture since he lives here full-time."

I nod, letting my heartbeat slow. "So you and Luke don't live here full-time like Mark?"

"No, Mark's the good son who followed in Pops's footsteps with running the ranch," he says. "Luke is a half timer, here for a few weeks, and then he's off taking a horse to show or to breed. Sometimes he's even gone for weeks at a time if he's got a training contract. This is his home base, and his horses are here, but he's in and out pretty regularly. I'm gone most of the year . . . big rodeo season runs January to April, then fall circuit to finals in Vegas a couple of weeks before Thanksgiving."

"Vegas? So you're riding most of the year?"

James shrugs. "Been that way since I was eighteen. Come home in the summer to help some, but this year that was even more important since Pops passed in April. Hard to believe it's really just been mere weeks, but as he always said, 'The work must go on!'"

"Do you really believe that?" I ask, and James sighs.

"He was old-school like that. Keep on keepin' on, no matter what, and he'd expect nothing less from us. Yeah, there's still a big chunk of hurt inside . . . but we're working through it."

"I'm sure he was proud of all three of you." There's a quiet moment, and I think James is reflecting, trying to decide if his father would actually be proud of him, and I realize something important in what he said. "So you're only here part-time too? You're going back to the rodeo in the fall?"

He must hear the flirty question in my voice because he looks at me before replying, "Yeah . . . sorta need to."

"Oh, that's just . . . good," I reply, hearing the lie in my voice even as it leaves my mouth. "I'm here for the summer, then back to school. You know, a summer internship."

He seems to catch my meaning, leaning in to give me a quick smack on the hip. "Just for the summer? Guess we'd better make it count then, huh? How about if tomorrow night, after you check on Briarbelle, we head into town, and I take you to dinner?"

I grin. "That sounds great. It's a date." I give him a saucy wink before continuing, "Oh, but FYI . . . I'll be dressed in work clothes for our date. It seems odd to change out here."

James laughs, nodding in appreciation. "What you're wearing now suits me . . . and you . . . just fine. And if you went and changed clothes out here . . . not gonna lie, I'd be peeking like a pervert, and we might never get to town."

He looks up and down my body one last time before he shuts the door, then thumps the doorframe twice, just to make sure I'm in tight. "Good night, Soph. I'll see you tomorrow. Even?"

I use two fingers to mime him walking into the house and reply, "Even."

I watch him walk inside before starting the truck and pulling a U-turn in the yard to head home. My brain races the whole drive, whirling in ways I never expected.

Wow, what just happened?

My initial impression of James was obviously wrong; he's been nothing but a gentleman since that first argument. And God, he's so hot! I don't think I've dry humped a guy in years, but I came harder with him than I have from full-on sex.

Best of all, he seems okay with a short-term deal and wants to take me out. I'm calling this day a ten on a scale of ten.

Helloooo, summer of my dreams.

CHAPTER 8

JAMES

Mama is pleased when I tell her that Sophie and I won't be at dinner because we're heading into town for a date and is blabbing to Mark and Luke before I even have a chance.

Of course, this means my brothers have to spend the rest of the day teasing and bugging the shit out of me about it. Luke gets started first as the three of us unload bags of feed for the horses before mucking out the stalls and laying down fresh hay.

"She gonna be a Bennett Babe now?" Luke asks as he sets down another fifty-pound sack of feed from the ATV trailer. "Just a tip, little brother . . . ladies like the ride to last quite a bit longer than the eight seconds you're used to. You up for the challenge or you gonna blow it too soon?"

Mark grunts, setting down the pitchfork that he's using to get the dirty hay out of the stalls. He even harrumphs a little, which for him is practically falling down in the dirt and rolling around laughing while holding his sides. He gets his own jab in. "I'll tell you, she seems like a nice kid."

"Kid?" I ask. "You need to get your eyes checked. She's all woman, Mark."

"Speaking of being blind, not sure what she'd see in a shit like you, but I guess everyone's got to go mucking about a time or two."

He winks, so I know he's not being serious. It's just his way . . . staid and serious, always in control and responsible for everyone and everything around him.

I drop my last bag and flip them both off. "Just for that, you two can play Dorothy in the barn. I'm gonna go check on the herd."

Mark gives me a wave while Luke laughs. I find the herd right where they're supposed to be, safely roaming in the pasture now that I'm done repairing and checking the fence. I spend most of the day just watching the sun race across the sky, biding my time until four o'clock when Sophie is supposed to be here. My watch beeps me a warning, and I head back quickly, tapping my horse into a loping trot I'm so eager.

"You know, I definitely prefer the horse," Sophie teases as I give her a quick kiss hello. "Something about seeing you trot along on horseback."

We go in for a quick check on Briarbelle and her still-unnamed foal, both of which are doing just fine. In fact, it's barely four forty-five by the time Sophie's finished feeding Briarbelle her last cookie and we give them both a brushing.

We go to the barn sink, washing up. "Wait here. I'll go grab my keys, and we'll head out."

Sophie smirks, raising a finely sculpted eyebrow. "You don't want me to come into the house? I should at least tell Mama Lou hello. Or are you worried she is going to see what you've been gettin' yourself up to?"

I sigh, knowing that if she goes in the house, we'll never leave. "Yeah, you could go in and say hello, but I'd like to get on the road. Besides, Mama will probably pull out baby books or some shit and we'll never beat the dinner rush."

She laughs, a naughtily playful look on her face. "Baby books? With little James, all nekkid save for his cowboy hat? Now *that* sounds like fun."

She moves to walk past me toward the house, but I step in her way, blocking her with the width of my body. I'm not a huge man—guys who are built like linebackers don't do a good job riding bulls—but I'm a full foot taller than her, and my shoulders are near twice as wide as her narrow waist.

Her petite frame is dwarfed as I intentionally loom over her, and I drop my voice deeper and quieter as I bend down to rumble in her ear, "You'll have to get past me to get up to the house tonight, Soph. I aim to take you on a date, and it ain't in that house."

Sophie reaches up with her dainty hands, pats my chest, and steps back, still smiling. "Alright, Cowboy. No need to get all bossy . . . yet. I was just teasing, so you can save the alpha bit for later."

She winks, and I get the hint that she's not really teasing about that part—that she really would like for me to be a bit heavy-handed in certain situations.

Sophie smiles, pointing toward the house. "Go get your keys. I'm gonna grab some girly things in my truck. Don't worry; I'll be ready as quick as you are."

Somehow, I doubt any woman, especially one as beautiful as Sophie, can be ready for a date that quick, so I go a bit slow grabbing my keys. I even take a moment to stop by the bathroom, where I swig some mouthwash and squirt some deodorant under my pits. Nothing crazy, but I don't plan on smelling like a horse's ass for our date.

Somewhere from the back of the house, I hear Luke call out, "You two behave yourselves, don't do anything I wouldn't dooooo . . ."

I chuckle a bit, knowing that leaves me plenty of damn options. Luke's no choirboy; I'm sure he's done more than breed horses on some of his cross-country trips. But I don't respond, not wanting to encourage him. Instead, I grab a fresh shirt from the laundry room and pull it on, then step outside. Sure enough, as I step into the yard, Sophie is ready, standing next to her truck.

I stop on the porch, taking her in. I just saw her a minute ago, but in that quick flash, she's pulled her hair out of its ponytail, and a dark curtain falls in large waves down her back, her cheeks look a bit flushed, and her lips are rosier than they were. It makes me want to nibble at them like berries, see if they taste as ripe as they look.

Striding toward her, I can't help but notice her eyes traveling up and down my body. I usually think of my body in terms of whether it'll do what I need it to do. Mostly that means staying on a bull and doing it with just the right type of showboating that gets good scores from the judges. But I'm glad that she seems to like what she sees, and I can't help but puff up a bit.

Stepping into her space, I grasp a wave of hair that's running down the front of her shoulder dangerously close to her full breast and twist it around my fingertip. "Your hair's longer than I thought it'd be all free like that. So soft too . . . like silk. So much of you is like silk; I just want to explore it."

I hear her tiny intake of breath, and my eyes lock onto her mouth, pink lips parted in invitation.

"Thought you were ready to go, Cowboy?"

Her voice is breathy, obviously affected by me, and it urges me to make her lose her breath in other ways too. I dip my head to find she's farther down than I thought. I have to bend my knees, but I need to taste her lips. Slipping my hands around her waist, I lift her up to her toes to meet me in the middle and press my lips to hers, inhaling to take in her scent as I take her mouth.

Strawberries. I don't know if it's her lip gloss or her shampoo, or even some perfume she spritzed on, but it suits her and makes me want to devour her like a juicy berry in the summer, biting into her flesh and licking every sticky drop as it runs down my chin.

Sensing that we could easily get carried away right here in the driveway, I pull back, and she chases my mouth a bit until I'm out of her reach, too tall for her tiny self to reach.

"Mmm, delicious. I believe that is what the French call an amuse-bouche."

"And you know French *how?*" she asks, biting her lip. I'm so tempted to go back for another round, but I restrain myself, popping my elbow toward her like usual and escorting her to my truck to put her inside like the gentleman my Pops taught me to be.

"I'm full of surprises," I tell her. I close her door carefully, and I smile as she gives me a raised eyebrow.

This isn't like Doc's truck. I won my truck during last year's finals, and it's big and tough, but with touches of luxury. It's easy and comfortable as we head into town, stretches of pleasant silence broken up by little bits of conversation. There's a little humming noise from Sophie's side of the truck, and I realize she's quietly singing along to the country song on the radio, Lauren Alaina's "Road Less Traveled."

Wordlessly, I turn it up a little, and she smiles at me before diving right in and belting it. She knows every word and is singing them, loud and proud and with feeling into her imaginary microphone. She's got spirit, this girl, and knows how to throw herself into it even if she's not exactly professional level. Actually, if my truck sounded like her, I'd take it in for a tune-up.

I grin . . . a private concert in the cab of my truck. I don't think I've ever experienced that, especially since Mark and Luke can't carry a tune in a bucket. Sophie's enjoyment is infectious, though, and I can't help but sing along since I know nearly every word of the popular hit too. We hold the last note for as long as possible but give in before it ends, dissolving in laughter.

I give her a little side-eye, turning the radio down as Rascal Flatts comes on. "You know what, Soph? You can't sing for shit, but that might have been the best concert I've been to."

She reaches across and shoves my shoulder, sticking out a very pink and very kissable tongue. "Yeah, I can't carry a tune, but after a few drinks, nobody in the karaoke bars seems to mind."

I laugh, betting she's probably right and that if she was onstage singing off-key, I probably wouldn't notice either since all my focus would be on her other assets. "Okay, I'll let you get away with that."

"You can actually sing, though, Cowboy," she says. "I'm surprised."

I grin back at her, giving her a devilish little wink. "I have all kinds of skills that'll surprise you."

She lifts one eyebrow at me, humming. "I've seen some of them."

"I've got more."

Sophie laughs, leaning back in her seat. "I bet you do."

Before I know it, we're already in town. I park the truck and shuffle around to the passenger side to let her out, grabbing her hand this time as we walk up to the best steak house in town.

A few minutes later, we're seated in some nice window seats and nursing a pair of beers, a local draft that doesn't go too froufrou. "What do you think?"

"Not bad," Sophie says, "but I have to admit, I liked the Negra Modelos last night more. I like the ambiance, though, and I'm looking forward to dinner."

I laugh, teasing her a little. "I'm glad you're not vegetarian. It didn't occur to me until Mama pulled out her food the other night that you might be vegetarian."

"Nope. I definitely try to get in plenty of rabbit food, but I'm not going to turn down a fresh-grilled steak, chicken, or fish," Sophie replies. "Or sushi. Or . . . well, much of anything. Jake and I even survived on Hamburger Helper for nearly a year before he figured out how to cook even the basics, and I crave it on occasion when I'm feeling nostalgic or need comfort food. Seriously, some people do chicken noodle soup when they're sick; just bring me some Hamburger Helper covered in Kraft powdered parmesan. But normally I'm adventurous with my food, willing to try anything once."

I wonder if she understands how even the little things she says have double meanings for me, some sweet, some dirty. "Does that adventurous streak extend to other areas of your life, or just cuisine?"

Sophie smirks, and I know the answer. She knows exactly what she's doing, and she's enjoying the hell out of it. "Oh, I'd say it depends on my mood. Sometimes I'm game for just about anything. Other times, I just hole up with a book and don't interact with humanity for days at a time. Better known as college life. Guess that's over for a minute, though, until vet school starts up, and then it'll be hard-core hitting the books again."

The playfulness drops from her voice by the end, and I'm reminded that she's right. Come fall, she's going to school, and I'll be back on the circuit. "Sometimes I wonder if I could have ever fit into that life," I say. "I went from the ranch to the circuit and never looked back. Been competing since I was a kid and went pro as soon as I was eligible. Honestly, knowing my personality, I'd have flunked out of classes at normal schools."

She tips the neck of her beer bottle at me, giving me a microtoast. "You'd be surprised. By the way, I want you to know, Doc told me to Google you, see what you were all about. I couldn't, though; I decided I wanted to know from the source. So, tell me all about James Bennett, Rodeo Star."

This is common ground, what every reporter asks me any time I get interviewed. But the person asking me is no reporter, and I know I'll let Sophie in a little more.

"Well, like I said, I've been competing since I was a kid. I started out on the county-fair circuit, moving my way up as I got older. I went pro at eighteen, right after I finished high school. I've ridden pro for the last eight seasons, with some decent results. Last season I placed in the top five at finals, and I think I could have gotten top three if my bull had been a bit better."

"What do you mean?"

I smile, reminding myself that while Sophie might know animals, she doesn't know rodeo. "Okay, thirty-second explanation. There are four judges, all watching me and the bull. They award each of us scores between one and twenty-five. The bull's four scores are added up and divided in half, with a total hopefully close to fifty. If I stay on the full eight seconds, my four scores get added and divided the same way, also hoping for up to fifty points. The bull's score and mine are added together for a final overall score for that ride. In round three of finals week last year, I drew a bull I thought would be great. Turned out he wasn't ready to fight that night, so I ended up number six."

"So how long do you plan to keep doing this?" Sophie asks. "Seems dangerous."

I nod, knowing she's right. "Yes, but I still plan to ride until I'm too old or they tell me I can't anymore. Which means I need to leave in late August to catch the fall circuits, make sure I'm in good competing shape physically and mentally for finals in November."

Sophie chuckles, sipping her beer. "Wow, that was very . . . practiced. You rehearse those sound bites in the mirror, Cowboy? Now tell me . . . why do you try to kill yourself via bull for shits and giggles?"

I laugh, but she's right; I slipped into my PR replies out of habit, and something about Sophie makes me want to give her more. I take a deep breath, making sure I shift my mind out of interview mode. Our steaks come, and it gives me another chance to calm myself, say things the way I really want to.

"It's not quite as suicidal as it sounds or looks. There's a science to it, but it's more an art. We get to know the bulls, and they know the riders; we read each other, trying to predict which way the other is going to go. It's like a dance, but instead of one leading the other so that it looks graceful, one is trying to lead the other through rip-roaring chaos, and it's up to the rider to find some elegance in the battle. That's why I do it, I guess. It's a challenge and it's fun."

Sophie is looking at me, hanging on my every word, so I continue, "Back when I was a kid, I always had all this . . . energy, I guess. Yeah, energy and chaos inside, and I always gave Mama and Pops fits, climbing trees so I could jump out, racing the train on my bike, never sitting still for even a second. But when I sat on the back of a creature with the same chaos but amplified with so much more power and I conquered it, it made me feel like I could conquer my own wildness too. When I ride, I feel centered and focused.

"When I don't get to ride for a bit, don't focus on my training, I have a tendency to get a bit lost. When I was a teenager, I got into trouble around town. Nothing major, just backfield parties that got a little rowdy or mudding through fields that didn't belong to me."

Sophie laughs. "I can see that. Teenaged James Bennett getting dragged home by the town sheriff and Mama dragging you in the house by your ear. What about now? You still get into trouble in the off-season?"

I shake my head, proud of what I'm going to say next. "No, not too much time off duty now. When you're in your prime age, you're fighting for the podiums, and if you're lucky enough to get there, you're fighting to put on a good show every night and keep the streak going. It's hard work, and you go in realizing that even on your best night, you might have only two or three scored rides in at most seven chances. Some nights you might only have one, so you have to make it count. Plus, the last couple of seasons, I sent a lot of my earnings back home to help out. Pops swore they didn't need it, and Mark even agreed that they were doing just fine, but it felt like the right thing to do."

"You've got nothing for yourself?" Sophie asks, and I shake my head, smiling.

"The only way I could get Pops to take dime one was to show him that I was saving some for myself. I fudged him a bit on some numbers to make him agree, but I'm doing fine. I've been able to put away a decent nest egg for when I'm done.

"Besides, I'm only able to help out here a few weeks a year now, so I figure my contribution to the ranch needs to pay for the ranch hand doing the work I'm supposed to do myself. It's the least I can do, and this is my way to help the family business. Somehow, riding bulls has helped me funnel that wildness, and now that I'm grown, I try to at least be responsible, even if I'm still a bit full throttle most of the time."

Sophie gives me an admiring look and takes another draw from her beer. "Well, you sound like you've got a little bit of Boy Scout in you after all, Cowboy. I'm not sure why Luke was teasing you about being a bad boy at dinner."

She looks at me skeptically, and I shrug. "Well, the circuit's not exactly known for being gentlemanly. It's more like a moving frat house with a brotherhood in Wranglers instead of popped collars, surrounded by what we call buckle bunnies. It's a bit unruly and, I'll admit, a bit like Candyland for an eighteen-year-old boy. I told Luke about some of my misadventures that first season, and he's never let me forget about it."

Sophie nods sagely, giving me an appraising look. "Perhaps a bit wild after all, then."

It's like I'm under a microscope, and for the first time in a long time, I want to pass inspection. It's weird, and I shift around in my seat. "I feel like I've been rambling all night. You done?"

Sophie takes one last gulp of her beer, finishing it off before nodding. "Yep, and I'm thinking I got a bit more insight than a Google search would've given me. Feel free to ramble away anytime."

I throw a few bills on the table to cover the meal and tip, and we head out. I take a side street out of town, driving toward Outlook Point.

It's to the north of town, on the way toward the resort area, but it's got some great views of town about halfway up the mountain.

I haven't been up here with a girl since high school, and I'm praying it's deserted on a weeknight, because I'm not ready to take Sophie home just yet.

CHAPTER 9

SOPHIE

It doesn't take me long to realize we're not exactly driving out the same way we came in, but I don't say anything. My interest in how things are going with James overrides my curiosity at what he has planned for our date. Besides, he's been honest and open. He could have lied, said he was a choirboy on the rodeo tour and that Luke's full of shit. He didn't, and if he only knew the details about my past, he'd understand he doesn't need to worry. I'm not one to judge.

We drive through a copse of trees and pop out the other side to a stunning view to our left, and James pulls off into a small field, driving forward until I can see all of Great Falls spread out beneath us. I lean forward in my seat, a delighted "Oh my . . ." escaping my mouth before the seat belt pulls me back. "Ow."

James reaches over and unclicks my belt as he puts the truck in park. "Come on. I want to show you something."

I giggle, leaning against my door and smiling. "I bet you say that to all the buckle bunnies."

He ducks his head, and I think I've stung him a little. Maybe there's a hint of truth in my teasing, but I honestly doubt James is the same kid who partied a bit too hard a few times at eighteen. I don't care if he is a bit wild, honestly. This is just for fun, even if I am more interested in James than I have been in anyone in a very long time.

His country-boy charm is damn sure working on me, especially when partnered with his lean, muscled body, occasional streak of growly bad boy, and teasing nature. He's one of the first men in a while who challenges me, and I respect that. He's a gentleman, a rogue, country smart, and sexy as fuck. All topped off with a sweet hat when he rides his horse.

And judging by the hard ridge of his cock I felt as I rode him last night, I want to get an up-close-and-personal visit with what's filling out those tight jeans he wears.

He lowers the tailgate on the truck and places his hands on my hips to help me hop into the bed. I realize that his hands nearly span the circumference of my waist; they must be huge. My waist's definitely narrow—I'm pretty petite—but I think the comparison more aptly highlights just how large his hands are.

I get lost for a moment, thinking about how those big hands could hold me just right, cupping my tits or my ass, his thick fingers filling my pussy.

He spreads a puffy, plaid sleeping bag out in the bed before sitting and pulling me down beside him.

"Not much a view of the city sitting down here," I say.

"It's beautiful," James admits, "but I think the natural sky is far better."

I look up to the sky, the darkness stretching far and wide above us, broken up by little sparks of stars. He's right; there's nothing here to distract from the light show Mother Nature is putting on overhead. "Wow. It's so gorgeous out here. You don't get to see the stars like this in the city. Even at the ranch, there's a little bit of light pollution."

James nods, putting an arm around my shoulders. "Tell me about the city, about your life there. Seems only fair after I told you about growing up on the ranch and rodeo. Even?"

He winks, and I can't help but giggle a little at what's quickly becoming "our joke." "Well, as a kid I grew up in a good-size house in the suburbs when my parents were with me. It was nice . . . trees, went to school with all the kids on our street, just a normal childhood.

"After . . . well, Jake moved me to a tiny apartment in the city to save money while he got his businesses up and running. Slowly but surely, he became more successful, and we moved up a notch every few years.

"Ultimately, we lived in a penthouse condo in the middle of downtown by the time I was in high school. It was my time to get a bit spoiled, even if Jake never is willing to admit it. He did a good job, changing his plans in ways I couldn't even understand at the time but always protecting me and guiding me. Somehow, he managed to stay my brother, even though he had a fatherly role for a lot of years."

James rubs my shoulder, and his voice is warm. "He sounds like a good guy. Must be to have raised you."

I nod, leaning against James and running my hand over his chest idly, enjoying the interplay of his muscles underneath the soft cotton of his shirt. "He is, and he put up with a lot. Like I said, I wasn't always the easiest teenager to look after. But I went to college, also in the city. So, my sum-total experience with country life had been on field trips and lab classes until last summer, when I worked on a ranch owned by one of my professors. I spent the summer there, just shadowing him mostly and being annoying with the number of questions I asked."

"And that changed you into a country vet?" James asks. "Brave."

I laugh, running my hand lower, over his stomach, and enjoying the feeling of his taut six-pack. "I guess. But something about being outside, far from the hustle and bustle of city life, just feels right. I wasn't expecting it—goodness knows Jake was expecting something totally different from his prissy little sister—but it's . . . home. In my spirit, it's home."

"I daresay we know how to hustle and bustle out here in the sticks too," he says, his fingers trailing over my shoulder, rubbing slowly and softly, making the heat in my body build without ever being lewd. "We gotta hustle to keep the ranch afloat, and there's always work to be done."

I nod, pressing my thigh against his and feeling more of his warmth. "You're right, but it's different here. There's a list of things that need to be accomplished, and at the end of the day, you can tell you've done a good job by the weariness in your bones, the happy sounds your animals make as they settle in for the night. And you know how to slow down, too, to enjoy a good meal and good conversation, or just the simple pleasure of sitting in a place like this. In the city, it's never-ending, and it's more like a rat on a wheel. People in the city are busy just to stay busy—no real reason other than that. Not better or worse, just different."

"So, now what?" James asks, his hand slipping lower and pulling me closer. "What's your next step?"

I'm slightly distracted, thinking about the steps I want to take in the next two minutes, but that's just part of the buildup I'm learning to enjoy. "Intern with Doc for the summer, then head back for vet school in the fall. It'll take me three years of mostly classwork, then one year of clinical before I can take the licensing test. I definitely want to work with large animals, so probably try to do as much clinical work as I can and assist vets like Doc, who work ranches, or maybe like the vet that travels with the rodeo. After that, I guess I'll see where I can do the most good, where I feel most at home. It'll be a while, and I'll be starting my real work older than some people, but I'm lucky. I've found what I really want to do."

James makes an approving sound, and for some reason I'm happy he seems to like my plan, not calling it a crazy dream or a wild goose chase like some people have. "Sounds like you've got it all figured out. Girl with a plan. I like that. Can't say I've ever been accused of having a plan, but I can appreciate that you do."

I grin, turning to place my hand on his belt buckle, which despite the stereotype isn't huge and brass. The huge, hard thing's a few inches lower. "Oh, I think you make plans, consciously or subconsciously. Did you think I didn't notice how you got me alone in the dark up here, in the bed of your truck with a blanket? That seems like a definite plan, I'd say. What's step two in your devious plan, Cowboy?"

He moves in, crowding me and urging me to lie down against the cushion of the sleeping bag in the truck bed, the long line of his legs stretched out alongside mine as he props himself on one elbow beside me.

His blue eyes smolder as he looks intently at my face, and I can't help but tempt him as I bite my lower lip.

"Step two?" James asks, cupping my face. "This . . ."

He leans down, meeting my lips with gentle, unyielding power, not devouring me yet but letting me know he's the man with the plan here. I'm thrilled to go along with him, giving myself over to him. He licks along my lower lip, and I open for him, letting him inside to tangle our tongues together.

I feel a vibrating tingle in my hands and realize that I've balled his shirt up in my fist and that he's moaning, rumbling through his chest as I pull him tighter to me. Apparently, while my mind is happy to play along, my body isn't quite ready to give James full control.

My body is demanding, wanting, needing more, and I whimper, licking his lip plaintively. James understands and moves his lips down, kissing and licking along my jawline, down the curve of my neck, and turning my whimper into a whine of desire. His free hand is busy, too, working my shirt up, exposing my belly to the warm night air.

I flinch as his fingertips brush along my ribs, tickling me for a split second before he cups my bra-covered breast, all ticklish thoughts evaporating as I arch into his touch. "Yessss . . ."

James lifts up, propping himself above me and pinning me beneath him. "Fuck, Soph, I need to see you."

I lift up slightly, letting him slip my T-shirt over my head as I reach behind my back to unclasp my bra. James lifts it off, slipping it down my arms, leaving me topless and exposed to his look, his touch. I feel sexy, powerful, and vulnerable all at the same time, a heady mix that intensifies with every heartbeat.

"You're beautiful," James says, glancing down at my breasts with their caps of pink nipples. "They're even yummier looking than I imagined, already hard and ready for me."

He reaches a thumb toward me, my nipple tightening up even more in anticipation as he strums lightly across the nub. I gasp, pulling him down as he rumbles throatily, ducking his head down to hungrily suck my breast into his mouth, drawing deeply as his tongue flicks across my nipple.

I inhale, arching my chest up to him, silently begging for more, before I give in and do it out loud. "Oh God, James . . . more . . . please."

He lifts up, reaching behind his neck to rip his shirt over his head before lifting my leg to reposition himself between my thighs. I spread wider to give him room before bending my knees to grip his torso, locking him in place against me as my hips buck with a mind of their own.

"You gonna rub that hot little pussy on me again?" James challenges me, pinching my nipple again and pulling lightly. "That's fine; take what you need, darlin'. But don't come. You don't come until I'm there to taste your sweetness as you come on my face."

I groan at his words, wanting his tongue right now, running my fingers through his hair to pull at him, direct him lower. Instead he holds his position, returning his mouth to my other breast, licking and nibbling as he drives me wild with want.

For a moment I think that I might come just from his ministrations to my breasts, it's that good, especially as I writhe against him—something about him holding me in place by the weight of his body doing delicious things to me. My pussy is throbbing, electrically chafed by my panties and jeans as I grind against him, desperate for more, desperate for skin-to-skin contact.

Just when I'm on the edge of losing my mind, he moves lower, nipping along the waist of my jeans as he undoes them and pulls them down. I toe my boots off, dropping them to the side with a thud and at the same time shimmying as I help him ease the tight denim of my jeans down and off.

I reach for my panties, too, eager to take them off as well, but James seems to have another plan. He lifts my legs, bringing me up until his face is inches from my panty-covered mound, inhaling my scent through the soaked fabric and humming in appreciation as he runs a finger along the wetness. "Even your sex smells good. Real. Intoxicating."

He blows an openmouthed, hot breath of air across me, and even in the warmth of the night air, the heat penetrates me, and I whimper, begging him for more.

"You ready, Soph? God, I need to taste you. I need to know if you taste like strawberries here too."

"Please . . ." I whimper, desperate. "Please, I need your tongue."

He nuzzles his nose against my cotton-covered clit for a split second before giving in to my original plan and pulling my panties down my legs. Before they're even all the way off, James is devouring me, licking with his broad, flat tongue in a long line that goes all the way from the bottom of my pussy to my clit. Fire and heat drip from his lips as his tongue rasps along my clit, rocking me hard. It's electric heaven, and I cry out, grasping for his head to make him do it again.

Whether my plan or his, he consumes my pussy with eager strokes of his tongue, pausing to leave light kisses along my soft folds and lapping up every drop as I get wetter and wetter.

James gets to his knees and, sitting back on his heels, pushes my bent legs open wide. It feels naughty, wanton, to be naked in the moonlight while he's still mostly dressed, and I fight the urge to spread them wider. I'm normally reserved, actually, but something about James makes me want him to see me, to drive him crazy like he's doing to me.

He smiles dreamily as he traces a fingertip along my inner thigh, and I slide my hips, hoping he'll slip it inside me, fill this emptiness in my pussy, so I have something to clench against.

He pauses at my entrance, teasing me with little strokes that have me whimpering in need again. "Is this what you want? You want me to fill your hungry little pussy with my fingers . . . or do you want my cock?"

The idea of his cock makes my body shiver in anticipation, and I grab the back of my knees, not caring if I look like a nympho or not. "Yes . . . God, yes."

James chuckles, reaching for his belt. "Hmm, that was an either-or, not a yes or no. Guess it's my choice. And I choose . . ."

I'm writhing, begging for his cock, knowing he'll tear me apart and I'll love every second of it. "Oh fuck, James . . . please . . ."

Without warning, he thrusts his finger inside me. I'm shocked, and before I can say anything, he pulls out before pumping two fingers this time, creating a pounding rhythm that makes my walls quiver. "Fuck . . . James!"

James's fingers never stop, and his voice is laced with the steely tones of command as he looks in my eyes. "Hold it, Sophie. Don't come yet. I can feel your tight pussy fluttering against my fingers, but wait. I'll make it worth it . . . right to the edge, but not yet."

He curls his fingers, rubbing me in a way that has me barely holding on before he touches his tongue back to my clit, swirling it in tiny circles that light my nerve endings on fire.

I grab handfuls of the sleeping bag, trying to ground myself to space, to time, to this moment because I'm floating away. The sparks behind my closed eyelids are no longer the bright stars of the night sky but flashes as the electricity races from my pussy through my whole being.

I cry out, warning him or asking permission, I'm not sure which, "Jaaaames . . ."

He growls into my clit, never losing pace with his punishing rhythm. "Do it, Soph. Come for me. Now."

And I explode, or implode . . . I don't know. All I know is that I've never felt anything like this before.

Whatever I thought good sex, a good orgasm, was before is nothing compared to what James does with two fingers and his tongue.

Fuck.

I'm thrashing about, trying to catch my breath and come back to Earth as I feel swept away again and again. I only come back when I realize James is leaning over me, an arm on each side of my face, watching every expression that crosses my face. "You're beautiful," he whispers. "Watching you . . . beautiful."

Feeling a little more whole, I smile dreamily at him, and he bends down to cover my mouth in a kiss. I taste myself on his tongue, and it turns me on even more. He sits back, bringing his fingers to his mouth to lick and suck them clean, stoking the heat inside me again as he moans in appreciation.

Everything about him is hot, and even though I'm still recovering, I'm ready to return the favor. I move to sit up, running my hands down his bare chest to his button, but he stops me. "Soph, tonight was about you."

"What?" I ask, and he nods. "But what about you?"

He shakes his head softly, smiling. "The best rides are the ones where you let the anticipation build. Besides, I don't want you to think I'm an easy lay."

I laugh, stroking his face. "You're terrible."

"Never claimed otherwise," he says, still smiling. "I did find out *almost* everything I wanted to know about you tonight, though."

"What do you still want to find out?" I ask.

He looks at my pussy, obviously in appreciation, and takes a deep inhale as he shudders. "Not yet . . . soon. But I need to know . . . what are you doing tomorrow night?"

CHAPTER 10

JAMES

The heat beats down outside as I take a quick minute for a sandwich lunch in the shady barn with Mark and Luke. Mama's always made good sandwiches, and preparing lunch in advance gives her a chance to go to town during the days to get her errands done. As the corned beef with Dijon mayonnaise hits my tongue, I moan happily.

My feet are propped on the desk in the corner even though Mark gave me an evil eye about daring to disturb his desk like this, but fuck it. It's not really *his* desk; it's a table that we keep the written details about barn stuff at.

"So, you going to start charging Sophie money for parking Doc's truck here all the time?" Luke jokes. "Or are you collecting payments in other ways?"

"I might be a bit of a shit," I reply, sipping on a big glass of iced tea, "but you know I'm not the type to kiss and tell." I answer Luke, but I look at Mark and give him a big wink.

Mark relaxes a little. He always does when I needle him; I think it's one of the reasons I do it so much. "Luke, I think our little brother is full of more bullshit than the east pasture."

"Kiss my ass," I laugh, reaching for my sandwich. "I'm keeping my trap shut, so you two gossip queens can go pound sand in your ass with your questions."

We laugh, and in the laughter I feel good. They're not jealous; it's just fun and what we do.

In a quiet moment, Mark's ear perks up a split second before we hear it too . . . a truck pulling down the drive. "You expecting Sophie early today?"

I shake my head, finishing off my sandwich. "Not until late this afternoon like usual. You?"

Mark glances at Luke, who shakes his head. "Not expecting anyone here either."

We all get up and line up in the opening of the barn door to see a shiny silver four-door dually. It veers toward the barn, spraying rocks a little as the driver hits the brakes a bit hard. The door opens, and we relax a bit, seeing that it's Paul Tannen, the owner of the neighboring ranch.

The Tannens and our family have had a decent relationship over most of my life. I wouldn't call Mr. Tannen and Pops friends, but where our lands touch, we've cooperated, splitting the costs of fence maintenance and on the rare occasions when something wanders one way or another across the line, giving a call and bringing it back. I haven't seen him since getting back, but like I said, he's a decent neighbor, not a friend.

Mark steps forward, offering a handshake. "Good afternoon, Mr. Tannen. Good to see you. Didn't recognize your truck; get a new ride?"

Mr. Tannen shakes each of our hands with a nod of greeting before answering Mark. "Sure did. Sweet little cherry on top of a shit sundae, I'd say. Right about the time we got the check for selling off this year's crop, which was dang good, if I say so myself, my son's truck died. Passed him down my old one; it'll get him at least another hundred thousand, I think, unless he drives it like he did the last one. And I got a new ride out of the deal. Wanna take a look?"

We all shrug, heading over because like most any men, we'll happily take a look at a truck, discuss towing capacity and horsepower as we ooh and aah over cushy seats and a good stereo.

"I see you put a fifth-wheel hitch in," Luke says. "Gonna use this for your horse trailers?"

"That's the plan," Paul agrees. "Now, my horses aren't as fine a line as yours, I'll admit. But they're strong and dependable. Good stock."

There's a lull in truck talk, and Paul jumps in. "Look, I didn't come over just to brag on my new truck today. I was hoping to catch you, Mark. But all three of you boys might be even better."

I read his tone of voice right away. Looking over at Mark, who has assumed his fuck-off stance, feet spread wide, shoulders down and back, and arms crossed over his chest, I see he's reading the same vibe I am.

Luke rolls his lips, hooking his thumbs in his belt loops and intentionally leaning against Paul's truck. He makes it look casual, but I know Luke; he's rattlesnake quick and can turn a man's lights out in one second from here. I keep my own arms crossed like Mark, deferring to him since he's the eldest, his role in the ranch more clearly defined. Mark rumbles, his voice dangerously low, "What's up, Paul?"

Paul puffs up his chest and says his piece. "Boys, I'm real sorry about your Pops passing on like he did. He was a damn fine man and a good rancher." He pauses, but Mark merely dips his head in acknowledgment. Seeing he's not cracked us yet, he continues, "This ranch meant everything to him, and you know as well as I do that he'd want to see it successful long after he's gone. I've got the funds and the crews to keep it running top-notch, and I'm interested in buying the land, even the cattle if you want."

I can feel my heart jump into my throat . . . we're not selling the BB Ranch. This is our land, our family home! Our own father dies underneath the tree in the front yard, and this motherfucker wants to just buy us out like this land has no meaning to us?

I hold on to my temper and tick my eyes over to Mark. I'm relieved, seeing that he's clenching his teeth and there's a coiled tension throughout his body. "And?"

"I tried to talk to Louise about it, but she wouldn't hear it at the time. Admittedly, it might've been a bit too soon, but I didn't know if you'd be in crisis mode or not, and I wanted to offer a neighborly deal to ease her mind if need be," Paul says, trying to sound like he's doing us a favor.

I can't take this anymore and interrupt his sales pitch, because that's what this is. All his niceties and neighborly care, it's just a façade so he can slick his way into buying us out, even taking advantage of a widow in her time of mourning. "We're not selling. This is our home. Not interested," I spit, fire and anger in my voice. "Anything else?"

I try to say it with finality, but Tannen knows I'm not the de facto family spokesperson here—Mark is. Mark looks at Luke and me before returning his hard look to Paul. His voice is civil and firm. "Paul, we appreciate your consideration, but it's not necessary. My brother's right. I assure you that we are doing just fine here and have no plans to sell our property in the near or distant future."

Paul looks taken aback a bit. I guess he thought we were going to be easy targets, or maybe it's just Mark's obvious coldness.

Still, he's got a hard-on for this sale, and isn't quite ready to give up yet. "Well, I understand how hard it can be to let go of family ties. You boys just remember that your Pops is not in this land; he's in your hearts, and he'll be with you anywhere you go, especially with money in your pockets and knowledge that his land is well cared for. You be sure to let me know if you change your mind and want to discuss some figures."

Every word sounds right, but there's an oiliness underlying them, belying his scavenger nature as he tries to take advantage of our unexpected loss. Luke speaks for the first time, looking up with ice in his eyes. "We'll do that."

Tannen touches the brim of his hat with a fingertip, nodding his chin down once in goodbye. Right before he gets in his fancy new truck, he turns and addresses us. "Make sure you tell Louise hello for me. Been a minute since I've seen her. Hope she's doing okay with all this stress and sadness. Lovely woman, your Mama. Hate to see her torn to pieces with all this . . ."

He gestures vaguely to the land surrounding us, then ducks into the truck to pull a U-turn out and head down the drive. We stand stock-still, statues until he crests over the hill out of sight. I barely resist the urge to chase the fucker down and beat the shit out of him for his disrespect and, hell, for even saying Mama's name like that, like he has some personal connection with her.

As he disappears, just a cloud of dirt remaining, we turn on each other. "What the fuck was that?" I ask. "What gives that fucking snake even a hint we might not be doing fine?"

Luke's voice is softer but no less intense as he grabs Mark's arm and looks in his eyes. "*Are* we doing okay?"

Mark looks skyward for a second, seeming to gather himself as he pulls his hat off and runs a big hand through his short hair, which makes me freeze. He's always calm and collected, so this must have set him on edge too.

"Mark?"

He resets his hat and pulls free of Luke's grip. "We're fine. I was already doing most of the business side even before Pops died; he was never much for numbers and spreadsheets. But the ranch has been running smooth and in the black for years, a little up and down some years, but always in the black. We don't need to sell unless we want to, and I can tell you right now . . . I don't want to, and I'm not."

He eyeballs both of us, daring us to say we want to sell. I can't speak for Luke, but as for me, I told Tannen the truth. "Hell no, I don't want to sell. Of course not."

Luke nods. "Me neither. I know I'm here and gone, but this is where I come back to every time. No way."

Mark looks around at the two of us, and for the first time in a while, I see a hint of a smile cross his face. "I didn't think so. But what worries me more is that he said he'd talked to Mama about this before. Either of you know about that? Because I sure as hell didn't."

Luke and I shake our heads. All three of us meet eyes for a moment before turning as one and marching toward the house. Mama should be back from town by now.

Busting in the front door, we all bellow, "Mama!"

Not getting an answer, we look around for a moment before Luke disappears down the stairs leading to the cellar. "She's in the pantry, boys. Mama . . . come on out here for a minute, please."

She comes up the old stairs, wiping her hands on an apron like I've seen her do a million times before, and it feels comforting. Everything's right in the world if your Mama can wipe her hands on her apron like nothing's wrong that a little bit of cleaning can't fix.

"What are you boys doing up at the house, yelling at me for? I've been downstairs for an hour, getting my jelly jars ready. Peach harvest's next month, and while our ranch doesn't have a lot, I do happen to like preserves on my toast come January."

Mark steps forward, ever the adult in any situation. "Paul Tannen from up the road just stopped by. Said some interesting things, made an interesting offer."

He leaves it hanging, waiting to see her take on Tannen's unscheduled appearance.

Mama's face says it all. "Ugh, that man. He's been a snake for thirty years—time ain't changed his scales. Never did see what Martha saw in that man, but I guess that's neither here nor there since she passed on when their babies were just little ones. John was polite with him, but he felt the same way I did."

It's been a bit since I've thought about the boys down the road, but once upon a time, we'd all been little hellions together. The three Bennett boys plus three Tannen boys more than once raised a little ruckus at Great Falls Elementary. I heard even their baby sister got up to shenanigans on occasion, but by then I'd stopped hanging out with them. They'd become jerks at an early age, and we drifted apart. The rift continued as we hung out with different crowds the rest of the way through school, even though we're the same age as a couple of the boys.

The last time I talked with any of them was when we mended a fence together, and it wasn't even working together. They just started at the south end of the fence while we started at the north, and we met in the middle. We exchanged barely a dozen words the whole time.

Funny how even in a small town, you can live in a different world from someone right down the street if your social circles never cross.

Mark, though, isn't totally placated. "He said he tried to buy the ranch from you? Why is this the first I've heard of it?"

Mama waves her hand, like Mark just "told a funny," like she says. "Pshaw. Boy, I didn't tell you because it wasn't no thing. I was in town, ran into him. He offered, I said no. That's it. Honestly, I was surprised he didn't try to sleep it out from underneath me."

We all flinch a little; nobody wants to think about their parents that way.

She smirks, reading my mind. "Relax, James. Like I said, your daddy never liked Paul either. Said he was always eyeballing me. I never noticed it, but John said no man should eyeball his wife, especially not in his presence, and expect to be friends with him afterward."

She laughs a little, wiping a stray tear from the corner of her eye. "He was a good man; always did right by me. I don't know if he ever said anything to Paul about it, but I know he was more than ready to knock that man's keister in the dirt if he got fresh."

Her attention refocuses on us, and she smiles. "I ain't sleeping the ranch away, and I ain't selling it away." She locks onto Mark, lifting an eyebrow. "We don't need to, right? You'd tell me if that were the case."

It's a statement, not a question, and we all know better than to keep secrets from her because she always finds out the truth somehow, and you pay twice as hard as if you'd been up front in the first place.

Mark nods, relaxing a hair. "Of course I would. We're fine, Mama."

She claps her hands, pleased. "Well, there you go. Crisis averted. Now you boys best get back to work. Sunlight's burning."

Dismissed, we walk back toward the barn as she disappears back into the cellar. Outside, though, we share our thoughts.

"I don't like it," Luke starts. "He saw us first today and made a beeline toward us to appeal his case. But what if we'd been out in the fields? Would he have propositioned Mama again . . . about the ranch? About more?"

Mark makes a grumpy noise, and I'm sure he's got thoughts along the same line as mine. Country justice is sometimes called for. "I don't like it either. Keep an eye out for his flashy truck. Give me a holler if you see him turning in our drive."

Luke nods. "Consider it done."

That settled, we all head back out from a decidedly longer lunch than we'd planned. My sandwich sits like a stone in my gut after all the drama. I don't like it, not one bit.

I wish I'd punched Tannen in his smug face when he offered to buy our ranch. Bet he wouldn't come back for another try after that.

And he can stay the fuck away from Mama. That's for damn sure.

CHAPTER 11

SOPHIE

I've been buzzing since waking up, on a high after my date with James last night. The way he maneuvered me, touched me, and made me come harder than ever before still leaves me shivering as I go about my duties with Doc, and more than once I've had to swallow the urge to just go monologuing about James.

There's a headiness to the way he mixes polite country-boy manners with that unique wildness that has me riled up, and I can't wait to see what he's planned for our second date. I haven't looked forward to a date like this in a long time.

Heading out to the parking lot of Doc's office, I decide to take a minute to freshen up. I can't do too much; it's hard to dress for a date when I'm going straight from working with animals to another barn. But I do take a minute to touch up my light makeup, slicking on the strawberry gloss he seemed to like and switching my dirty T-shirt for a tank top, still modest but sexy enough to show a little skin as it skims my curves.

As I drive out, the sun feels nice on my skin, and I'm humming with excitement. Everything's great . . . until I pull in the gate.

James is there like always, swinging the gate open, but he doesn't hop down from his horse to dip in the cab for a kiss like he did yesterday.

"Hey, something wrong?"

James half turns in the saddle and nods. "Nothin' you need to worry about. Just business and family stuff."

James is quiet as we get to the barn to check on Briarbelle and her foal. Both are still doing well, and I'm glad to see the baby is looking a little antsy even. At this point, I don't think they even need the antibiotics, but it's always best to finish the course. It'll also be good for mama and baby to get some time in a pasture, walking and playing like they're supposed to.

As I finish up my notes, James watches me, hands in his pockets and one boot heel cocked up on the stall railing. Still, there's a tension inside him that's impossible to miss. He's not comfortable with me right now, regardless of what he said about his mood being down to "business stuff." Maybe he's having some second thoughts after last night?

I thought things went well. Hell . . . way better than *well*. And I tried to reciprocate, but he didn't let me. Maybe that was for a reason?

Only one way to find out, I guess. I cap my pen and tuck it away, snapping my notebook closed. "So, we still going on that second date tonight?"

James startles, seemingly not even aware that I'm here. "Yeah, about that . . . can I get a rain check? Maybe we can go out tomorrow night, and tonight we can just do dinner here? It's been an interesting day."

I'm disappointed, but whatever. This is supposed to be casual, and maybe he really has had something of a day. I usually prefer a night out to rinse away the stress, but maybe that's not his style?

And he did specify tomorrow night for our date. So, while we've got a rain check, it's not a dismissal. He's not totally trying to blow me off with a "maybe sometime," and I don't know any sane man who would try to get rid of a girl by inviting her to have dinner with his family. So . . . it's all good, right?

"Sure, that's fine, I guess," I reply, trying to keep the disappointment out of my voice. James notices, and he at least looks a little chagrined, but says nothing as we walk toward the open doors. Along the way, I pause to pet each animal as we pass, unable to resist their neighs at the stall doors as they beg for some love and attention.

Near the door, I see a stunning huge chestnut stallion with a white diamond on his face, who wiggles his upper lip as I pet him. "He's beautiful. And a flirt, it looks like. Must be yours."

James walks over with a carrot, and for the first time today, I hear his voice soften a little. "That he is. I've been riding Cooper recently because my buddy here had a sore hoof. But this is Hunter, named because he's always hunting a treat and an unsuspecting person to charm out of said treat."

I take the carrot and feed it to him carefully. The stallion takes the treat with almost dainty movements before chomping down with a twinkle in his eye. "Seems to have his act down to a science, especially since it worked on us."

James smiles, but it doesn't reach his eyes. "He's . . . unique."

I try to take advantage of the opening to ask him what's wrong, but before I can, a loud bell sounds. I guess dinner's ready.

After washing up, all of us sit around the table, taking the same seats as we did before.

Luke and Mark share James's stony face, which while making for a tense dinner atmosphere, at least reassures me that James wasn't lying. Something's going down, and while it sort of sucks to not know what it is, I realize that it's probably not my business.

Mama Lou is a great host, though, passing around a serving dish piled high with slices of meat loaf followed by a big platter of freshly fried onion rings.

She gives me an amused look as the dish comes my way. "I grew these onions right out in the garden, you know? But I'll tell you a secret . . . I don't even like onions. That's why I fry them up. Everything tastes good battered in flour and fried in butter, even onions."

I laugh at her joke, but the guys all barely grunt. Well, okay then. I get things might be cloudy somewhere, but this food smells delicious.

"Well, I'll let you in on a secret of my own," I stage whisper back. "The only way I like onions is fried . . . or in a good meat loaf. So I guess we're both lucky tonight."

Dinner progresses as the conversation is mostly just between Mama Lou and me. Mark's especially grumpy, grunting more often than forming words, eating his dinner like he's in the army or something, head down and machinelike.

There's an odd tension brewing, too, and I wonder if it's because of my date with James last night. We were out late, and James must have slept in at least a little. I know I was dragging ass to pick up Doc on time, and my day starts a lot later than his.

All my thoughts or worries dissolve, though, as James sits back in his chair and slides a hand under the table to rest on my thigh. I resist the urge to jump, but the heat from his touch immediately makes my pussy wet, and that feels wholly inappropriate at Mama's dinner table.

His thumb starts drawing lines, no . . . shapes on my thigh, and I try to focus on what Mama Lou is saying, while at the same time trying to decipher what he's tracing.

"So, anyway, after digging out all my jars, I realized that I had a box that I hadn't opened yet. And lo and behold, there were my missing quart jars I thought I'd broken last year! I'd thrown a fit then, going out and buying new ones . . . well, of course I had to use them. So I did a test run. My friend Patricia brought over about five pounds of strawberries and blackberries that she grows wild on her property. Normally I put them in a pie, but I decided today to make a little bit of jam. So I sterilized a half dozen of the jars, and they're downstairs now. Tell Doc—"

In the middle of Mama's story, I finally realize what James is repeating: *S . . . J . . .* a star . . . and a heart. My heart stutters as my thighs clench. Fuck, I need him.

To look at him, you'd never know that his mind is rolling through last night. In fact, he's still just as tense as Mark and Luke, but somewhere inside, he is thinking about us, and that eases my nerves a bit.

Mama finishes her story, and I realize I've missed a question. "Sorry, what was that?"

"I asked if Doc would like blackberry or strawberry jam. Well, never mind, I'll send you back tomorrow with a jar of each. You just keep which one you like, and Doc can get the other. Now, who's up for dessert?"

Dinner finishes, and I half hope that James will want to walk down to the pond again. Maybe if we're alone, I can figure out what's bugging him and help him handle it . . . either directly or by distraction.

I'm sure I could come up with at least one or two ways to distract him, and only one or two of them involve me getting on my knees.

Instead, he escorts me back to Doc's truck in the drive, opening the door for me like usual. He presses a hand to the door and one to the cab, and I turn in the cage he's created for me.

Well, I guess I'm just going to have to try it the hard way. "You sure you're okay tonight, James?"

"I'm f—"

"Come on," I whisper, cupping his face. "Something's eating at you. Your brothers too. Mark was doing his best caveman impression all dinner, and even Luke wasn't his normal chatty self. I gotta ask . . . did I do something? Is there tension because of me?"

"You?" James asks, surprised. "Of course not. It's just . . ."

He sighs, looking down at his boot where he's grinding it in the dirt. "Okay, here's the deal. We had a so-called friend of the family and neighbor offer to buy the ranch today. Found out he'd made the same offer to Mama before, but she didn't tell anyone. We're all protective of her, and it kinda set us on edge."

I stroke my thumb across his cheek, the day's worth of stubble tickling my skin, and lift his chin to look in his eyes. "It's good that you three protect her. Does she want to sell? Do you guys?"

He hisses, stepping back like I just asked him if he wanted to quit rodeo to join a boy band. "Hell no. As the fucker drove off in his fancy truck, it was all I could do to not chase after him and punch him out."

I laugh a bit and step closer. "Well, then . . . no harm, no foul, as they say. This guy made an offer, you refused. Nobody got assaulted. Everyone goes about with their lives. Don't let it tear you up, Cowboy."

He grins, scratching his lip with his thumb in the way that draws my attention right to his mouth, and nods. "Maybe you're right, city girl. Just business, you say? I'm thinking we had some business planned for ourselves, and I've gone and mucked it up tonight."

I smile, kinda glad that he realizes that bailing on our date is a downer after I'd been excited all day. "Perhaps . . . but no harm, no foul."

James laughs quietly and pulls me in close, where I immediately feel warm and safe. "I tell you what. How about if I pick you up tomorrow at your place like a real date? Finish up with Briarbelle, and head home to get fancied up. A dress even; I bet you wear dresses better than any girl I've ever seen. I'll drive us up to the resort, and we'll eat like city folks. What do you say?"

Before I even think about it, I throw my arms around his neck and pop up onto my tiptoes to lay a smacking kiss on his lips. "That sounds lovely! Just to be clear . . . I was fine with our date by the pond and fine with the local steak house, too, but I'm not going to miss out on a chance to get dressed up and show off a bit for you, Cowboy. You're in trouble now."

He grins at me, his hands sliding down to cup my ass and hold me close enough to kiss some more. "I just bet I am, Soph. Something tells me that if I see you in a dress, bare legs exposed to my wandering hands,

I'm gonna want to shove you back in your house, and we'll never make it to the restaurant, but I bet I'm satisfied on dessert alone."

I bite my lip, shaking my head. "Yeah, I noticed those roaming hands at dinner tonight. But we're going on a date, and that's the bottom line. By the way, Mama Lou might not be okay with you getting me all wet at her dinner table."

He hums, pulling me flush to his hard body, my breasts squashing against his chest and sending tingles from my nipples to my pussy. "Your sweet little pussy was getting wet just from me putting my hand on your thigh? I wonder what would happen if I did this . . ."

Without warning, he squeezes my ass in his hands, pressing me against the side of Doc's truck, and I have no choice but to wrap my legs around him and hang on to his neck for dear life.

Not that I mind, especially as he attacks my mouth in a fiery kiss. I weave my fingers through his hair, thankful his hat has been hanging on the hook by the back door since dinner started. This is what I've been looking for all night, the intense passion and desire that James has shown me before.

Grasping his hair and pulling hard, I use the leverage to kiss him back as thoroughly as he is kissing me before nibbling along his jaw. Yes, this is what I want, to focus on and be the focus of this man's power and need.

He growls into my ear as he squeezes my ass hard, hopefully leaving his fingerprints to mark my flesh for the next couple of days. "How about now, Soph? Does your pussy want to be filled with more than my fingers? Fuck, I know I want more. I want to fill you up and have you scream my name, begging to come on my cock. You'll scream for me, right?"

"God, yes . . ." I moan, and he grinds his cock against me, bucking back and forth as he kisses me again. I swear I'm on fire from the inside, getting close to coming right here against Doc's truck in full view of the house in the dim light, fully dressed.

But that's what he does to me. In every touch of our skin, every kiss, even in the way he looks at me, he makes me hotter and hotter, to the point that I feel like I'm going to explode if I don't give it right back to him.

So I do, spreading my legs more to press the crotch of my jeans against his cock. James groans, the tension in his shoulders apparent as he pulls me tight, lifting me away from the truck and letting me slide oh-so-slowly down his body until my boots touch dirt again.

Both of our chests are heaving, my body's trembling, and James has to inhale deeply before he's able to say anything. "Tomorrow night," he finally gets out between breaths, "a real city date. And Soph . . . don't you dare come without me. You're going to drive home like the good girl you *sometimes* are, and go to bed without doing a thing about how you feel. We worked up all this fire together, and I'm gonna be there when you ignite. Wait for me. Wait till tomorrow."

I bite my lip, not sure if I can promise him that. I'm so close that even the vibration of Doc's truck through the seat could have me careening off the edge, but eventually I nod. "Okay, it's gonna be hard . . . but I'll wait. On one condition—you wait too. Tomorrow night . . . that cock is mine. Judging by what I feel in your jeans, Cowboy, every long, thick, hard inch of it. It's mine. Even?"

He grins at me. "Even. If you don't mind, I'm going to go skinny-dipping in the pond before bed. That might just be cold enough."

He offers a hand to help me into the truck and watches as I pull down the drive. As I drive, I let my mind wander, and all it wants to think about is James's naked body in the pond and the way the water's going to be glistening all over his body.

"Goddammit, James," I growl, cranking the air conditioner to the max, "you knew exactly what you were doing with that last comment."

In my mind, I can almost hear his gravelly chuckle.

~∿~

It's only a half hour later when I get home, the promise of a fancy date replacing the disappointment of the change in tonight's plan. I'm half debating with myself over breaking my promise, the tingles between my thighs near unbearable. I was right, Doc's truck has too much engine and not enough suspension to prevent the seat from becoming a tantalizing torture device.

I glance toward my bedroom, where I know I've got something that can bring me some relief . . . when my phone rings.

Ah, saved by the bell, I suppose.

I fish it out of my purse and see that it's Jake. "Hey, Jake. What's up? Roxy treating you right?"

His laughter comes through the line, and I realize how much I've missed that. "Hey, Sophie. Yeah, we're doing good. Us and the kids. How about you? Any animals kicked you yet?"

I laugh, flopping down on my sofa and yanking off my boots. "Sorry, big brother. So far the only horse's ass to kick me in my life has been you."

He laughs back, likely flashing back to our younger days, when he'd carefully wrestle and goof off with me, our rambunctiousness getting a little carried away once or twice. Even after our parents died and he had to be father as well as brother, we still goofed off.

I grin, thinking of all the fun times. "But really, I'm doing great. The vet I'm working for is a great teacher, always quizzing me, but lets me get my hands dirty and actually do the work too. I did a red-bag delivery for the first time, and I've been doing follow-up care on the mare and foal—"

Jake interrupts, groaning, "Please, for the love of God, do not tell me what a red-bag delivery is. I don't need to know, just congrats on . . . stuff. Yay you!"

I laugh back. "Well, you see, Jake . . . when a mommy horse and a daddy horse love each other very much, they make a baby horsey . . ."

Jake gags. "Hold it right there, Sophie! Really, don't wanna know. What else is going on? Are you working nonstop, or are you making some time to relax too?"

I hear the meaning behind his words, and it touches me. Jake spent a lot of years buried to his eyeballs in work, making sure that he was successful—for himself, for me, and for our parents' memories. It was a lot of pressure, and in some ways it led to the biggest fight of our relationship. But that fight and his wife, Roxy, have led to him discovering there's more to life than business suits and bank accounts, and he's chilled out a lot. Now that he and Roxy have their own kids, who he's without a doubt a stellar father to, he's suddenly found a new focus. And not a conversation goes by where he doesn't check that I'm creating some work-life balance for myself too.

"I've made some friends, and a local family has kind of adopted me after I delivered their foal. That was the red-bag delivery. Their mama is sweet, reminds me of Mom some, just doesn't put up with any shit and does what she wants. The boys are good guys, I've seen one of them a couple of times. Nothing serious since I'm just here for the summer. Actually he is too."

Jake's voice is curious, but I can still hear that same protective streak that he gets whenever he's reminded that I do have feminine interests. "Just the summer? Why's he leaving?"

I bite my lip, wishing maybe I hadn't shared that fact, because Jake isn't going to like this part. "Well, he's a professional bull rider . . . in the rodeo. So he leaves for training before finals in the fall."

There's definitely a bit of shock in Jake's voice, which I guess I can understand. "A bull rider? In the rodeo? Are you serious, Sophie?"

I laugh, trying to lighten the parental tone his voice has taken. Jake's always been picky about who I see, and he's been right more often than not, especially one time in particular when I was in high school. "It's nothing, Jake. Just hanging out. I'm off to school in the fall; he's off to

Vegas. He's fun and sexy as hell. Tips his cowboy hat at me like a lady before he fucks me bowlegged."

Jake groans, and I can imagine him clutching at his heart, or maybe his stomach. "Sexy? Tips his hat before he fucks you? Oh God, tell me you're fucking with me. Roxy . . ."

He calls out, and in the distance I hear my lovely sister-in-law talking. "She's an adult now, honey. There's going to be guys, and she's going to . . ."

That's Roxy, always plainspoken and giving zero fucks . . . okay, she's rubbed off on me a little bit. Her voice gets closer, and I'm sure Jake's set his phone down on a table or something. "Sophie . . . is he hot? Treat you well?"

"Yes and yes. Much to my brother's frustration, he's the hottest thing on two legs I've ever seen!"

Jake sighs, and if it wasn't for Roxy's laughter, I bet he'd be headed out here right now to talk some sense into me . . . and maybe to try and beat the shit out of James.

Roxy, though, sounds amused. "Then have a good summer, honey! Hey, Jake . . . can you help me for a minute?"

Jake sighs again, the long-suffering husband who still spends most of the time with a look on his face like he's died and gone to heaven. "Two against one. Why did I think she was going to be on my side? Really, Sophie . . . I'm just going to assume you're trying to teach me a lesson here to stay out of your personal life. But take care of yourself and be careful, with the four-legged critters *and* the two-legged animals."

I smile, nodding even though he can't see me. "I will, big brother. And Roxy? Thanks for helping get Jake off my case."

"No problem, hon. Next time we get together, I want alllll the details," Roxy says.

Jake laughs, his mood restored, at least for the moment. "Okay. In the meantime, love you, Sophie."

"Love you, too, Jake."

We hang up, and I laugh, leaning back on my sofa.

Well, at least one of the good things to come out of that conversation, besides needling my brother, is that the heat between my thighs has settled to embers. Maybe I can wait until tomorrow after all.

But James better make it worth the wait.

CHAPTER 12

JAMES

I pull up to Sophie's address, a cute little house not too far from Doc's office in an area that is filled with what the people on TV like to call "starter homes." It seems to suit her, yellow and sunny with crisp white trim, the yard still green and lush even with the summer heat.

It's obvious the owners take care of their property, and it makes me happy that she's in a good neighborhood, in a house that won't fall down around her.

Nothing about her says she'd even put up with living in a dive. In fact I get the impression from hearing about her brother that she's used to some of the finer things in life. Still, I'm pleased it's as well kept as it is.

I climb the three small steps to her front door, knocking on the frame as an unexpected blast of nerves swirls through my gut.

Hell, I don't know that I've ever actually done this . . . pick up a woman for a date where I get all dressed up in my best non-shit-kicker clothes? In my teens, it was just parties and good times, and now that I'm grown . . . well, usually parties and good times, just now they're after some rodeo.

I feel like an idiot in this suit, which I've worn exactly twice before, once for a meeting with the Stetson people before I signed my endorsement contract and once for the end-of-year awards because I was nominated for "Rookie Rider of the Year." It's a nice suit, but I'd rather be in my jeans.

All my nerves, all my thoughts disappear in a whoosh, though, as Sophie opens the door, and I get my first look at her dressed nicely.

She's a vision . . . hell, she's a fantasy come to life. Her dark hair is curled, loose waves dipping in front of her shoulders to curl under her full breasts, framing her face, and making her look angelic.

Her makeup is subtle, too, giving her a little extra glow but not disguising her natural beauty. The light pink of her lips complements her dress, a body-hugging pink thing that caresses her curves and highlights each swerve, showing plenty of leg and just on the right side of the line between ladylike sexiness and blatant raunchiness.

It's longer than I would've thought she'd choose, just a few inches above her knees, but I realize the last several inches are made of lace, her creamy thighs peeking through as she shuffles about in sky-high heels.

She's an angel, with a body built for sin . . . and she's unafraid to show me both sides. In my pants, I feel a stirring, and I remind myself that I promised her a night on the town, city-style.

She smiles, saucy and vulnerable all at once. "You certainly clean up well. So, what do you think?"

She's just as gorgeous done up head to toe as she is when she's barefaced with a ponytail in barn clothes, but right now, seeing her like a fantasy for my pleasure is making the blood rush to my cock, and I stammer for a moment before answering, "God, Soph . . . I was right. You look stunning. You're the sexiest fucking thing I've ever seen." I move in to greet her with a kiss, but she presses one pink painted nail against my chest, and I realize she really has gone all out.

"Whoa there, Cowboy. You promised me a dinner. Let's go." With a swish and a smirk, she struts past me, closing the door as she goes.

My jaw drops at her gall, and then at the glimpse of the way her dress perfectly lifts and frames her grabable ass walking away from me.

Hoping to relieve a little bit of the tightness in my pants, I adjust myself and take a steadying breath. "You play fucking dirty, but I'll admit that I like it if that's the view I get when you walk off."

I catch up with her, walking her to my truck as she smiles, knowing that this is just the first move in what's going to be hours of foreplay.

She moves toward the passenger side, but I pull her back. "Ain't you ever been on a date with a country boy? You aren't sitting over there."

"Is that so?" Sophie asks as I guide her back to the driver's side, helping her in and making sure she sits flush up against me in the center of the bench seat after tossing my suit jacket to the other side of the cab. "Well, this I could get used to."

Roaring down the street, I rest my hand on her thigh, and she does the same to me, one hand on my thigh and one scratching up and down my forearm. I've been told they're sexy, but what do I know?

All I care about is that they're strong enough to help hold the ropes so I can stay on a bull, but I guess the muscles and veins that give me a good grip do a little something extra to women, and it seems Sophie isn't immune.

I squeeze her thigh, thankful for the handful and knowing it'll flex the muscles under her fingertips. Sophie hums and scratches my forearm a little harder, her breath quickening. We don't say anything; there's no need for words as we take the road up the mountain, past Outlook Point and climbing higher.

Too soon, we reach the resort, which is impressive. I'm not one for skiing, but I could go riding in these hills for a long time in the warmer months.

"So, have you been here before?" Sophie asks as I help her out. She smooths her skirt over her ass, tugging a little and smiling, watching as I slip my jacket back on. My temporary debonair image is back in place as we head toward the front door.

"Only once," I admit. "It's not that I don't like the mountains, but when I'm in town I'm normally too busy. What about you—ever been to the resort when you're in town?"

Sophie nods, blushing a little. "Well, oddly enough, through a Six Degrees of Kevin Bacon sort of deal with Jake's in-laws, I actually know the owners a tiny bit. Let's see if I can get this right . . . my brother, Jake, is married to Roxy. Her sister's best friend and her husband are the owners. I've really only met them at weddings and such, though."

I take it in, surprised at just how wide and how moneyed Sophie's connections are. Every other woman I've met who runs in circles like those has a tendency to "put on airs," as Mama likes to say. I never would have guessed it about down-to-earth, honest, and spunky Sophie, though.

I laugh, relaxing. "Does that mean we can get a discount on our appetizers?"

Sophie lets out a big breath and laughs quietly. "Nope. But it does mean if you're not a gentleman during dinner, you'll have a former All-Pro football player turned resort financier paying you a visit."

I smirk, nodding. "Well then, I'll behave . . . in the restaurant. No promises otherwise."

We go inside, where we're seated with a stunning view of the mountains, and our waiter takes our drink orders. Sophie's surprised. "Wine? I figured you'd have asked for some JD and Coke."

I shake my head, sipping my water. "No way. I'm driving, and I expect to maintain control of my truck as we go down the mountain. Second . . . there's a time for JD, but I never mix it with Coke. I have culture."

Sophie laughs, giving me a smoldering look. "So . . . I know the basics about you. But I'm still interested in knowing more."

"So am I. You seem so well put together; tell me one of the craziest or stupidest things you've done."

Sophie laughs. "Okay. Probably the biggest fight my brother and I had. Jake and his business partner, Nathan, went in halfsies and opened up a night club in town."

"Okay . . . so where do you come in?"

"Well, one night, just after I turned eighteen, I snuck in with a fake ID and happened to get a little tipsy. The night ended up with me half-drunk and Jake nearly punching out the bastard I thought was my boyfriend. I was so mad at Jake at the time, but he was right about that asshole all along, although it got worse before I realized Jake had my best interests at heart. It was, well, my bad-boy phase. I'm glad I outgrew it."

"Oh, you have?" I ask. "I'm not exactly a choirboy."

Sophie laughs, leaning in. "I may not be totally out of that phase, but you're different. But . . . your turn. Even."

I can read the challenge in her voice, and I understand what she's saying totally. She's not into bad boys . . . but she's not ready for Mr. Nice yet either.

"Well, I'd say the stupidest thing I ever did involved a bull, way too much beer, and not much else," I tell her, chuckling. "It was my second year on tour, and I'd just gotten my first win. It was a huge achievement for me."

Sophie hums, nodding. "So, what did the wunderkind do?"

"Well, that night, after I'd made sure my prize check was locked away, a couple of the guys threw me a party. Someone got a couple of kegs of Coors Light, and we started drinking."

"Coors Light?" Sophie asks, wincing. "Kidding; it'll do."

"Oh, it gets better. About a keg and a half in, one of the guys, a real old hand named Fred Livingston, says there's a traditional challenge for first-time winners . . . or else you're deemed a pussy for the rest of your life. Of course with me being nineteen and drunk, I wasn't going to back down."

"I'm guessing that's where the bull comes in."

I nod, laughing. "They found the biggest, baddest bull in the pens that night and set him up for me, and five minutes later, I was on his back . . . naked. No hat, no boots, nothing but my glove that everyone wears unless you want to lose the skin off your palm. They pulled the gate, and . . . it was the worst pain I've ever had in rodeo."

"Really?" Sophie asks, laughing. "Why?"

"Things got . . . crunched between me and the bull," I explain without actually explaining. "There's a reason we wear tight jeans. At least, those of us who want to have functioning equipment later on."

Sophie's eyes twinkle, and as our dinners arrive, she sips her wine. "Well then, I'm glad you only did that stunt once."

⌁

This is a new sensation, walking Sophie up to her front door at the end of our date. I'm fighting with myself. Half of me wants to be the not-quite-bad-but-naughty guy that she's played around with and keep last night's promise to shove her in her house, rip that pink dress off her, and fuck her until she screams my name and walks funny for three days. But there's another side of me that knows she deserves more than a hard, fast fuck before I burn rubber and drive home.

The revelation hits me like a punch in the gut. Regardless of what she deserves, I want more than that with her. I want both the naughty and the nice, to fuck her, fill her, and then hold her in my arms till she's ready to do it again. I don't need to go home to sleep before tomorrow starts; I just need to possess Sophie, and I'll have energy for days as she electrifies me from my cock out to my limbs.

I'm shaking with need as she unlocks the door and turns to face me, biting her lip. In her eyes, I can see the same war in her mind, and it answers my questions. Don't care how, I want the whole world now.

"So, you coming inside, Cowboy?" Sophie asks, playing with her keys.

106

I smirk and take her keys away from her. "Darlin', I'm coming anywhere and as many times as you'll let me."

Even though I probably shouldn't, even though this isn't the respect a woman like her deserves, I push her inside. She goes willingly as I shut the door behind me and attack her with my lips, cupping her face in both hands as I devour her.

Pushing her against the wall of her tiny entryway, I pin her with my body, growling in her ear, "Where?"

Sophie twists her head away enough to take a big breath, the lust visible in the light from the lamps she's left on while we went to dinner. I'm just about to ask if she's okay when she pushes me away, lets out a big whoop, and runs off down the hall. "C'mon, Cowboy!"

I can't pass up a chase this much fun, and I take off after her, laughing all the way. Barreling through the last door on the right, I freeze in the doorway to see Sophie standing in the middle of the bed, her heels kicked off somewhere along the way and her pink dress riding up her thighs so that the lacy bit at the hem shows me the black panties she has on underneath.

Her face is flushed, a playful, seductive light dancing in her eyes as her chest heaves, more from anticipation than the quick sprint down the hall. "Well, you found me. Now what?"

My cock hardens instantly, lust overwhelming me as I shrug off my suit coat. "Soph . . . I ride bulls for a living, but you in that pink dress, looking all bright-eyed and sexy, knowing that your pussy is wet just for me," I rasp, my voice overcome with lust and desire, "you make me want to charge at you like *I'm* the damn bull, grab you, throw you to the bed, and pound into you . . . wild like an animal."

As I talk, I stalk her, slowly walking into the room to get closer to her, get her within arm's reach. Her eyes follow me, her thighs trembling as her body's caught between wanting to run and wanting to give in. Suddenly, she freezes like the prey she is, holding up a hand. "Stop."

It takes all my self-control, but I fucking do it. I stop exactly where I am, eyes meeting hers, my plea silent but just as loud in the room. Sophie reaches a hand up along her side, finding a zipper I hadn't even noticed along the seam of her dress, and tugs at it slowly, her eyes never leaving mine.

"What are you doing, Soph?"

"Preparing myself . . . this bull ride is going to be naked too," she says, slipping her arms out of the little sleeves at her shoulders, and the loosened dress falls to her feet, where she steps daintily out of it, leaving her in the middle of the bed in a black lace bra and panty set.

The first things I notice are the bows. There are tiny pink bows at the center of her cleavage and on the sides of her panties, with a larger one right above her mound. Little bows, like presents waiting to be unwrapped. I realize she is a precious gift, but one that isn't supposed to be treated gently. No, this is a precious gift that's supposed to be taken to the limit and then pounded into total submission. It makes my cock swell . . . and I know I'm the man she needs.

"You're fucking gorgeous, Soph. Like a real-life sex dream."

She blushes even more, and I wonder if she's never had someone tell her just how amazing she is. I reach down to undo my belt, a smooth black leather one that I've only worn with this suit. Next I unbutton my shirt because if she's getting naked, I'm damn sure getting naked too. Just polite, after all.

Her eyes roam my body, and she licks her lips unconsciously as she looks over my chest and stomach, all the muscles tight and highlighted against my skin. Dropping my shirt to the floor, I move to the closure on my pants and hear her breath catch, and she whispers to herself, "Showtime."

"This what you want to see?" I ask, letting my pants drop, leaving me in just my underwear. "Say the word; it's all yours, Soph."

She nods her head, her eyes wide and her chest heaving sexily in her bra, the bow shaking in the movement. "Show me, James. Let me see your cock, all hard for me tonight like it was before. But this time, we're gonna be even, you hear me? I want it, and I want you."

"Then get ready." I hook my thumbs in the waistband of my underpants and slip them down, tugging the elastic out to let my cock pop free. Sophie's eyes widen as I take my shaft in hand, giving myself a few strokes, precum already glistening on the tip. "What do you think?"

She nods, unable to form words as she bites her lip again in that way that has my cock pulsing in my grip. Sitting down on the edge of the bed, I shuck what's left of my boots and pants, virtually springing across the bed for her the instant I'm naked.

She giggles and bounces as she plops onto the mattress. I reach for her. "Even time," I growl as I gather her in my lap to straddle me, my arms wrapping around her and kissing her mouth quickly before moving down her body to slip the strap of her bra down and plant kisses all along her shoulder. "You're not playing fair."

"Guess you'll just have to help me then, Cowboy," she purrs, running her hands over my chest. "I'm busy."

I unclasp her bra and toss it to the side of the bed before pressing our chests together and growling at the feel of her smooth skin against me. She bucks, rolling her hips as she starts riding my bare cock through her lacy panties, and I need to be inside her.

Reaching down, I find one of the bows on the side of her pretty panties and pull, feeling the thin lace and silk rip from her body. Sophie gasps, her fingernails scratching at my chest. "Oooh fuck. I liked those . . ."

"I'll buy you a new pair," I reply, tugging them the rest of the way free. As soon as they're out of the way, though, she goes back to slipping and sliding against my cock, teasing me. Knowing I'm just on the edge of entering her, I reach down, stopping her hips with the last of my will. "Soph? You ready?"

She nods, and I lift her hips, positioning myself at her entrance and letting her coat me with her honey again before pulling her down, slowly making her take every inch of my cock in one thrust.

Sophie sits back, her fingernails digging into my chest as she moans thickly. "Oh my God, James. Yes . . ."

She stays still for a moment, letting my cock stretch and fill her totally before lifting her hips, moving up and down along my length and driving me crazy as she rides me. I lean back, not lying down yet to keep her close, one arm behind to support me and the other free to roam and tease her nipples and her clit. Sophie whimpers, and I reach around to smack her ass, making her cry out in pleasure.

I bend my knees to get some leverage as I pound into her from below, our hips meeting in loud slaps with each driving thrust. Sophie's body quakes, and she grabs my shoulders, rolling her hips and grunting deep in her chest as she lets her desire flow.

"Ride me, Sophie," I command her, smacking her ass again before putting my hand on her low back to help support her. "Take my cock just like you want it. You're gonna ride me so hard that you're going to come harder than ever before. You want that?"

She cries out, nodding, and I can tell she's getting tired, but I'm not done with her, not by a long shot. I reach under her arms, wrapping my hands up to her shoulders, and pull her to me, pumping my hips slowly and forcefully, grinding her clit against me at the bottom of every stroke.

Sophie is keening, groaning as she breathes in and out, begging. "Please, James . . . I'm so close."

I nibble on her neck, rasping in her ear, "Touch yourself, Soph. I'm gonna fuck your sweet pussy, let your silk walls squeeze me tight, but I need you to rub that needy little clit so I can hold your shoulders and pump into you. Rub it and come all over my cock, and I'll fill you up like you want. Do it, Soph."

She wails, both hands reaching into the tight space between us, one hand pulling herself open wide, and I feel myself sink inside her just a little more before her other hand blurs across her clit. I hold her tight, hammering into her and trying to wait for her, but I can't, it's too good.

"Oh fuck, Soph . . . I'm coming!" I cry out, and I feel her walls squeeze me even tighter before starting to flutter as her own orgasm takes her, her voice raw as she moans my name in my ear. It draws me out, making my pleasure even more, and I hold her, bucking my hips hard as my cock erupts. I keep going, helping her ride it out as long as possible before she collapses onto me and I hold her tight.

"Shit, woman," I rasp, stroking her dark hair softly as she's overcome with shudders. I can feel it, too, that type of orgasm that's so hard it was more than physical—it was emotional too. "That was . . . that was . . ."

I'm speechless, not knowing what to even call . . . that. Sophie does, though. "That was fucking perfect. Wow."

I laugh lightly. She's right. It was wow, it was perfect, and I can't wait to do it again. "Hope you're not done yet. I've got plenty of energy saved up for you."

Sophie grins and climbs off me, removing the little that was left of her panties. "You kidding? I'm not done; I'm just going to get some water and a warm washcloth to clean us up."

We spend the rest of the night tussling and wrestling and laughing in her bed before fucking and coming over and over. The more we go at it, the more we please each other. Finally, we collapse sometime in the early morning hours, sated and exhausted and smiling.

Fuck it. Luke can let the cows out in the morning.

CHAPTER 13

SOPHIE

"You sure you have to go?" I ask as James adjusts his pants. "I think you look good even in a day-old suit."

James, who rolled out of bed a half hour ago to grab a quick shower, chuckles. "I'm already late. If I'm not there in time to help with the barn work, I'm never going to hear the end of it from Luke."

"And Mark's going to frown so hard his ass is going to crack," I joke, making James laugh and nod. "Okay . . . well, can I at least get you a coffee?"

"I don't know—"

"In a thermos," I promise him, heading for the kitchen. "You can drink it on the way."

He chuckles warmly. "Woman, keep it up, and you're going to domesticate me."

His answer makes an unexpected flurry of warm tingles in my belly, and I hurry a little bit more. I figure it's the least I can do, considering we were both up damn near all night.

After he leaves, giving me another thrilling kiss in the doorway, I try to nap for another hour before I have to get up to get dressed for work.

Today's the last day I need to attend to Briarbelle and her foal, and I'm not sure what's going to happen after that.

It makes me a little nervous. After today, I'm not going to have a built-in reason to go see James every day, sit at Mama's dinner table, and catch up on the day. I don't even know if Mama Lou will be so welcoming when I go from "vet helping out" to "hussy who's taking up her baby boy's time and probably corrupting him."

It hits me that in just a short week, I've come to depend on that routine, the connection with the Bennetts being the sign of a day well worked. Can I adjust back?

James had just whispered that he'd see me this afternoon after that quick, albeit steamy, kiss goodbye this morning, so I guess I'll see what he says today, because I definitely want a repeat of last night.

Getting myself ready finally, I swing by Doc's house and pick him up. He hops in, already spry and awake, apparently having gotten much more sleep last night than I did.

Doc is at least polite enough to overlook my double yawn as he puts on his seat belt and turns to me, a very satisfied look on his face. "Good morning. Guess what?"

I barely restrain my juvenile response of "chicken butt," automatic after years of college with twelve-year-old boys trapped in twenty-year-old men's bodies, but luckily my brain not firing on all cylinders serves me well in the moment, and I manage to respond more appropriately. "What?"

"We're out in the field today!" Doc says, a note of glee in his voice at the prospect. "You ready?"

I grin. There's nothing better than getting out of the office and working a day in the sun. "Absolutely! Where to?"

After a quick trip to the office to grab our supplies and for Doc to change into boots, I follow his directions to a farm on the other side of the mountain. Along the way, he fills me in about a rancher who bought a group of pigs that need exams before he mixes them in with his other swine.

"He bought them from a supplier that he hasn't worked with before, and he wants to make sure he's got good stock on his hands. Full checkups on six pigs, ranging in ages from piglets to full porkers, two males and four females. You should be an expert on healthy pig exams by this afternoon . . . assuming they're all healthy."

He says the last part with a little bit of a question in his tone. I glance over at him, feeling mischievous. "Is it evil if I want something to not be one hundred percent? Just a little challenge to my skills, an extra bit of training? Nothing serious, mind you. I'm not a monster. Besides, I love baby pigs; they're just too cute with the way their noses wrinkle up and everything. Just want to test myself."

Doc laughs, shaking his head. "No, that ain't wrong. Keeps us all fresh. If all we ever saw were healthy animals, we wouldn't know what to do when one needed help. These will likely be just fine, though, but don't let preconceived ideas taint your exams, because you never know what you'll find."

"Good advice. Gotcha, Doc."

"One other piece of advice," Doc says, looking me over. "Get yourself a set of hip waders like fly fishermen use for days like this. Pigs aren't like horses or cows . . . those jeans of yours aren't going to be any good for the office after today."

"Damn," I grumble, looking down. "I liked these jeans too."

We spend the day in the barn, hip high in hogs as we check them over, snout to hooves, scanning paperwork from the previous owner and vet and updating some vaccines for the animals. There's nothing wrong with them, and the farmer, a rather truculent old sot named McAndrews, questions everything. "You sure, Doc? That sow just don't look right to me."

"Angus, that sow is just fine," Doc reassures him, just as he has for every other pig so far. "Her having brown patches on her teats is just her normal coloration, not a sign of disease, I assure you."

McAndrews nods. "Alright, I trust you. I'll get out of your way so you can do your job," he says, and he leaves us.

Picking up a bright-pink baby with the world's most angelic eyelashes, I coo, chuckling. This is my favorite part, just petting them and giving the animals a little love and affection. I've been lucky that most large animals seem to respond to me, calming and settling even as we handle, poke, and prod them.

It's for their own good, but they don't know that, so a comforting and soothing presence helps them not be so scared. It's late in the day by the time we finish and head back to town.

I drop off Doc, and as he gets out, he stops to lean in the open driver's side window. "Great job today, Sophie. Today's Briarbelle's last dose, too, right?"

"Yes sir, it is. No signs of infection in her or Polka Dottie. I don't think they'll need any further care."

Doc hums, pleased. "Polka Dottie, huh? I like it, suits her just fine. Alright then, you've worked hard and done great all week. Head out there today to check on Briarbelle. Sorry it's so late today."

"Might be a bit later," I admit, looking down at my jeans and boots. "I feel like I've been dipped in pig shit."

Doc laughs, looking over my soaked lower legs and boots. "Told you. Okay, take the weekend off; you've earned it. I'll call you if there's an emergency."

I grin, pleased at the praise. "Will do, Doc. I plan to Netflix and chill all weekend."

Doc rolls his eyes, probably because nothing I said involved watching sports on TV. "Keep the truck; I'm not going anywhere all weekend. If there's a call, swing by and pick me up. Deal?"

Nodding, I reach through my window and give the old guy an unexpected and slightly awkward hug. "Deal. Call me if you need anything, even it's just doughnuts and coffee!"

He steps back and I pull out, driving home quickly and changing before pressing against the speed limit to get to James . . . and the BB Ranch. Even still, the sun is setting low by the time I pull up to the gate, with James nowhere in sight.

"Well, what did you expect?" I mutter to myself as I fish out my phone. "The man's got more work to do than sit around by the front gate all day waiting to open up just for me."

Thankfully, we exchanged numbers earlier this week, and James picks up after only two rings. "Hey, woman, where the hell have you been?"

From behind him, I hear Mama Lou, her voice sharp and iron hard. "Boy, now you know I didn't raise you to talk to a young lady like that."

I laugh, both at the humor and at the unexpected insight into Mama Lou. James is right; she might be sweet to me, but she's got iron in her spine. "I've been in McAndrews's barn with swine all day, Cowboy. Probably smell like it too. You'd like it, you pig. Come let me in the gate."

There's a click, and in a short few minutes, I see him striding over the hill on foot. He swings the gate open and then hops in the passenger seat of Doc's truck. The first thing he does is lean over to give me a quick kiss before recoiling. "Damn, girl, you weren't kidding, were you? You smell like shit."

"Well hello to you too," I tease, driving up. "You should count yourself lucky I changed my boots and jeans at least. Good thing I came out to see Briarbelle anyway. I'm sure she won't be so picky as to the company she keeps."

He laughs, and once we pull up, he disappears into the house while I do Briarbelle's check and administer the meds.

Finishing up my paperwork, I sniff my pits and recoil myself. It's not just BO, although I am certainly ripe after a day of sweating. There's an overall aura of pig-shit funk clinging to me like a miasma, something strong enough I wonder if I'm going to need to bathe in rubbing alcohol and turpentine to get it out of my hair. "Oh well," I say, laughing to myself. "Cowboy can take it, or I can go home. His choice."

I'm packing up my gear in the truck when James comes back out, a bag in his hand. Saying nothing, he disappears inside the barn for a moment before coming back out on his horse, Hunter. I look up curiously, leaning against the truck. "Where are you going?"

James leans down, cocking back his hat as he smirks. "*We* are going on a ride to the pond, let your stinky self air out a bit. Told Mama she didn't want you at her table tonight anyway. She understood when I explained why. So I made us sandwiches for dinner. Hope that's okay?"

"Sunset ride with a picnic by the pond? I guess it'll do. Would've been more romantic if you'd left out the part about me stinking," I tease him.

"Can't help that bit," James says as I swing up into Hunter's saddle. We ride toward the pond. It's a pretty ride, not too far considering we walked it a few nights ago, but it's more private than I'd realized, the small hillocks and mounds providing a natural barrier and blocking sightlines all the way around unless you're standing almost right on top of the pond.

It gives me an idea, and as we loop the reins over a low shrub's branches to keep Hunter in place, I step back and quietly toe my boots off without James noticing. The soft grass feels great between my toes, and as quickly as I can, I slip my jeans and undies off before pulling my smelly shirt over my head and throwing it at James's head with a whoop. "Race you, Cowboy!"

My bra drops a split second later as I run for the water, naked as the day I was born. Hitting an outcropping, I leap, pulling my knees up and trusting in blind luck that I'm not about to go ass first into a rock. Unleashing a whoop that startles the birds in the nearby trees, I hit the water, plunging deep before kicking back up, sputtering and already shivering. "Holy shit! It's cold! How is it this cold in June?"

James laughs, but he's pulling his boots off too. "I told you it was spring fed. What did you think I meant, hot springs?"

"Yeah but . . . fuck me, this is cold!"

James shucks off the rest of his clothes, his eyes gleaming like he's got a surprise for me. "That's one way to warm you up. Let's see what else comes to mind."

He wades in, the water glistening on his torso just like I dreamed of, and I defiantly splash him, daring him to come after me. "You think you're getting some action after telling me I smell like shit?"

"The idea crossed my mind. Especially since I think I've got a fix for that stench . . ." Suddenly, he dives at me, pressing my head underwater before grabbing me around the waist. I fight back, giggling and laughing the whole time, and we tussle for dominance, each trying to dunk the other.

After a short few minutes, sputtering and drenched, my hair a stringy mess in my face, I cry out, clinging to him, "Okay, truce! Truce."

James stops, his eyes gleaming in the dim violet light of near darkness, and growls, "So I can take what I want?"

Instead of answering, I dip my head backward, my hair sleek along my back now, offering myself to him. There's a split second of anticipation, his calloused hands against my hips under the crisp water before he bends down and kisses me. It immediately takes us back to where we were last night, no slow build or foreplay, just instant need, hot and deep at my core.

I drop my right hand to his cock under the water, wrapping my seemingly small fingers around his thick length. The water may be icy cold, but his body is hot, his cock stiff and pulsing as my pussy heats up, too, the delicious interplay of cold and hot making things even better.

The water easing my way, I move along his shaft, pumping him through my fist and rubbing the head of his cock along my belly. "Mmm . . . if what you want is to come hard, then yes."

James gasps, his fingers never stopping their exploration of my skin. "Fuck, Soph. You always surprise me."

I keep fisting him, looking up at him. "Tell me when you're right about to come, just before. Promise?"

He nods, and I watch him, my hand pumping his cock, creating ripples that spread outward from our joined bodies as the crickets start to chirp in the twilight. I can feel his stomach tighten, his fingers growing rougher as I tease him, bringing him higher and higher. It's powerful and addictive, knowing that I can do this to such a handsome stud of a man with just my lips, my body, and my hand.

He groans, and I feel his cock swell in my fingers. "Oh shit, Soph, I'm coming . . ."

Quickly I take a big breath, releasing my grip from his cock to hold my nose and dive down, my face under the water as I slide my lips around his cock and take him deep in my throat. I don't have a lot of time, thirty seconds maybe, so I swallow and moan, hoping the vibrations push him over the edge.

He grabs at my head, somehow both holding me under and trying to pull me up at the same time, but I fight to stay down as he comes, filling my mouth. It's amazing. I can't hear him because of the rush of water in my ears; all I can feel is the chill against my skin and the warmth of his cock in my mouth, the taste of him on my tongue, and I want every last drop before I come up.

At last, I pop through the surface, gulping oxygen and laughing as I wipe the water from my eyes.

James looks at me, incredulous. "Holy shit, Sophie. Are you okay? I've never . . . I didn't even know you could do that."

I grin, still breathing deeply and licking my lips. "Never done it before either, just wanted to taste you. And here we are . . . besides, the shore seemed so far away."

He laughs and gathers me in his arms. "God damn, you are maybe more wild than I am. I need a break after that. Come on . . ."

He lifts me up in his arms, pressing a sweet kiss to my lips as he carries me toward shore. Even after I'm out of the water, he doesn't let go, holding me like I'm as light as a feather as he sets me down on the soft grass. Plopping down next to me, he opens the bag he's brought and hands me a sandwich. "Here . . . not that I don't want to return the attention, but you look famished."

Naked and somewhat satisfied, we chat and I tell him about my day with the pigs to explain my stench.

"So they're all healthy, and Doc said I have the next two days off, too, on account of my good work. Well, and because it's the weekend."

James thinks, then reaches out, taking my hand. "Stay here, stay with me. I'll do chores in the morning, and we can ride around and check on the herd during the day. What do you say? Wanna be a cowgirl for a weekend?"

I study his face for a minute, surprised at the invitation, but he's dead serious. And it really sounds like a fun experience . . . horses, cattle, and my very own cowboy tour guide.

Finally, I nod, making a decision. "Sounds great. Um, just one thing . . . didn't you say that you and Luke share the ranch-hand house? Will he mind me crashing your cowboy pad?"

James laughs, waving his hand dismissively. "It's a big enough house. And if he doesn't like it, he can take his ass to the barn. I don't need him hearing you scream my name all night anyway. Might give him an inferiority complex."

"And what if I decide to start screaming 'Oh, Luke, that's it! Use the Force, baby'?"

James laughs, not taking the bait. "Then I'll just have to fuck you harder."

CHAPTER 14

JAMES

I sneak out of bed while it's dark and early, leaving a naked Sophie curled up like a little kitten. We ended up chasing Luke out of the bunkhouse with plenty of laughs before turning the night into a wonderful experience, alternating naps between rounds of going at each other like a pair of horny rabbits.

It was amazing, having Sophie in my bed. Every time I woke up, she was ready for another round, another position, another . . . anything. She keeps me on my toes, that's for damn sure.

Getting to the barn, I do my first round of chores, brushing down and feeding all the horses before I slip in the house to get cups of coffee. Mama's got breakfast waiting, hash browns and sausage ready to be sandwiched between johnnycakes.

"Morning, son," Mama says, just like she does every morning. "You need a spare cup today?"

"Yes, ma'am," I answer sheepishly, making myself a "cowboy breakfast." Obviously, Mama knows that I have a sex life; she's no fool, and I'm a grown man after all. But I've never brought a girl back to the ranch before, and I have never had to kick my brother out of his bed so we could go at it.

Mama, though, is taking it totally in stride. "Mm-hmm. Well, tell Sophie good morning for me."

Instead of replying, I stuff a mouthful of sausage and johnnycake into my mouth, humming noncommittally. I'm not trying to be rude; I just don't know what to say.

Mama gives me a few moments to twist and turn in the breeze, then sets her spoon down and turns to me. "James, I'm going to say this only one time. She's a nice girl. Just make sure you know what you're doing."

There's no anger, no condemnation in her voice. In fact, if I had to give it any sort of vibe, she's just looking out for me. "I know. We've talked. She knows I'm back to the rodeo in the fall, and she's back to school. We understand the limits of what this has to be."

Mama nods and hands me a big thermos of coffee. "Well, tell her whenever she wants, I've got breakfast for her too. And I could use a little help in the garden; my strawberries are looking ready to harvest, and I might make cobbler tonight. That is, if she doesn't want to go out in the fields with you."

I nod my thanks and slip out, caffeine in hand. As the screen door bangs closed, I hear Mama mutter, "Best-laid plans . . ."

Back in the ranch house, Sophie is just waking up, stretching her arms wide, her breasts peeking delectably above the blanket, and I'm sorely tempted to hop back into bed with her and spend the day hiding from responsibilities.

But that won't do. It's just not how I was raised; Pops taught me better than that, so I keep my distance, lest her sleepy temptation pull me back into the nest of blankets. Setting the thermos on my dresser, I tug on the edge of the blanket. "Up and at 'em, sleepyhead. Cows won't wait."

She climbs out of bed, no shyness in her sexy curves as she walks over and grabs her clothes from yesterday. I wince at the mess, knowing that while she's claimed the jeans were fresh, there's no way I can put up with sweat-soaked pig-shit funk for a couple of hours in today's heat. "Here, let me loan you a shirt; we can get that shirt washed later. I mean, to keep you ladylike and all."

I wink at her, and she blows a raspberry at me. "You weren't complaining last night."

"Nope," I agree as I grab an old T-shirt of mine and toss it to her. "But last night you were the one who took a flying leap into the pond. I don't want to have to throw you in today."

"Thanks," she says sarcastically, but she's still smiling as she slips the blue T-shirt on. I got this shirt years ago at some fair or another on the fried-chicken circuit, and it's emblazoned across the chest with the name of a car dealer, probably the guy who sponsored the show. It's way too long, so she ties it in a knot at her waist, preventing it from swallowing her whole. "How do I look?"

"Sexy as fuck," I tell her honestly. "Although I think the *F* and the *D* are sticking out a lot more than I could ever make them stretch to."

Sophie looks down, laughing. "Yeah, well, if you want another chance to *F* these *D*s, you're gonna behave yourself. My body needs at least a few hours' break."

She grabs her hair into a ponytail, pulling a band off her wrist, and with a tug of her boots, she stands up, posing for me. "Ready for duty, Cowboy!"

I whistle, glad I'm on the other side of the room. "I don't know that I've ever seen a woman go from bed to ready in two minutes flat and look as fucking sexy as you do right now. No pretense, just you, ready to ride and work with me on your day off."

"It's a special talent," Sophie jokes with a wink. She walks past me, grabbing the coffee as she goes, and I'm gifted with another fantastic view of her ass in those painted-on jeans she wears. "So, where to first?"

"First, we're going to go check on the herd in the far pasture," I tell her. "Then we'll head on out to the eastern pasture to check on the critter situation."

"Critter situation?" Sophie asks, raising an eyebrow. "What's that?"

"Not much," I reply, shrugging. "Just that after we move the cows from one field to another, there tends to be an influx of burrowing animals who want to tear the shit out of the fields. I guess it's because the dirt's softer, more riled up maybe. I don't know. But we need to check on them, and if there's a problem . . . well, we'll deal with that when we come to it."

We get our horses and ride out, Sophie stopping in first to grab a sausage-and-johnnycake sandwich that she eats while we ride. It's not far, just a half mile until I see the first of the cows. "Here we are," I tell her, indicating the herd. "Three hundred and fifteen head by last week's count. That's a bit high for us, but we'll be selling off some of the—"

I stop, my words cut off as I see something I certainly don't want to see. "Son of a bitch!"

"What?" Sophie asks, but I'm already kicking my horse up into a light gallop as I close in on the problem. I give Sophie credit; she's not that far behind.

"Get away from there, you stupid bovine!" I yell. Sophie pulls up but quickly sees my problem. The new fence, which I just put up, is down in a big section almost five yards wide, and some of our cattle have already drifted. "What the hell?"

"What can I do to help?" Sophie asks. "Do you want me to get Luke and Mark?"

"No, I can get this," I growl, knowing that if Mark and Luke helped out, I'd never hear the end of it. This section of fence was my responsibility, and now I've got ten cows across the line between our land and the Tannens'. Just fucking perfect. They had to break through on this section.

"Stay here," I tell Sophie, maneuvering my horse through the gap in the fence and cutting around the cows. It doesn't take long—cows aren't exactly the type of animals to get riled up unless you threaten their calves or their herd, and with most of the herd on the other side of the fence already, they head on back through amiably enough. Following the last one through, I take off my hat and wipe my forehead.

"Anything I can do?" Sophie asks.

I nod, giving her a smile. "Most helpful thing you can do is to stay here. Keep your horse between them and the hole in the fence. I'm going to ride back to the barn and grab some supplies. With a little bit of luck and maybe your help, we should have this fixed by lunch."

Sophie nods, and I wheel my horse around, breaking out into a trot as I head back to the barn. Luke's inside, giving me a raised eyebrow as I pull up. "Fence problem," I say simply. "Got it handled."

"You sure?" Luke asks as I unsaddle my horse. "I can—"

"Sophie's with me; we've got it," I assure him. "Can you handle the brushdown?"

Luke nods, and I give him a thumbs-up as I jog over to the other barn, where the repair supplies, along with the ATV, reside. After loading up the trailer, I'm back out there before even a half hour's passed.

It's not a long gap, but as I rumble across the field, I see two riders on the hill, Sophie and someone else. As I get closer, I hear a voice piercing the still morning air. "So, Daddy always says that if one of the cows break through, the first thing you have to do is lead it to the far side of the pasture or else they're gonna—"

"Shayanne, is that you?" I ask, pulling up closer and interrupting the monologue. "It's been ages!"

I've known Shayanne Tannen since she was born, hers the first diapers I ever saw getting changed back when things between our families were a little better. She's all grown-up now, though, and her long light-brown hair streams out from under her hat.

"The one and only!" she says, throwing a hand up. "And James Bennett, as I live and breathe. I'd recognize you from being on TV even if I hadn't grown up next to the BB Ranch. By the way, if anyone asks, you didn't see me. I snuck out to get a ride in while the pie I cooked for dessert tonight is cooling."

She gives a little wink but looks behind her deeper into her side of the property like she might actually be a bit nervous about being out when she's not supposed to be. It makes me wonder just how old she is now, and that's saying something because she looks to be no older than nineteen, maybe twenty if you fudge the numbers to one side because of healthy country living.

I look at Sophie, who's looking like she's got sand in her boots, and remember my manners. "Sophie, this is Shayanne Tannen," I say, introducing the two. "Shayanne, this is Sophie Stone. Shayanne's the annoying tomboy little sister who would tag along with us boys back when our idea of raising hell was shooting at tin cans with BB guns."

I'm just teasing, and Shayanne seems to take it in stride, laughing. "I seem to remember beating you in a contest once. All of you, in fact."

She conveniently leaves out that it was the one time her father let her participate. He was the one doing the aiming while she kind of just helped hold the BB gun, but I don't remind her of that. Sophie raises an eyebrow, and I quickly hurry on. "She's got three older brothers around the same age as my brothers and I. Sophie's my . . . friend."

I hesitate a little, uncertain about how to label us, but neither woman seems to notice too much. Instead, Sophie reaches over, offering her hand to Shayanne, who shakes daintily. "Pleased to meet you."

"Same here," Shayanne says. "So, why the ATV?"

Sophie, who knows why, interjects her own question. "Did you get the supplies?"

"Sure did," I reply, stepping out. "Tie your horse off on the handlebars, and you can help. I grabbed a spare pair of gloves for you."

There isn't much in the trailer; the main reason I brought the ATV was for the post driver, a homemade contraption Pops got from his time as a ranch hand when he was younger. I pull it out and hand a set of wire cutters to Sophie as she comes over. "Go ahead and cut me four lengths of wire about five feet long. Don't need to be perfect, just enough to cover the gap."

Sophie nods, while Shayanne looks on sagely. "Oh yeah, I see the breaks in the line. Daddy says you can tell a lot about how good of a rancher a man is by the state of his fence. Well-kept fence, well-kept herd. Broken fence, well . . ."

She glances at the fence a bit haughtily, and I bite back what I think of what her daddy says.

"Yeah, but James said he repaired this section not too long ago," Sophie says, grunting as she squeezes the wire cutters until a sharp metallic *twingk!* fills the air. "Maybe the cows got to messing with it?"

I can hear the defensiveness in Sophie's voice, and I like that she's on my side, even in something so minor as a critique of our fence. I say nothing, though, being a gentleman as I cut the fence free from the wire and realign it, using the post driver to quickly bury one end two feet in the ground. I wrap the remaining wire around it, fixing it while the ladies talk over me.

"So, what are you doing on the BB Ranch, Sophie?"

Sophie, who's been attaching her lengths of wire to the strands still on the ground, doesn't look up from her work. "Well, I'm working with Doc Jones this summer and have been coming out to check on Briarbelle after a rough delivery. But today I'm just hanging with James, tagging along while he does chores."

Shayanne has a flirty tone to her voice as she answers Sophie. "Ooooh, that kind of 'friend'; I see now. You know the saying, you can tell a lot about a person by the company they keep. Bennetts are good people, so you must be too. Even if Daddy's not too happy with them right now."

That perks my ears up. Attaching the last strand of fence, I tuck my pliers into my pocket. "Huh? Why wouldn't he be happy with us?"

In my head, I'm thinking we've got a damn good reason to be pissed at him since he's trying to take advantage of us, and I can only hope that Shayanne, who seems sweet and young, isn't wise to her father's shenanigans. "Well, he says he tried to help you guys out, but you just shooed him away like a pesky gnat," she says. "He took offense. I over-heard him mouthing to my brothers about it."

She shrugs like he gets pissy on the regular. Who knows, maybe he does . . . but that doesn't mean he's got a right to be pissy about us not wanting to sell.

In an attempt to keep calm, I shake my head, forcing my voice to remain even. "Not exactly what happened. He came over and tried to buy the ranch from Mama when Pops was barely in the ground, and then thought maybe us boys would be pushovers and take his deal too. Just so we're clear, my family's not interested in selling our land."

Shayanne holds her hands up, palms toward me in a plea for peace. "I ain't trying to get under your hat, James. Just telling you what I heard."

I go back to repairing the fence, noticing something a bit peculiar. At first glance, it looked like the section of wire had pulled free from the post. It happens; cows push against the wire, a twist slips, and boom . . . gap in the wire.

But looking at the section that Sophie's been working with, I can see that it's been clipped—cleanly. The end also has plier marks, ones that Sophie hasn't put in yet, like someone untwisted what I did here.

There's no reason for a stranger to undo the wire; the gap is big enough that a lost hiker can slip between the strands. And there's only a few people who'd be out here in this back pasture, Bennetts and Tannens. I know we didn't clip our own damn fence, so that leaves . . .

"Hey, Shayanne? You said your dad was mad and mouthing to your brothers?" I ask, wiggling the end of the wire so that Sophie can see but Shayanne can't. She looks, raising an eyebrow as she sees the same thing I did.

Shayanne, though, is innocently oblivious. "Sure was. He was on a roll, too, not hollering, but just going on and on and on. Why?"

"Oh nothing; just thinking," I reply. "We got a lot of acres lined up next to each other, don't we? I'm usually checking our fences and herds out this way. Your herd pastures out here sometimes too. One of your brothers or your dad check your side?"

Shayanne nods, leaning on her saddle horn. "Usually Brody does that since he's our animal caretaker, but they all do every now and then. Bobby and Brutal do more farm work since that's our primary income. Hey, speaking of animals, did you know that Brody got a herd of goats?"

I'm only half listening now as she jumps from topic to topic, trying to reconcile that our fence has been cut and it's likely one of the Tannen boys who did it.

Sophie, who's trying to help out while also being nice, looks up. "Brutal?"

"That's what we call him," Shayanne says. "His real name's Bruce, but back in high school he played nose guard for the Great Falls High defense . . . one game he knocked out three guys in a single half! After that, well—"

She dissolves into background noise again, and I go back to working on the wire. I get that maybe Paul Tannen is mad, but what good does cutting fence line do? The most he would end up doing is making a few of our herd wander over onto his land, and to what point? We'd just get them back, like we did today. They're all tagged, so it's not like he'd be able to steal them from us—every buyer in two hundred miles knows our brand and tag.

Maybe just ornery acting out? Could be it. For me, that usually consists of less destructive things, though.

As I drift, luckily Sophie seems to be listening to Shayanne, keeping her off my back. "You know, I love goats. Maybe I can come see them sometime? Have you seen those videos of goats in pajamas and people paying to do yoga with goats jumping all over them?"

Shayanne looks aghast. "People pay for goats in clothes to jump on them? People are weird. Daddy says that's why we stay out here where folks are normal and sane, just good old country folk. Oh, but the goats . . ."

I go back to finishing up the repair, and I want to do a bit of checking along the rest of the fence and report in to Mark for his take on the damage. Tossing my tools in the back of the trailer, I turn to Shayanne, dusting off my hands.

"Hey, Shayanne, it's been good seeing you, but we'd better get back to chores, or we won't make it to the dinner table on time this evening."

Shayanne smiles brightly, nodding. "Oh I understand! I should head back in soon, too, or else the guys are going to holler about dinner not being ready tonight. Good to see you."

Shayanne seems a little shy as she turns to Sophie and offers her hand again. "Hey . . . you really want to come see the goats sometime?"

Sophie nods, shaking Shayanne's hand. "Absolutely. Unofficially, of course, not as Doc's assistant. Just as a fellow goat and animal lover."

I can see that Shayanne is beaming, excited that Sophie would visit. "Here, put my number in your phone and text me," she says. "We'll figure out when the boys are all gone and you can come over to see the goats. My favorite's named Baaaar-bra—Barbara for easy's sake."

Sophie smiles, and pulls her phone from . . . well, I'm not quite sure. It's a skill I think all women have, the ability to hide a phone, makeup, pencils, and other stuff on their bodies like a ninja or something. Makes me wonder why they need a purse at all. "That's super punny. I approve."

"And remember," Shayanne says as she wheels her horse around, "you never saw me. I've been baking a pie alllll day."

She grins and heads off at a trot, leaving me and Sophie alone. I school my face, not wanting to worry Sophie with my inner thoughts about the exact cause of the fence vandalism, and thinking a long ride sounds like a great idea. "Hey, let's check out the fence along the property line with the Tannens' land. It'll probably take all day, but it'll get us closer to the house, just in time for dinner. Hop on the back; we can ride tandem. The horses are trained to head back to the barn on their own, and Luke'll take care of unsaddling him."

Sophie settles in behind me, wrapping her arms around my waist.

"So, seems like you made a new friend," I say as we pull off.

Sophie laughs, shaking her head "Maybe. She sure can talk, but she seems like a nice girl."

CHAPTER 15

SOPHIE

After patching the fence, I spend the rest of the day with James, riding along the fences as he tells me story after story of his adventures as a kid growing up in this idyllic place.

I laugh as he relates tales of a mini-James who was bursting at the seams to try everything, do everything, *be* everything. "Thankfully, my little rocket pack was put out when I splashed down in the pond . . . although getting my bike out of there was a major pain in the ass."

There's a touch of sadness underlying his story, one I've felt through a lot of his little anecdotes. For most of his childhood, he felt trapped by the small town, needing to explore and create his own destiny beyond what was preordained by his family's land and legacy.

"So, now what? Back to the rodeo, and Mark and Luke take care of the ranch?" I ask as he wraps up a story about a Winnebago he rented last year for the tour.

I don't mean it to be accusatory, but his shoulders tighten, and when he speaks again, I can tell he's a little upset. "Yeah, I guess. That's always been the plan. Maybe someday I'll come home and settle down, but I've still got some crazy left in me; too young to let go of my gypsy nomad life just yet."

I smile a little, relieved. His comment started off serious, but the end of it had a thread of laughter and irony. He's still enjoying the rodeo, but part of me thinks he'd be just as happy riding the fences here and building a future for himself and his family.

Still, it's not all out of him yet. "You miss the fast pace while you're here?"

He throttles down the ATV until it's nearly at a walking pace, thinking harder than I'd expected him to. "Yeah, it gets repetitive sometimes, but this week has been a little more exciting than usual." He looks over his shoulder, his eyes twinkling. "Guess I have you to thank for that."

I duck my head, smiling. "Glad to add a little crazy to your wild."

In that moment, I think we might jump off the ATV and go at it, right here in this field in the dirt. My arms wrap tighter around his waist to explore the chiseled washboard of his abs, then run up his hardened chest. Before I can do more, though, from far away I hear Mama's dinner bell, and the moment is broken.

James's voice is still a little husky as he looks back. "Guess we'd better head into the house. See what Mama's whipped up for dinner."

Whipping? I must be in hormonal overload, because even James's innocent comments are causing me to think about sex. "Sounds good."

He throttles up the ATV, and we ride back to the barn. My mind's still whirling about sex with James, and I'm half-distracted when he jumps out and starts putting the tools away. "Hey, wanna make it interesting?"

I smirk at him, thinking he did a pretty good job of making dinner interesting the other day by rubbing on my thigh. If he touches me right now, I know for damn sure we're not leaving this barn. "Sure, what have you got in mind, Cowboy?"

"I'm thinking if I beat you inside, you're mine to do anything I want with for the night. If you get there first, I'll do whatever you want."

I act like I'm considering it, before taking off at a sprint across the barn, my yelled agreement blowing behind me in the wind. "Deal!"

I hear James curse and give chase, gaining ground fast. Even with my semicheating head start, it's a close race, but he reaches the steps before I do without question.

Pulling me close to him, he lowers his lips to brush against my ear, sending another thrill down my spine to spread through my body. "Oh, woman, you are so mine tonight. I'm thinking my fantasy about fucking you as you bend over the truck seat is a go tonight."

He looks into my eyes as he strokes a tendril of hair that escaped my ponytail behind my ear. "I could be up for that," I whisper, trying to keep my voice low enough that the rest of the family can't overhear us. "If we move the truck."

James laughs silently, nodding. "Maybe even smack that ass, since you seemed into that. I know what I'll be thinking of all dinner . . . your curvy little ass bare in the sunset, pink with my handprint, my cock driving into your sweet pussy as you try to be quiet so we don't get caught. Is that what you're gonna be thinking about while you eat at Mama's table tonight, Sophie?" he asks, and I can't help but nod. "That's my naughty girl."

I reach up to his neck, pulling him down to me, but instead of the hot kiss he's expecting, I bite at his bottom lip, near growling into his mouth as I tease him back. "Cowboy, yeah, that's what I'll be thinking about. You fucking me so hard I have to lift up to my toes as you grab handfuls of my ass for leverage to get in deeper. I'm gonna squeeze you so damn tight that you come before I do."

He growls at me, reaching down and squeezing my ass as his hard cock presses against my belly. "How do you do it? I'm teasing you here, winding you up, and you turn it around on me, and somehow I'm the one going into a nice family dinner with a raging boner."

He moves in for a kiss, but I drop back down to my flat feet, scooting away to keep the game of chase going. "C'mon, James, can't be late for dinner or Mama will give your plate away to your brothers. You've got to behave properly at her table, all gentlemanlike, you know?"

James chuckles and reaches down, adjusting himself visibly. "Gentlemanlike? This better be a damn fast dinner because I need to be inside you as soon as fucking possible."

I smirk at him, leading him by the hand to the house, giggling inside as I watch him rush to the sink before pausing to take a couple of big breaths, seemingly trying to will his dick to calm down.

Dinner is a welcome break, chatting about the day's happenings on the ranch, even as James and I do our best to drive each other crazy with little touches here, brushes there, and maybe I do suck the spaghetti a bit suggestively when he's looking, but, c'mon . . . it's spaghetti. He should be lucky I don't make him share a plate and nose a big meatball over to me.

The whole time, I know James is struggling to control himself, but he's forgetting a little fact. Sure, the tent in his pants might be showing his arousal . . . but he's not the only one turned on. I'm just lucky that his T-shirt is loose enough that my hard nipples aren't showing.

About halfway through dinner, James looks over at Mark and sets his fork down. "Hey, Mark, just to let you know . . . there was a fence break out on the back pasture. A few head got through to Tannen land, but we shooed them back over, and I fixed the fence."

"That's good," Mark says, not worried.

James gives me a look, and continues, "Funny thing was, the wires looked cut, definitely not from wear and tear considering I checked it myself a week ago. And the fence post wasn't bent . . . it was like someone pulled it up instead of a cow leaning on it."

Mark's face immediately goes into boss mode. It's similar to his usual demeanor, but there's something a bit extra about him when he clicks into that mental space, assuming the mantle of command and not just big brother.

James doesn't flinch, but to me it seems rather intimidating as Mark fires off questions at rapid-fire pace. "Which side? How big of a section? Did you really check the whole fence or half ass it, and now you're covering up? Any proof it was the Tannens?"

James raises a grumpy eyebrow at the half-ass remark but otherwise keeps his cool. "It was a solid stretch a week ago, and this was probably a fifteen-foot section laying flat in the dirt, letting the herd come and go as they wanted. We did see Shayanne up there—"

I interrupt him, trying to lighten the mood. "Oh, but she said 'we never saw her,'" I say, using air quotes to show her reluctance to be spotted. "And I saw the same spots. It looked like fresh tool marks on the wire, not week-old ones."

James gives me a grateful look, while Mark looks both more and less pissed. I guess it'd be easier to just know his little brother might have fucked up, but at the same time it's good to know he didn't. He rumbles, looking at James, "Shayanne?"

"Yeah, she said she'd slipped out from chores, but that her dad had been mouthing to the boys about us being disrespectful and not taking his offer."

Mark's face clouds, and he strokes his chin while looking at Mama and then Luke before saying anything. "Nothing concrete, I guess, but definitely something to keep an eye on. Those boys have been bullies since they were kids, and when Paul Tannen gets all riled up, I don't know that I'd put it past him to do something like that either."

Mama interrupts, probably hoping to keep the peace at least through dinner. "I think we'd best let it lie for now, boys. No way to be sure it was a Tannen, and if we engage, they're gonna get more hot under the collar. If it happens again or anything else, I'll go over and have words with the man myself."

I see the guys all give each other pointed looks, and I have no doubt that if it comes to that, there's no way they're letting Mama go over there, at least not alone.

As she gets up to get dessert, James pushes away from the table. Patting his belly, he gives her a smile. "Mama, I'm going to have to take a rain check on dessert tonight. I was planning on Sophie and I heading into town."

It's news to me, but getting alone with James sounds like a great idea, so I happily play along.

"Well, I guess I'll just have to have a few more leftovers tonight," Mama jokes. "And I just want to say it now, in front of everyone. Sophie, I know Briarbelle doesn't need your care anymore . . . but you're more than welcome in my house for dinner anytime you want. Or breakfast, or lunch even. Whatever meal you happen to turn up here for, I'll feed you right."

She makes it obvious that she knows about me spending the night but gives me a wink, so she seems to be okay with it. Still, it's hard not to blush furiously, especially as Luke rolls his eyes, obviously not looking forward to being kicked out of his bedroom more often.

In fact, Luke can't pass up a chance to get one little jab in on his brother while James gets his hat. "Does that mean I can sleep in my own bed tonight? Oh, and don't worry about leftovers—I'm taking James's dessert!"

Mark growls as we leave, and I hear him mumbling, "Like hell you will." Mama hushes them both, though, with a laugh, reminding them there's two extra servings.

We hop in Doc's truck, and I fire up the engine, but James directs me to pull over off the main driveway and park behind the barn on the other side of the house. I turn in my seat to look at him, raising an eyebrow. "This doesn't look like town to me. What are we doing over here?"

Giving me a wink, he quickly climbs out of the truck and rushes around the front to open my door. Leaning in, without preamble he devours my mouth, taking our dinner-table teasing from a simmer to a bonfire in an instant. I grab his shirt, pulling him closer as my ass slides along the seat and my breasts squash against his body.

He pulls me out of the truck, whispering in my ear, "I figure we've got thirty minutes while they're eating dessert. Are you already slick and wet for me, or do you need a warm-up? God knows, I'm ready to be inside you, but I'll be more than happy to have your apple bottom with a side of pussy for dessert first."

"Tempting," I tease, tracing a hand along the outline of his cock in his jeans until he groans. "Maybe I didn't have enough meat for dinner myself."

James gasps, cupping my breast through my shirt and sucking on my neck hard enough that I know I'm going to have an epic hickey there tomorrow. "Fuck it, Soph. You'd better be ready. Unbuckle your jeans, now."

I nod, grinning like a loon, or maybe like a horny woman about to get exactly what she wants, and do as he says, pulling my jeans and panties down to pile on top of my boots. James does the same before spinning me in place and pushing my head down to the bench seat.

James stops, and when I glance back over my shoulder, I can see that he's staring at me, and I hope I look just like his fantasy. He steps closer, kicking my feet as wide as they'll go and caressing my bare cheeks. He grabs me and pulls me open, and I feel his eyes taking in every inch of my wet pussy and my asshole. "Mmm . . . you look sexy as fuck right now, Soph.

"You are ready for me," James says, his voice near incredulous, like he can't believe that I'm ready to go, but he does that to me. Just one word or look, and I'd gladly take him.

"Of course I am," I tease, wiggling my ass for him. He lets go, and I momentarily wonder what he's doing, and then I feel it—a sharp, stinging slap on my right ass cheek, bright and hot and wonderful.

I gasp at first, but it quickly turns into a moan as I wiggle my ass for more. I've never really experimented with spanking before, but right now, I'd happily and willingly go along with whatever James wants. It all just turns me on more. "Please?"

He obliges, reaching across to smack the other cheek and then tracing a fingertip across each cheek, soothing the sting. His right hand dips down to my pussy, now dripping wet, and he chuckles.

"Oh, you definitely liked that, didn't you?" he asks cockily. "Even your pretty little asshole is quivering. I could fuck you any way I wanted right now, and you'd love it, wouldn't you?"

I'm wanton at this point, so I just grab the seat in front of me harder, pushing my ass back in invitation. James pulls my cheeks apart again, bending down slightly to slip his cock to my entrance. He pauses for a moment, and I can feel myself involuntarily pulsing against him, trying to pull him inside my body.

James runs a finger along my spine, his voice pure gravel. "I'm memorizing this moment, right here. My fucking fantasy—hell, better than anything I imagined—come to life."

The sweetness mixed in with the sexy is my undoing, and I squeeze my eyes shut before an emotional tear can leak out. My heart tightens in my chest, and I'm caught up. This is supposed to be just a fun fling, but when he says stuff like that, I can't help but get my emotions tied up too.

Before that thought can take root, though, he rears back and slams into me in one powerful thrust. All thoughts except overwhelming lust are obliterated from my mind as James immediately starts pounding me relentlessly, giving me no time to adjust to his size or the fullness he creates inside me, and it feels overwhelming and awesome.

One of James's hands tightens around my hip, his fingers digging in hard as I lift to my toes as predicted, arching even more to offer him as much access as possible, wanting him as deep as he can go.

His other hand grabs my ponytail, firmly pressing my cheek to the seat as I press back against him, fighting for more and more.

It's too good, and I start to make instinctive, primal noises, moans and cries escaping my lips until he shushes me. "Gotta be quieter than that or you'll have the whole family out here wondering what's happening by the barn. I'm gonna make you come so hard, all over my cock, but you gotta keep it down."

I nod, biting my forearm nearly hard enough to draw blood in an attempt to mute myself before I remember my earlier challenge. *Give it to me, James . . . but I'm going to give it right back to you.*

I start to clench my inner muscles in rhythm with his driving thrusts, milking him with every thrust. Smiling, I meet his thrusts, pushing my ass back and making our hips smack together.

James feels it immediately and leans over me, growling in my ear, "No way, naughty girl. I'm not coming before you do. Go ahead and keep squeezing my cock tight, it feels so damn good, but I know it drives you crazy too. Keep doing it, and we'll both go . . . together. Even?"

It takes all my self-control to not abandon myself again, and I turn my head, giving him a short nod. "Even."

We create a punishing pace, pushing and pulling, squeezing and releasing, and it's only moments before I moan from deep in my chest. "Now . . . I'm coming, James."

He pulls back and slams deep into me harder than ever, sending me hurtling off the edge, lost in the pleasure. Through the haze of it all I hear him gasp. "Me, too, Soph. Fuuck—"

The feeling of his cock pulsing inside me, filling me with his seed and laying claim to my entire body heightens my orgasm, a delightful warm sensation coursing through me. Collapsing over me fully, his weight makes me lose my tiptoe touch with the ground, and my legs slide on the gravel behind me as we pant for breath.

"Mmm, I think we'd better get moving if we're gonna make it back to my place before dark," I finally say as James pulls out, my pussy immediately wanting more. I feel a slight chill as he steps back; I want more than his cock. I want his warmth, the shared experience with him, and the chance to be held in his arms, safer than if I was in Fort Knox. Still, I have to tease him a little. "If we don't go, Luke's liable to catch us, and I don't think I could stand your brothers teasing you about us having truck sex while we sit at your Mama's dinner table. You know they'd do it."

James immediately pulls me up, turning me to face him for a tender kiss, our lips smacking together three times before he looks down at me, smiling. "Not a chance in hell. I'd punch them or leverage one of their dirty secrets before I'd let them embarrass you like that. Now hurry up, woman. That shower of yours is gonna get some use."

I laugh as he runs around the front of the truck, yanking up his underwear and pants as he goes. He's already seated inside, drumming on the dash to speed me up when I move to pull my undies and jeans in place. "How'd you do that so fast?"

"I'm used to doing things in eight seconds or less," James reminds me, before smirking as he cranks the engine. "Aren't you glad I take longer on some things?"

"Yep . . . but I'm also glad rodeo taught you something else."

"What's that?" he asks, and I smirk.

"To be ready for six or seven rides a night."

CHAPTER 16

JAMES

Stretching my arms over my head, I glance at the calendar on the wall, somehow amazed that weeks have passed since Sophie and I first met. We've found a good balance, her working all day with Doc, and me around the ranch, before meeting up for late nights and early mornings, sometimes in town, sometimes her joining my family for dinner at the ranch before . . . well, moving on to other things.

It's not perfect, we both know. If she stays at the ranch, she has to drive to town before the sun comes up to get Doc. If I stay at her place, I have to drive back out to the ranch even earlier, but somehow neither of us seems to mind the run of sleepless nights, as long as they're spent together.

It's fun, playful, and sexy as hell to fuck her into exhaustion and then do it again in the middle of the night before we truly crash, needing a few hours of shut-eye to keep up our crazy pace.

But tonight will be different. Tonight . . . we're playing house the right way, with an overnight date and a long and lazy, and hopefully naked, morning. Pulling on fresh-pressed jeans and my favorite button-down, I holler at Luke, who's sitting in the main room of the bunkhouse with his boots up, reading *Sports Illustrated*, "You sure you don't mind covering for me tomorrow?"

Luke hollers back, not missing a beat from the sound of a page turning, "Nope. Go have a good time with your woman. I'll cover for you . . . just like I always do."

I hear the teasing note to his voice, but he's not entirely joking. Luke has covered for me in more ways than one over the years, taking care of my chores when I flaked or once even telling Sheriff Bishop that I'd been camping in the back pasture with him all night so I couldn't have possibly been over at the bonfire party that left a hundred bottles of beer behind. Empty, of course.

Afterward, Luke still questioned me thoroughly about that one, though, to make sure I hadn't done anything particularly stupid. Luckily, this time his covering for me isn't quite so serious or last-minute. And, since he seems to approve of Sophie, he knows I'm not doing anything foolish.

I adjust my boots and walk out into the main room, clapping him on the shoulder. "Alright, if you're sure then. Thanks a lot, Luke. I'm off to pick up Sophie. We'll see you at the Fourth Festival in town?"

The Fourth Festival is one of the biggest summer events in town, where everyone shuts things down early in order to kick back and party a little. Luke nods, and I continue, "We'll be at Sophie's all night, then I'll be back tomorrow afternoon sometime to finish up for the day."

"That's fine . . . but you owe me a barbecue sandwich," Luke says, glancing up. "One of the king-size ones too. None of that lite and healthy mustard sauce shit."

I laugh, nodding. "Okay. See you later."

I run out to my truck, where I can almost smell the light scent of Sophie's bodywash as well as the headier, earthier scent of her arousal from the last time she was in here with me. It reminds me of what's in store for today, and I'm humming along with the radio as I drive into town.

I'm mumbling along to some George Strait as I get to Sophie's house. I get out and knock on her door. "Soph?"

"Close your eyes, Cowboy," she calls from inside. "I want it to be a surprise!"

I back up, putting my hat over my face as I hear Sophie unlock her door and step out.

"Okay, Cowboy . . . how do I look?"

I take my hat down, but I'm so shocked and turned on by what Sophie's wearing that it tumbles from my fingers.

The first thing I notice is the shorts . . . and *shorts* is the only word to describe them. Tight, denim, and hugging her hips, they're cut high enough to make Daisy Duke herself blush. They're sexy, like Sophie. *And* like Sophie, they're not trashy at all.

Dragging my eyes upward, I notice she's wearing a white cutoff tank top underneath a checked shirt that she's tied off to expose her flat, tanned stomach and highlight the swell of her breasts. Her hair's pulled into twin ponytails, and she's got a hat on that nearly matches mine, shading her eyes but revealing the bewitching bow of her smirking pink lips.

She's the perfect cowgirl for the Fourth, and I confirm it by looking down, forcing myself to ignore the sexy length of her legs to find a pair of relaxed high-heel cowboy boots. "My God."

Sophie grins and comes over, squatting down to pick up my hat and giving me a nice look down the inch of hollow between her breasts before standing up and plopping the hat on my head.

"I'll take that as James-grunt for you like the outfit," she says cheekily, patting my chest. "You look pretty good too . . . if you can stop drooling and close your mouth."

I pull her close, hooking the belt loops on her shorts to press our bodies together as I look into her eyes. "You . . . are the sexiest woman I've ever seen," I growl, running my thumbs over the soft skin on her sides. Thankfully, Sophie isn't ticklish. "I'm going to have the best-looking girlfriend in all of Great Falls for today's festival, and I don't care if anyone wants to disagree with me. They're a blind idiot."

"Girlfriend, huh?" Sophie asks, cupping my face. "I like the sound of that. By the way, you shaved."

"You said it makes it easier when we kiss . . . no skin burn."

Sophie nods, biting her lip. "Yeah . . . but you look damn sexy with a day's worth of stubble," Sophie sighs. "Guess you'll just have to start shaving right before we start kissing and foreplay."

I laugh and walk her over to my truck. It's not a far drive to the festival, which is being held this year in the touristy part of town at the Little League baseball complex. We find parking and get out, and Sophie takes my hand.

"Wow," she says as we enter through the fence, which has been festooned with plenty of red, white, and blue. "I've never been to a place like this before."

"Really?" I ask, looking around at the rides, booths, and tents that I've grown up with all my life. "This is your first fair?"

"Well, yeah," Sophie says. "I mean, I've been to fairs before—one time Jake had a business trip out to San Diego, and he took me to the Del Mar Fair, but it was nothing like this. The rides were bigger there, but . . ."

"I gotcha," I assure her. "Nothing quite like dirt and grass and a little country charm, is there? Come on, let's see what we can do."

Sophie nods excitedly, and for the next two hours we wander the booths, playing some of the nearly impossible-to-win games. "Come on, I thought all you cowboys knew how to shoot!" she teases me after I leave a shred of black on the star-shaped target, failing to win her a big teddy bear. "What happened?"

"What happened is the gun shoots faster than nearly anyone can adjust their aim to punch the shape out," I admit. "Now, gimme a decent lever action, and I'll shoot the feathers off a duck's butt at two hundred meters."

We keep going, playing games, riding rides, and just generally enjoying ourselves. It's refreshing, seeing all this through Sophie's eyes. For her, all this is new: the tired, old Viking swing ride with its squealing motor is new and refreshing, the mostly rigged games a challenge instead of a waste of a dollar.

"So, ready for some food?" I ask as we get off the Ferris wheel. "Maybe some funnel cake?"

"First . . . I want to get you wet!" Sophie says, grabbing my hand and dragging me toward a big blue sign. "Come on, you're a celebrity!"

I'd hardly call myself a celebrity, but I see where Sophie's dragging me. "You're serious?"

"You go up, I go up," she promises me, but I have a feeling she's fibbing. "Come on, Cowboy, don't you want to see me in a wet T-shirt?"

The dunk tank is an annual standard of the Fourth Festival, run by the local high school to raise money. This year the sign says the funds are for the music program. As I approach, I see Doc Jones throwing a ball at the target, dunking the high school principal to cheers from the small crowd. "Nice throw, Doc."

He turns, smiling. "Well now, James and Sophie. Happy Fourth. You enjoying yourself, Sophie?"

"This is great!" Sophie exclaims happily. "The Ferris wheel was awesome; I could see over most of town at the top."

"Well, you two have fun. Just don't overdo it," Doc adds in his quiet way. "This is the sort of town with sharp ears and long tongues. Don't get caught misbehaving."

"Will do, Doc," Sophie says, her smile never wavering. "You might want to stick around and watch me dunk James, though."

I roll my eyes, playing along a little as she negotiates with the dunk-tank people. In the end, it takes a guaranteed fifty-dollar contribution and a few whispered promises from her to me, but I soon find myself bootless, sitting on the platform with my hat on my head.

"You sure you don't want to lose that Stetson?" Sophie taunts me, tossing the softball up and down in her hand. "I guess this is the wrong time to tell you I used to play sports in high school."

"Sorry, you can't get me with that," I taunt back. "You already told me you were a total girly girl in high school."

"Yeah, well . . . I still think you're taking a bath," Sophie says. She rears back and throws the first of four shots, missing the target by a good foot.

"Oh, so close! At this rate, I'm gonna have a great seat up here for the fireworks!"

"Keep talking, Cowboy," Sophie says before unleashing another throw. This one's closer, clanging off the target arm, but too far inside, and my seat's still secure. "One more shot is all I need!"

Suddenly, she switches the ball from her right hand to her left and rears back, uncorking a fastball that clangs on target. I don't even have time to protest before I'm plunged into the water, dousing myself all the way and getting water up my nose before I come up.

"What the—?" I cough, grabbing my hat, which is floating jauntily on top of the water. "I didn't know you were left-handed!"

"I'm not, but I can throw lefty," Sophie says, smiling. "You're right, I didn't play ball in high school . . . I played Little League a year or two, though."

I climb out of the tank, grab Sophie, and pull her close, letting her absorb some of the water that's still streaming off me before kissing her deeply. "Well, I'd say you played me well," I purr in her ear. "I guess you get to be in charge for the rest of the festival . . . after a stop by the truck to change into some dry clothes, you ringer."

"Great," Sophie says, stepping back. I watch a drop of water race down her flushed chest, disappearing into her cleavage, and I'm struck by an urge to chase it with my tongue, lapping it up to make her squeal. But before I can follow through, she teases me, "Now that my diabolical plan to get you wet was victorious, let's get some food."

After a quick change behind the door of my truck, where Sophie peeked more than she acted as guard, she leads me over to the food area. Looking around, she chooses homemade corn dogs. "There. I want one of those, please."

We enjoy our food, run into Luke, and I buy him a sandwich like I promised. As the sun starts to set, everyone moves over to the big grassy area, where they've set up a bunch of the Little League bleachers. I have another idea in mind and grab a blanket out of the back of my truck before taking Sophie's hand, pulling her toward the street.

"Where are we going?" she asks as I lead her toward a small alley near the back of the field complex. "I'm into a lot of things and willing to try even more, but a dirty alley isn't really my taste."

I grin at her as she looks around like the few bits of trash on the ground are gonna jump up and bite her. "Prissy aren't we, Princess? Trust me, I'm not fucking you in the alley. I just want to have a little privacy. C'mon."

I can feel her eyes boring into my back as I lead her to the far end of the alley and a small cinder-block building. The door's tightly secured, so I hand her the blanket and give the doorknob a firm lift before banging it to the right.

It pops open in front of us, and she gasps. "James Bennett, are we breaking into this building? Didn't you hear Doc say to behave ourselves?"

She's joking, fake indignation in every word, so I grin, taking her by the hand again. "Yep, he said don't get *caught* misbehaving, so you'd better sneak your fine ass in this door before someone comes and catches us."

I peek over her shoulder, forcing my eyes wide and basically shoving her inside the dark space on the other side of the door.

"Oh my gosh," Sophie whispers, scared. "Was someone coming? Did they see?"

In the dark, I grin, knowing I've gotten her. "Did who see what? Nobody was there but us."

She growls, a false sound of frustration as she presses in tight to me, swatting my chest with her tiny hand. "So, is this the big plan? Breaking and entering and then hanging in a dark . . . closet?"

I take her hands, turn my back to her, and place them on my waist. "Follow me. There's another door, and that's where we're going."

I feel her hands clenching my belt loops, but she follows me step for step as I lead her out the door, up a flight of dark stairs, pausing at another door.

"Thank you for trusting me," I tell her when we reach the top. "This is what we're here for . . ."

With a twist of my hand on the knob and just a bit of dramatic revelation, I expose the rooftop space where I plan for us to watch the fireworks.

On Saturdays during Little League season, it's a lounge or loft for volunteers who just want to relax a little after a hot day of organizing, with old patio furniture sitting against one wall. But tonight, with the fireworks show being overhead, I spread the blanket and guide Sophie to sit down.

"So, uh, how exactly did you know we'd be able to get up here? Seems like you've done that a time or two before. Was this your special spot to take all the Bennett Babes in high school?"

Even in the dim light from the festival below, I can see her batting her lashes as she jokes around. "No, actually this was my spot. I discovered this place one time when Pops volunteered to be an umpire for Little League. It sort of became my place to hide when I'd raised a little too much hell in school. Later, it was just my cooldown place when I needed to get away. Being up here let me see far beyond the scope of town. In the daylight, you can see all the way into the city, to the world beyond . . . this town, the responsibilities, the expectations. I could see a way out."

She cups my face, the banter gone as the seriousness of what I just shared settles into the air around us. "And you did get out," she says softly. "You've gotten out and had wild adventures, traveled the country, tamed beasts, and generally just embraced that wild child inside you. You did it, James. And you did it while still being a good man, taking care of your family, and being here when they need you."

I huff a laugh, taking her hands and shaking my head. "But I wasn't here. I was halfway across the country when Pops died, had to rush home for the funeral. And I'll be honest, I chafed against the routine here, same day on repeat for infinity. But I learned something while I was away too."

"What's that?" Sophie asks, the festival ignored as she focuses totally on me. It's something that makes her special; nobody else does that.

"On the road, it's kinda the same thing. We roll into a nameless town, do our rides, party, train in every free minute. I've been across the United States multiple times, and I've only been to the Grand Canyon because they were shooting a commercial there. I saw Mount Rushmore only in glimpses in between a photographer taking shots. I've been to Nashville, and didn't even have time to see a single concert because I was too busy riding a bull, then loading up for the next town. Most of the time, I never eat at anything fancier than the local greasy-spoon diner or a protein shake to keep myself lean, or really see beyond the windshield as I drive through to the next bull ride. It's repetitive, too, just in a different way."

"But you love it, right?" she asks, concern in her voice. "You've got friends on the circuit, a type of family there too."

"I have always loved it. And I'm in my prime, riding better than I ever have before," I agree. "Of course, we're like a family since we spend every waking hour together or following each other down the highway like a gypsy caravan made up of custom-stickered Winnebagos. But they're not my brothers, not really, not like Mark and Luke. The guys on tour, we're close, but at the end of the day, you know that the guy you're having a beer with today is the same guy trying to outdo you and get a bigger check tomorrow. They'll gladly watch you fail if it means they can win. Mark and Luke aren't like that. As for Mama, she was always fine when Pops was here, but this year . . . I just don't know. It feels different to be here without him, feels different to leave in the fall. Like I'm leaving her alone, even though she's obviously not. Just those same old responsibilities and expectations pressing down on me, trying to force me to take root here."

Sophie hums, thinking to herself for a moment before she nestles against me, her body warm and petite and comfortable in a way that I'm coming to look forward to more and more. "James, has Mark or Luke said anything to put that pressure on you? Have they made any assumption that this year will be any different than every other? I know I'm not around all the time, but from what I see, they seem to think you'll ride your way to finals in November, come back for a Christmas visit, and then be gone again in January for the season. Are you sure . . ." She hesitates like she's unsure if she wants to say whatever is next, but continues, "Are you sure that it's not *you* who is feeling an urge to stay, to put down roots with your family? Things are different now; of course they are with your dad being gone. And it's okay to reevaluate and see what you want. It doesn't have to be the same thing you've always wanted."

I'm quiet, letting what she said sink in. Is she right? Am I putting this pressure on myself? I clear my throat, ignoring the sky and looking at the concrete roof below me. "I know when I left at eighteen, it was with drama and duress, Mama begging me not to go when I was so young, to wait until I was twenty or twenty-one at least. It was one of the only big fights between her and Pops, with Pops having the final say in stating that I was a man, and while he may not have cared for the rodeo, I had to go out and make my own life, good or bad. Mama didn't speak to him for days after that.

"Maybe I've just always thought she still felt that way about my rodeo career, but if I'm honest, she's never asked me to stay home again.

Instead, she's supported me, cheering me on, proud of what I've accomplished. And having the world's best pie ready for me when I come home, no matter if I win or lose."

"Mama Lou's a good woman," Sophie says, wrapping her arms around me. "Very loving."

"Mark and Luke too. Minus the pie, and with a few more sarcastic comments and grunts," I add, making Sophie chuckle. "They've always had their shit together, and it's been hard. Mark knew from a very early age that he was going to take over the ranch and worked to learn everything he could, his path clear. Luke's always said he wanted to work with horses, and he's made that a successful reality for himself. Me? I was the wandering, aimless one whose only goal was to chase adrenaline and conquer it."

And I have, I think, going silent. Maybe it's time to reevaluate for myself. I am in my prime, but I don't have to ride. I could be in my prime at home, doing more to help in Pops's absence.

Is that a better, maybe more adult, course of action?

Sophie seems to sense the rising anxiety of my whirling thoughts because she sits up to straddle me, pushing me to my back and locking eyes with me.

Planting her forearms on my chest, she crosses her arms and looks me in the eyes. "This is not a decision to be made tonight, Cowboy. You've said a lot, and I'm honored that you let me see so far inside that handsome, yet oh-so-thick skull of yours. Turn it around in your head while you're out on those long rides like a movie montage scene, but tonight, right now . . . be here with me. Watch the fireworks and celebrate a lovely summer day, a hot July night, and the sexy cowgirl at your side."

Knowing she's right, I lift to kiss her, letting my hands run along her back to her thighs where they frame my torso, tracing up her inner thighs to skim along the edge of her shorts.

She sighs in pleasure for a moment before she jumps, the boom of the first firework scaring her for a moment before she's backlit with sparkles.

She laughs and slides off me, curling up between the V of my spread legs on the blanket with her head on my shoulder as we watch the light show above.

I can't help but do as she says, focusing on this moment . . . this perfect moment with Sophie in my arms, my family somewhere below us watching the fireworks with the townies, the ranch steady and safe, and Pops watching us all from above.

I get the feeling that he'd be smirking at me, telling me that for all my nomad desires, maybe I've done what I set out to do and it's time to grow up and be a man now . . . for my family and for his legacy.

And while Sophie and I will, barring something weird or crazy happening, get hot and heavy tonight . . . she's given me a lot to think about. Like the proverb about the horse, she's led me to water without trying to make me drink. Just letting me consider what I actually want to do. She's surprised me again, with her heart and her mind.

CHAPTER 17

SOPHIE

The sky is inky black, and the lights from the baseball fields barely cast a dim glow as we sneak out of the building, bubbly and childlike from oohing and aahing over the spectacle. While there was a lot of touching between us, we focused on the fireworks show for the most part, knowing that after this . . . we'll make our own fireworks.

From behind us, I hear a shout. "Hey, Bennett!"

James pauses, turning. I think for a minute he's about to introduce me to another old friend in town like he's been doing all day. But the guy approaching doesn't seem particularly friendly. In fact, he looks downright pissed and has the size, in both height and width, to do something about it.

I move a little closer to James, who subtly steps in front of me, protecting me a little with his body. "Hey, Brody," he says stiffly. "Enjoying the fireworks, I see."

As Brody gets closer, I can smell the beer not just on his breath—an overall aura of hops and barley surrounds him. Looking closer, I make the connection. Brody . . . Shayanne's brother. Other than sharing a similar shape to their chins and the same color hair, they're nothing alike. Good for her.

Luckily, Brody seems to only have eyes for James, not paying any attention to my presence. Stopping about two feet away, he stabs a thick finger in James's direction, swaying a little on his feet. "Fuck you, Bennett. My dad tried to help you and your family, but you just go shitting on him like you always do. Think you're better than everyone else, Mr. Thousand-Dollar Stetson Big Shit Pro Rider?"

James seems a bit shocked by his outburst but doesn't budge an inch. "Look, man, I don't know what your dad told you, but someone really smart once told me that business is business. He made an offer; we chose to not take it. Done deal. As long as nothing else happens"— James pauses dramatically, giving Brody a fierce look—"it's all good."

Brody's face pinches, and I can read it in his half-drunk face. He understands that James has guessed about the fence damage, and he's not too happy to get called out on it either. "Just tell your brothers to leave us Tannens alone," he finally sputters, trying to keep the initiative. "You stay on your side of the property line, and we'll stay on ours."

"Fine by me," James says, keeping the peace but not backing down either. "Make sure your dad keeps away from Mama too. No more visits trying to catch her alone. We don't need him sniffing around like she'd have his ass."

Brody puffs up even further, getting right in James's face, but James doesn't flinch. Brody's a little shorter but easily fifteen to twenty pounds heavier. James just tilts his head, solid as a rock and with ice in his veins. I imagine this is what he must be like when he's getting seated on the back of a pissed-off bull, because right now, Brody might as well be a raging bull himself.

Brody isn't backing down either. "Just what are you saying, Bennett? You think my dad's trying to fuck Louise? Whatever."

Brody starts to turn away, but it's a feint, and he whips back around, catching James with a mean right hook across the cheek. James barely stumbles, nudging me back before he brings a punch straight from the shoulder in a return hit that crashes into Brody's nose. They tussle for a moment, punches and shoves flying so fast I can't even tell what's what.

I consider if I should do something, anything to stop their fighting, but I'm afraid if I get too close, I'm likely to get knocked in the head myself. Brody's punches are wild, swooping country-boy haymakers, and one of those things could put me in the hospital.

Thankfully, Doc appears out of nowhere, giving an earsplitting whistle and catching both guys' attention. They push off each other, both winded and bleeding. "Cut that shit out, you two!"

Brody points a thick finger at James, wiping at his lip with the other arm. "Fuck you, Bennett."

He turns, striding away with his back stiff and straight. Doc eyeballs James a minute, then turns to me. "Now's probably not the time for me to butt in. Seems like this is something you can handle. Got a first-aid kit at home?"

I nod, touched. Doc understands—this doesn't need the law involved, and tensions are probably still high. "Yes, sir."

He claps his hands, absolving himself of the matter. "Alright then. I'll see you Monday."

With only a slight nod to James, he walks away like grown men fighting for no damn good reason is just a normal, everyday occurrence. Hell, I don't know . . . maybe it is out here? I turn to help James, but he pops his elbow out at me like he's some sort of gentleman, except there's blood trickling from his nose and a bruise already forming below his eye.

I sigh, taking his arm. "Well, guess I'll be playing doctor tonight, and before you make some sex joke, I don't mean in the fun way. C'mon, Cowboy."

"Can I get a naughty nurse at least?" James asks hopefully.

"No. You're going to get some antiseptic, a bag of frozen peas for that eye, and if you're good, a hug. Don't push your luck."

James seems content with that as we go back to his truck and he drives us home, the fight with Brody Tannen already seemingly forgotten. I relax some when we get back and I get a good light on his wounds . . . no need for stitches, luckily—just some cleanup and a bag of frozen peas for the shiner.

It's been a long day. The festival, the fireworks, and the fight have all taken their toll, and as we climb into bed, there's only one thing on our minds. And for a change, it's not sex.

James spoons up behind me, making me feel tiny and enveloped in his warmth as we drift off.

It's quiet for a while, and I'm nearly asleep when he kisses the back of my neck, whispering, "Sorry about ruining our night."

I let a small sigh escape and take his hand, wrapping his arm around me, and he gives me a tight, squeezing hug that feels like another apology. "You didn't. We had a great night, before . . . Look, I'm not one of those girls who wants to see her man in action, fighting for her and shit. You don't need to put on that strutting-cock alpha act to impress me."

"I know," James says softly. "That wasn't about impressing you."

"I know, and I don't know that you could've handled that any differently. He was spoiling for a fight, and he got one. You handled yourself, you handled him. Maybe after a good night's sleep and some sobriety on his part, it'll be an almost-forgotten tale about 'the Fourth of July we got into it' that you tell your kids someday, especially when you're going to be neighbors for the next hundred years or so."

James bristles behind me, his voice stiffening as well. "As long as he stays on his fucking side, I got no qualms with him."

I smile, patting his hip behind me to settle him, and curl back up, letting sleep overtake us both. "I know. Good night, Cowboy."

CHAPTER 18

James

Walking out of the theater, I can't believe the unbelievable fun I've had spending the day with Sophie. It started off with some very delicious pancakes that I actually prefer over Mama's, although I'll go to hell before I tell her that. Fed to me mouthful by mouthful in bed, oozing syrup and butter, it was the best breakfast I've had in months. Of course, soon after the last bite was shared, the plate ended up on the floor, and I ended up pouring maple syrup over the soft, creamy mounds of Sophie's breasts before we spent an hour having sex, slow at first before the sweet melded with the heat to create something that left me shaking as I came deep inside her.

Of course, with pancake crumbs and syrup all over her sheets, we had to strip the bed and do some laundry. I'm not normally that domestic, but it was fun being silly with Sophie before propping her up on the washer and kissing her all over. I just can't get enough of her, and we nearly ended up having sex again right there in her laundry room.

Finally, just as the sun was passing noon, we got dressed and headed out. After my fight yesterday, I've got a pretty nasty little shiner; Brody's first punch caught me a good one, so I didn't want to walk around town inviting questions. Thankfully, Great Falls has a decent little theater, and so we caught an afternoon matinee, some sci-fi action flick where the guy with a thicker country accent than me is, of course, an engineering genius who "figgers out" how to "get dem durn aliens" without killing off any of the big stars.

It's cheesy, it's silly, there's a ton of explosions . . . so it was a perfect cool escape from the summer heat. And it was at least interesting enough to keep our attention for the most part, especially with the wandering hands we both had throughout the movie keeping a fire burning as we teased and taunted each other, letting our hands roam closer and closer to the prize.

Somehow, we manage to not get kicked out for our inappropriateness, and we're laughing as we sit down to a late lunch. Sipping at my vanilla milkshake, I give Sophie a little toast. "Thanks for last night . . . the talk, and after the fight. I appreciate your thoughts and your almost-vet first-aid skills. Seems fitting since I'm mostly animal anyway."

Sophie snickers, raises her own milkshake, strawberry for her, and toasts me back. "No problem. And thank you for the festival date and private fireworks show. You definitely know how to court a girl."

"Courtin' you now, huh?" I ask, smirking. "Now where did you learn a word like that?"

She stops, eyes dancing with concern and a little bit of worry as she shrugs. "Back in high school, I watched a late-night movie with a cowboy trying to catch the girl he wanted, and he told her he was 'courting' her, and she didn't know what that meant. It stuck with me because that's definitely not a word I'd ever use to describe the guys at school. Did I use it right?"

She's being silly, so I grin, laying on the accent a little thicker than normal. "Well now, Miss Sophie, I do reckon you used it correctly."

She laughs and flicks a little bit of milkshake at me. "Smart-ass!"

I wipe the droplets away, laughing. "Okay, yeah. Although usually that's a bit more old school, when a guy is pursuing the woman he wants to marry. Last time I really heard it being used would be with Mama's generation. And let me tell you, to her, courting is serious business."

She smiles anyway, and it strikes me that she is the type some guy is gonna court someday. It makes my stomach roll to think of some other guy chasing after her, marrying her, while I just keep riding the roads and the bulls.

Suddenly, I have a flash of her standing on the porch of a country house, a dark-haired baby on her hip, and in my mind's eye, I see myself come out to stand behind her, wrapping my arms around her to highlight the plain gold band on my hand.

The image is so shocking I nearly drop my cup. Hell no. I'm way too young for that—too many more years on the road, too many more bulls to ride, chaos to conquer.

"You okay?" Sophie asks. "You look like you just saw a ghost."

"Uh, yeah . . . just drank a bit too fast; ice cream headache, you know," I lie, unsettled to the core. I move the conversation to lighter topics as our food arrives, but that quick image of us as a family sticks in my head, unwilling to be dismissed as readily as I'd like.

Wrapping up, I walk Sophie home, a piece of me wanting to go inside the house and continue this with her, whatever this is. Despite my misgivings, there's a huge part of me that just wants to be with her, whether we're talking or playing or having sex. I just want to spend time with her.

The thought that this is becoming a lot more than I thought it would be a few weeks ago makes my stomach flip-flop.

"You sure you're okay?" Sophie asks as I stop, looking up at me. "You're not looking too good."

"Yeah . . . I mean . . . no. Just being hit by a sudden wave of guilt for throwing all my duties over on Luke again," I say, sputtering. "I think I'd better head on home, make sure he's okay handling all my chores."

Sophie looks disappointed and confused. "I thought he was taking care of everything for you today?"

"He said he would," I say with a shrug, feeling like I'm digging deeper and deeper into the bullshit and not sure when I am going to stop.

She nods, but it's obvious she can feel that I'm not exactly being transparent about everything. She lets it go, though, testing the waters. "No problem. Should I come with you?"

I shake my head, waving airily. "Nah, I'd better take care of my duties, and I need to talk to my brothers, maybe Mama, too, about Brody last night. We need to be on the same page about the Tannens to make sure nothing else happens. Can I call you?"

"Sure. Of course. Just, uh, let me know, I guess . . ." she says, trying not to look disappointed. It's awkward, and it's my fault, but I need to focus on what I know . . . the ranch, my family, and getting out of here to get back to the rodeo. What I don't need to focus on is the sudden realization that I've developed feelings for a girl who's going to be leaving town in less than two months.

After giving her a soft kiss on the cheek, I head out to my truck and drive like a maniac to get home, away from Sophie and her tempting confusion. Dammit, I can't have this. I'm supposed to be focused right now. I get my shit done on the ranch, and come the end of the summer season, I'm punching out, working my ass off for finals.

What I'm *not* supposed to be doing is thinking all sorts of domestic things about Sophie. We're from different worlds, going in different directions. When I'm going to be strapping on my chaps to see if one of Bodacious's grandsons has my number, she's going to be in a classroom learning things I could never understand. How could we ever be together . . . how could we ever have a family?

Shutting that train of thought down with a screech, I pull in the drive at home like there's a demon on my tail. Luke comes out of the barn when he hears my truck, lifting a hand in greeting.

Before I can even get my door closed, I can already hear him giving me shit. "What are you doing home early? Sophie kick you out of bed for eating crackers, man? Let me guess, you played Eight Seconds with her, didn't you?"

He's grinning at me, but when I look up and he sees my face, bruised and starting to scab, the smile drops immediately, concern replacing the teasing. "What the hell happened to you, James?"

I try to make light, waving him off. "You should see the other guy. If the sheriff comes looking for me, I'm not here."

But Luke's not having it; he's already gone into full big-brother mode before my very eyes. He grabs my shoulders, shoving me against the front of my truck, worry and surprise letting him get the better of me. "Who did this? And why didn't you call?"

"It's fine!" I half yell back, shoving him back a step. I brush off my shirt and run a hand through my hair. "I'm fine. Brody Tannen got a little drunk at the festival last night and decided to take out his anger at our handling of his dad's offer on my face. I really did get a couple of good shots on him, too, before Doc stopped us. Sophie doctored me up, and it's fine—just gonna be ugly for a couple of days."

Luke soaks it all in, then breaks out laughing. "I hate to tell you, James, but you've been ugly for a lot longer than a day or two. And nothing Sophie can do is going to change that, unless she decides to be a plastic surgeon." He gets serious again, and looks my face over. "Really, you're okay? I don't know why I'm asking this, because fuck that guy, but is Brody okay?"

I nod, amused at Luke's last question. "Yeah, we're both fine. Just stupid shit. By the way, thanks for those defense skills you taught me way back when we were kids—it helped. We agreed for them to stay on their property and us to stay to ours."

Luke nods his agreement with me, and I continue, "I wonder, though . . . what has Paul been telling those boys of his to make them so damn-fired mad at us? Shouldn't be a big deal, should it?"

Luke shrugs and leans against the bumper of my truck. "There aren't too many ranchers out here now, just farmers and those artisan types who charge way too damn much for cheese out near the resort side of things. Guess we were always going to be in each other's way at some level. I say we stay clear of them, and it'll all be fine. We're a little like the Hatfields and McCoys now. I wonder if the Hatfields were just as confused as we are about how they got locked into some feud, though? Maybe the McCoys were just as grumpy as the Tannens?"

We laugh, heading in the house to relate the whole story again to Mark and Mama. Mark is furious, although an outsider probably wouldn't see it, his calm façade locked into place. But I've been his little brother long enough to recognize the twitch at the corner of his eye as the sign of impending doom it always has been. "I see," he says quietly, stroking his chin. "Okay, then."

Something tells me this won't be the same as when he tackled me and pounded me into the dirt when we were kids because he'd caught me spying on him and his girlfriend.

Nope. I think that while Mark's not opposed to some physical damage and more than capable of dishing it out, right now he's thinking of some more serious strategies for dealing with the Tannens if there are further issues. Of the three of us, that's Mark. I'm the Viking, charging off and running headlong into the fight more often than not. Luke's Switzerland more often than not, calm and neutral but with great pride. Mark, though . . . Mark's our Caesar, cunning and smart.

Mama wipes her hands on her apron and gets up from the table. "Well, now that we've got that whole story sorted out, I guess we'd best finish up before dinner. You boys head on out, and stay out of trouble.

Don't go looking for it, and if it finds you, you do what your Pops would expect of you and behave yourself like a Bennett."

We mind her, going outside and striding far enough away that she can't hear us or see us through the back door. We head over to the horse corral, where we lean against the wooden fence, just watching Briarbelle and her baby walk and chew on the scant grass that grows along the edges.

Luke looks at Mark, who's scratching his cheek. "What do you think?"

Mark eyeballs me, giving my shiner a good look before replying, "I wish I would've been there. But I'm glad you're okay and held your own against Brody. Let me do some asking around, see what's up with the Tannens. You two just watch your backs, especially when you're in town." He directs the last part to me, knowing that I've been coming and going at all hours to see Sophie. "If you can, do as much as you can out here."

I nod, while Luke looks resigned to the fact that he's going to be kicked out of the bunkhouse more often. "Will do."

Mark looks at my truck in the drive and seems to realize for the first time that I'm alone. "Sophie not come back with you tonight?"

I swallow, making sure that none of my earlier emotional tornado shows on my face. "No. Figured this conversation was better had with just family, so I told her I'd call her."

Mark frowns a bit, then shakes his head. "She's welcome in family matters if you want her to be. Besides, Doc has business with the Tannens, too; it wouldn't be right for her to get shoved into a situation she's not prepared for. But your call. She seems like a fine lady. Is she okay from the fight, no collateral damage?"

I nod, proud of that fact. "Yeah, I don't think Brody even saw her. He was laser focused on me and jonesing for a fight. Sophie stayed back, too, although I think she was ready with a trash-can lid if I'd gotten caught."

Luke grins, slapping his thigh. "Knew there was a reason I liked that girl. Still, one thing."

"What's that?"

"Y'all need to help me set up a cot in the barn or something for when she's around. I'm not sleeping in the house again. You know I love Mama, but you also know she snores like a grizzly bear."

CHAPTER 19

SOPHIE

James doesn't call that night, or the next morning either. I consider calling him, but since he seemed a bit flustered, I think maybe a day to calm down from whatever ruffled his feathers is in order.

I'm ruffled too; the festival was amazing. Playful and full of wonder when we walked around, but tender and intimate when we were talking on the roof. Not to mention the hot pancake-syrup-covered sex after breakfast. Other than the fight, it really was the perfect day, and that makes my head spin a bit considering he's dangerously close to ghosting me.

With my thoughts running, I try to decide what to do with an unexpectedly free day. Doc had to get his annual physical. Though he proclaimed himself "healthy as a horse," I assured him that he couldn't fully diagnose himself like one of his animals, and he'd begrudgingly agreed to keep the appointment, closing the office. Right now, though, I wish it were a regular workday and I had something to keep my mind busy . . . and off James.

Suddenly, my phone rings. It's a number I don't know, but it's local at least. "Hello?"

The female voice immediately starts talking in one long run-on sentence, and I recognize it immediately. "Oh my gosh, Sophie! Is James okay? Brody came home the other night all busted up and wouldn't say nothing about what caused it and Daddy said that Brody shouldn't be . . ."

I grin, cutting off Shayanne before she talks herself into breathlessness. "Yeah, Shayanne. He's fine. What about Brody?"

"Who cares?" she says, before sighing dramatically and starting up again. "He's okay, I guess, just an asshat. Daddy says he needs to quit acting like a tantrum-throwing toddler if he ever hopes to take over the ranch. Told him there was 'more than one way to skin a cat.' Now, it took me almost two whole days of badgering him before he even told me what happened . . . and well, I just had to give you a call."

"I appreciate that. Glad Brody's okay, too, I guess."

Shayanne chuckles. "Forget about him. That's not really why I'm calling, anyway. I'm calling because all my menfolk went to the next town over to check on something then go fishing, and I'm home alone."

She's squealing by the end, and I'm not exactly sure why she's so excited. "So that means you can come see the goats!"

A little taken aback by her exuberance, I am barely able to stammer a little "Oh" before she keeps going. "I mean, if you're not busy, I guess. It's just that they hardly ever all leave, and it'd be awkward if you came while they were here. And I really do want to hang out with a girl for a change. Guys are nice but they're all my brothers and stink like cows and goats all the damn time."

I grin. What the hell, I do need more of a social life than just hanging out with James and working with Doc. "I'd love to, Shayanne. Let me get cleaned up, and I'll be right out."

It's not hard to get out to the Tannen ranch. After all, they're on the same dirt road. Still, as I pass the BB Ranch, it strikes me how easy it'd be to turn into James's drive, but I press on. I'm not exactly experienced in matters of relationships, but I do know that coming off as the desperate party isn't exactly the best move.

Shayanne is basically jumping up and down when I pull up, dressed in jeans and a Luke Bryan T-shirt, grinning. "Hey, Sophie! Glad you came!"

Her energy is infectious, light and bright, and you can almost see the words racing across her mind, too fast for her mouth to say everything she's thinking. "Glad to be here! You promised me some cute baby goats?"

"Absolutely," Shayanne says. "Daddy says you can judge a man by his word and how strict he adheres to it. So I'd better get you over to these goats before the babes get too big for cuddles. Come on . . ."

I follow her across the yard to a small fenced pasture, laughing inside at her Daddy's pearls of wisdom. She whistles, and I hear answering bleats that make me grin, but I don't see the goats yet. "Are they shy?"

"They just like the grass over by the trees more, I think. It's nice and cool over there. Come on, we've got about twenty minutes before my show comes on. Steffy's got herself in trouble again, and I so want to see what happens."

I follow Shayanne over to find an adorable collection of goats lying in the grass. Some of them approach curiously, including one of the babies, who bleats at me before licking my palm, and my heart melts. "Oh gawwwd, you're so cute!"

"They're all friendly with people," Shayanne says, kneeling down and scratching the little one behind his ears. "I've fed all of them by hand, because I've been promised that these babies aren't going to be sold for meat."

"No?" I ask, touched. "Milking?"

"Oh yeah, we milk them, and I make goat's milk soap to sell at the farmer's market. Helps the herd pay for themselves. Daddy says everyone's gotta earn their keep."

I sit down in the soft grass, and a small brown-and-white fluff of a goat curls up in my lap. I'm delighted and immediately start cooing and petting the softness along its back.

Shayanne laughs. "Looks like Troll there likes you. I know someone else who likes you . . . what's the deal with you and James? Y'all serious?"

I laugh at the goat's name, catching the reference to Billy Goats Gruff, and renew my loving scratches behind his ears, procrastinating as long as possible before answering Shayanne's transparently gossipy question. She could definitely use a lesson in subtlety. "No, we're both just here for the summer. I'll go to vet school in the fall, and he's back to the circuit. But he's a great guy, and we've been having fun this summer."

Shayanne sighs dreamily, her eyes fluttering. "Oh, I thought you two were all lovey-dovey, the way he kept looking at you when we were at the fence. I just . . . I wanted to see something romantic, like my shows. Maybe there's a chance for long distance in the fall?"

"I don't know," I reply, setting the baby goat in my lap down and standing up, brushing off my hands. One bad thing about goats . . . cute or not, cuddly or not, I'm going to have to wash my hands. "I guess I hadn't really thought about it too much; just enjoying the ride. But he's really something. Makes me crazy just being around him, always teasing and . . ."

I pause, this close to saying he's amazing in bed, but by the look on her face, Shayanne already knows what I was gonna say. She quirks an eyebrow playfully. "So, it's all just sex and games with you two?"

I bite my lip, thinking before shaking my head. "No, there's, um . . . that, but we talk too. About the rodeo, about our families and our childhood, what we want to do with the rest of our lives. Just bigger life stuff too. It's comfortable, easy to be together, he makes my heart race with even the littlest thing. And his family is amazing."

Shayanne nods, looking a little sad. "Yeah, I don't know the Bennetts that well. I was still little when the boys stopped hanging out, but I know they're close. You close to your family?"

It's a casual question, but it makes my heart clench a little at how welcoming the Bennetts have been with me, inviting me into their family dinners and their inner circle time and time again. It's a sweet and addicting feeling to be a part of a family again.

"Hard to say. It's complicated, it's just me and my brother. I mean, he's married, and her family's great, and Jake's a great brother who raised me by himself for a long time, but it's different when it's just the two of us versus a whole family like the Bennetts have or like you have here with your dad and brothers."

We start heading out of the goat pasture, Shayanne making sure we close the gate behind us. "With how you light up when you talk about him, it sounds a bit more serious. I mean, meeting the family is pretty big, right? If it was just casual, he'd just sneak into town, take care of business, and sneak back out. Isn't that how it goes?"

I pause as she double-checks the lock, her simple questions hitting home, and I realize that even though Shayanne is younger than me with even more to learn, she's right. Somewhere between our initial promises of casual summer fun, I started having some more serious thoughts about James, about *us*.

Maybe that's why he left so fast yesterday? Was I acting clingy? Maybe he somehow knew and ran in fear?

Does it really matter, though? I'm only here for such a short time, and he is too.

But maybe Shayanne is right. Could we actually do a long-distance thing? I don't know; I've never tried to do something like that. Could that work? With us in different states, buckle bunnies at every turn, just a phone call to connect?

It sounds . . . impossible.

There's a long pause of silence as I reflect on it all before Shayanne speaks up. "Sorry! I didn't mean to get so deep—just making conversation. But . . . it's time for Steffy!"

It's been years since I watched any daytime soaps, but once *The Bold and the Beautiful* is over, I'm surprised when Shayanne shuts off the TV. "Wait, that's it?"

"Well, yeah . . . just enough to keep you watching," Shayanne says with a laugh. "Want to see *my* soaps, though? The ones I make with the goats' milk?"

I follow her into the kitchen, where she spreads her hands wide, gesturing to a sideboard cabinet with stacks of multicolored blocks. "Here's the batch I made yesterday. What do you think?"

It's . . . I can't believe this. They're amazing. I find myself liking each soap more than the last, oohing and aahing over the scent combinations and packaging with funny puns. Finally, I laugh over For-Goat-Me-Not. "You should totally make a website and sell these online!"

Shayanne shakes her head uncertainly. "I don't know. Brody sells these for me at the local fairs and farmers markets, but Daddy says it's just a fun hobby to keep me out of trouble and mostly out of his way."

Ugh . . . I don't want to say anything bad about her father, but the more I hear about the man, the less I like him. "That's not true! You've got some real skill here . . . beautiful soaps, some really cute graphics on these wrappers you printed out, and engaging jokes that make you stop to read them all before deciding. And you know what happens when a customer picks them all up to read them?"

Shayanne is rapt, caught up in what I'm saying. "What?"

"They buy more!" I tell her. "Look at that guy, Dr. Bronner. He fills his labels with gibberish that doesn't even halfway make sense, and he sells a ton of soaps! Maybe you could offer a buy-two-get-one-free deal and sell even more?"

"It sounds like a good idea," Shayanne says. "But . . . I'm not sure Daddy would like that."

"Well, you're an adult," I remind her gently. "Does he really decide what you do? How old are you, by the way?"

Shayanne blushes. "I'm nineteen, but yeah . . . Daddy says he's in charge of me until I'm self-sufficient or married off. Of course, then he laughs and says nobody would ever want to marry me anyway."

I'm shocked, and move Paul Tannen from my "maybe I don't like" list to my "fuck this guy" list. "Shayanne, why wouldn't someone marry you? You're gorgeous, sweet, caring, creative, and kind. And fuck that, you're only nineteen. Go into town and get a job so you have your own money and be independent. You don't need to worry about getting married for years!"

Shayanne shakes her head. "You don't understand. Since my Mom died when I was a girl, all I've ever done is take care of Daddy and the boys. If I weren't here, who'd cook them meals, clean the house, pay the bills, run the house? This place would fall apart. I couldn't just leave them like that."

She shakes her head like the idea of being on her own is foreign, and I'm struck by just how different we are. I can't possibly imagine the life she leads, where she's a working part of the whole, but somehow she's less than her brothers and her father. It reminds me of just how special my brother is. He never, ever discouraged my pursuits, and if it had been me who had the idea of making soaps . . .

"Well, maybe you can start small. Post some soaps on Etsy and see what happens. You could try it out and see if it's worth the time and trouble."

Shayanne seems to consider the idea, then nods. "Maybe I'll try that. I'll have to look into it, but either way, thank you!"

I smile, and clutch the bar of Goat-Tee-Tree Oil to my chest. "And I'd like to buy a few bars today, if you don't mind? I'm happy to be a customer." I gather two big stacks and give her cash from my back pocket. "And I was thinking . . . if you need help, give me a call. Doc's office is just down the street from the post office. I can drop off packages for you or something?"

Shayanne blinks, then reaches across and hugs me tight. "You're awesome, Sophie. Really."

We head back out to say goodbye to the goats, and I'm strangely hesitant to leave Shayanne here alone, protective of her somehow since she seems so sheltered, innocent. "You gonna be okay until everyone gets back?"

Shayanne looks at me strangely, like I've maybe been sniffing something besides soap for the past half hour. "Of course. I may not be in charge, but there isn't anything that happens on this farm that I can't do myself. Daddy says that I might be slower than the boys at just about everything out here, but I'm a damn good farmer. And I'll tell you a secret . . ."

She leans in, putting a hand up like she needs to disguise what she's about to say, and it makes me grin at her as she continues, "I can outshoot, out-rope, and outride any of my brothers. On a good day, Daddy too. I ain't all pies and soaps, mind you."

I laugh, realizing that my earlier judgments about her might not have been entirely accurate. She's certainly a little sheltered, but she sounds like she can handle herself. She's definitely got a different life than I do, but maybe it's not as bad as I'd feared, just different. "Alright, I'll definitely keep that secret. On one condition . . ."

Shayanne raises her eyebrows at me questioningly. I point a finger at her, menacingly dropping my voice into a growl. "Every time you say *Daddy says*, I'm gonna smack you solid, and you're gonna let me. I don't give a rat's ass what your Daddy says—I care what Shayanne says. Deal?"

She laughs, nodding sheepishly. "Deal. Do I say that a lot?"

I mock glare at her. "Only every other sentence! I haven't even met your daddy, but I've talked more about him than I want to."

She laughs, and I'm glad she takes it well. "Fine, I won't say *Daddy says* anymore around you. Might be a hard habit to break; he's always been such a presence since I'm mostly just out here with him and my brothers. God knows they love me fiercely, but good Lord, they smother the hell out of me sometimes."

Spontaneously, I give her a big hug, and she hugs me back. "You be good, Shayanne. Call me anytime! Maybe you could come to town sometime? Maybe even do a spa night at my place with your soaps, and I'll stop by the salon, get some good shampoo and conditioner and all that other stuff. We could do a girls' spa night with facials, hair goop, mani-pedis, and lots and lots of junk food."

Shayanne laughs. "That sounds great. Let's do it!"

I nod. "Alright, then, you tell me when you can get away, and it's on!"

CHAPTER 20

JAMES

"James, got a minute?" Mark asks. It's been three days since I ran out on Sophie, each day worse than the last. By the look in his eye, Mark has had enough of my pissy mood, which is saying a lot considering how grumpy he always is.

"Yeah," I reply, setting down the shovel I'm using to scoop cow feed into their troughs. I'm covered in sweat; it's a lot of work, even if they are mostly grass fed. "What's up?"

Mark tosses me a bottle of water from behind his back, leaning against the trough. "What's up is you. What's your deal, James? You and Sophie have a fight or something?"

I try to ignore him, turning back to my truck bed full of feed and wishing Luke was here to do it, but he left early this morning to go visit a neighboring ranch about training their latest barrel racer. "No."

"Uh-huh," Mark says, and I know he's not going to let this go. He'll sit there all fucking day if need be—the man's got the patience of a marble statue. Hardheaded as one, too, and I sigh, giving in. "No, we didn't have a fight. We're . . . fine, I guess."

Marks grunts and pushes back the brim of his hat to look up at me. "You ain't fine. You've been grousing here and testy there since you came home after the festival. Hell, you didn't even notice when Mama was teasing you last night at dinner. What happened?"

I jam my shovel back into the pile of feed, leaning against the truck. "Nothing, really. We had our date . . . the festival, fireworks, even the fight. You've heard about all that."

"Yep. Go on."

"The next day we uh . . . well, you know . . ." I pause. There's limits to what I'm going to tell Mark, but he just nods, assuming my meaning. "And the movies, and lunch. But at lunch, I just got spooked."

Mark crosses his arms, studying me for a minute before hopping up in the truck and sitting down next to me. "Spooked how? She say something, she looking for more from you? I thought she was heading back to school in a few weeks anyway, so what's the big deal?"

Instead of answering, I walk away before leaning on the fence and yanking my hat off to run my fingers through my hair.

Mark follows, silent but seeming to know everything. I'm reminded of Pops for a minute, how he'd stand over me when he'd deliver a lecture about something I'd done. I guess I've always known it, and Mark's shown it plenty of times over this summer, but he's the one who's meant to take over this ranch. My role in life . . . well, it's less defined, which is just one ingredient in my current mood.

I look over at Mark, who to a casual observer would look like he's studying a cattle stall, but I can feel his attention from out of the corner of his eyes. "Alright, so don't laugh, 'kay?" He grunts, and I take that as the standard Mark agreement, so I continue, my voice halting from time to time. "So, we're sitting at lunch, and she makes a joke about a man courting a woman from some movie. She thought it meant just dating, and I explained that it's a bit more serious than that. As soon as I said it, the thought hit me like a lightning bolt . . . some guy is gonna court her, marry her, have babies with her."

I pause, and while Mark doesn't move, I can tell he's been listening. "And you think you want that to be you?" he asks, before spitting out onto the dirt. "Or are you thinking you *don't* want it to be you?"

I swallow, and half shrug, half shake my head. "I had a flash of a picture . . . her with a baby on her hip on the porch, me standing behind her, hugging her tight. Like I said, it spooked me."

Mark nods, pushing away from the fence to look at me directly. "Has she made any mention that she wants anything like that? She's got big school plans, right? She's definitely the type of woman with a plan."

I shake my head, sticking my hands in my back pockets like I used to when I'd get in trouble with Pops for doing something stupid. "No, she's happy working with Doc, but she's already admitted for school in the fall."

"So, what you're saying is, you're scared that you might want more and maybe she's leaving you behind?" Mark asks, but doesn't really ask. "Because if she's not asking for more from you, and is in fact making plans to leave, you're the one putting pressure on yourself. You always have these ideas about what people expect from you and bristle at the least bit of restraint, but most of the time, the only one with those expectations of you . . . is you. Maybe the Rodeo Rider is ready to settle down after all?"

I snort, toeing the dirt at my feet. "No way. I'm in my prime, with rodeo *and* with women. I'm off to the fall circuit, headed to Vegas, and then spring circuit shortly after that."

Mark snorts, just like Pops used to always do when I said something foolish. "That's what you've always done. Doesn't mean it has to be what you always do. Things are different this year . . . for a lot of reasons. I'd never ask you to stay, but I think we both know that whenever you're ready to settle, you're probably gonna do it right here with us. There's enough land, you can build yourself a respectable house that you could easily raise a family in, or we'd figure out a way for you to get a place in town if that's what you wanted. Whenever that is . . . now, later, whenever . . . that's up to you. I will say that whatever damn fool life crisis you're having, Sophie didn't do it. She might be the focus of your questions, maybe making you want different things, but the only one changing here is you. Sounds like you need to decide what you want and where it's at. Go there and do it."

His piece said, Mark reaches out and punches me in the chest, just like when we were kids, and walks away from the fence, leaving me to my thoughts. Just before he rounds the back of the truck, he turns back. "And get the rest of this damn feed spread; those cows don't know how to shovel!"

After he leaves, I sit for a bit on the tailgate of the truck, mulling over everything Mark said. There was a lot of wisdom in his words, but I'm still unsure what I should do. One thing's for sure: I need to man up and call Sophie.

I jump down and go to the cab of the truck, pulling my phone out to dial her before I can wimp out.

When she comes on, it's like a balm to my nerves, even if she does sound a little nervous. "Hello?"

"Hey, Soph," I greet her, like calling her in the middle of the afternoon while covered in dust and sweat is something I normally do. "Whatcha doing?"

"Oh, not too much," she says, sounding relieved I didn't say *we need to talk*. "Doc's taking a half day today, so I'm just cleaning the house a bit, and then I was thinking I'm going to get me cleaned up a bit too. I got some of Shayanne's soaps to try."

I grin, knowing I could use a good shower myself. "It's really good to hear your voice, I've missed you the last few days . . . wait, did you say you have Shayanne's soaps? How'd you get those?"

"I went over there to see the goats the other day, when you were all radio silent on me." She isn't trying to sound angry with me, but it still stings enough that I wince inwardly and decide to quickly cover this problem.

"Oh yeah. Sorry about that. There was just some stuff I needed to deal with. Um, personal stuff, if you don't mind me being a bit secretive on it. But I think I'm good now . . . so . . . any chance you might want to go out tonight?"

"Uh, I guess. As long as you're sure you're okay leaving the house for a bit. Everything fine there?"

She's obviously aware that my excuse to run home was just that—an excuse. But I don't want to discuss too much over the phone; I want to hold her in my arms when I tell her I'm a scaredy-cat jerk who ran at the first sign of something real, even if it was only real in my head, and in my heart.

Instead, I laugh, a big fake laugh that sounds bad even to my own ears. "Yeah, it's all good out here. Can I pick you up at seven?"

"Seven it is. That'll give me time to get all fancied up for anything you'd like. Plans?"

"Just casual, you know how I am. Okay, I'll see you then. And Sophie?"

"Yeah?"

"Thanks."

We hang up, and I lean against the truck, smiling foolishly. There's a knot in my throat and a tension in my chest, but most of my blood seems to be in my cock, knowing that in a few short hours, I'll be seeing Sophie again.

"First things first, though," I say as I hear a far-off moo of a cow. "Gotta get my damn work done."

CHAPTER 21

SOPHIE

Looking in my closet, I regret not packing more for this summer. I used to have a closet bigger than my current kitchen, with enough clothes for any occasion . . . well, except for a rodeo, but that was a whole other life.

Now, looking at my collection of work shirts, T-shirts, a few workout clothes, and a single dress that I've already worn for a date with James, I'm feeling very short on options.

Sighing, I shake my head, enjoying at least the scent of raspberries that Shayanne's soap gave me. "Well, he said casual . . . guess he'll just have to be happy with casual then."

I get a clean pair of jeans out of my dresser along with one of my cuter tank tops, a light-blue, clingy, ribbed top that has some sparkly decorations around my boobs and hugs my figure nicely. It's casual, and since I have no idea where the hell I'm going, it'll do.

Clothes picked, I try to decide on my footwear. My sneakers go almost immediately—I'm only wearing those for workouts I do when James and I haven't been working up long sweats with intense, passionate sex—which leaves me with my work boots, my sexy boots, and my sexy set of heels.

"What the hell, let him sweat a little," I decide. "I'll stay barefoot until he tells me what the fuck's up, and then decide on nice boots or slutty heels."

Decisions made, I touch up my hair and makeup a final time, making sure to choose my strawberry lip gloss that I know James likes. Besides, it complements the fruity smell of the raspberry soap.

"Well," I tell my reflection as I purse my lips to give my gloss a check and then blow myself an air kiss, "time to find out what he wants."

I'm actually feeling really nervous, for some reason. Something obviously spooked James last time, and I have a sneaking suspicion it was him picking up on my growing feelings. Even if I hadn't quite realized it, I must've been telegraphing them somehow. What if he's trying to back out before things get more mixed up? What if he figures it's better to cut our losses now rather than wait until next month, where we'll have a whole new depth of feelings to get over?

Alright, chickadee . . . cool, collected, definitely not crazy and clingy. That's the play tonight. Let's just ride this out and see what happens. "Besides, if it goes bad, you'll have plenty of time to get studied up for fall classes," I tell myself. "You know you're just a big nerd inside."

My little pick-me-up talk finished, I hear my doorbell ring, and I hurry over, my heart fluttering in my chest as I open up to see James. He's dressed like he said, casually, in jeans and a nice but not too fancy shirt and, in a rarity for him, lace-up boots.

"Hey . . . wow, you look great," he says, greeting me.

"Thanks," I reply, feeling a flush in my chest. "You look . . . awesomely normal."

James laughs and steps inside, pulling me close to give me a kiss on the cheek. "I'll take that as a compliment since I left the hat and boots at home. I can be seminormal sometimes."

"I'll take semi," I joke, deciding in my head on my casual boots. He's going casual; I don't need to wear a set of fuck-me heels. Besides, he's still got something to say. I can see that in his face. "So, we're off?"

"Yeah . . . let's go. I missed you the past few days, and I want to make up for it," he says, taking my hand instead of offering me his elbow as he leads me out to his truck. I remember to go to his door and settle into the middle of the bench, flush against him and already getting a bit tingly just from the feel of the long line of his body beside mine.

Jeez, three nights without him, and I'm already thinking of what I can get away with while he drives. *Down, girl!*

James puts his arm around me, rubbing my shoulder as we drive down the street. "You hungry, or can you wait a bit?"

"Actually, I am kinda famished. This morning Doc and I did cleanup of the kennels out back at the office, the ones we keep the sick pets in or the ones recovering from surgery. He said that he could use the spare set of hands, so we spent most of the morning lugging them out back and power washing them. That is one gross, smelly job!"

He looks at me, laughter sparkling in his eyes as he takes a big cartoonish whiff of my hair. "Can't tell now. You look like a lady, and smell like one too."

His compliment warms me inside, and I nestle closer against him, my lap belt digging into my hip, but I don't care. "Well, I did shower and scrub and scrub. Point being, feed me, Cowboy!"

He laughs, drives us to a diner on the main street of the tourist district, and hustles inside to sit down right as the dinner rush hits. Two quick orders of chicken-fried steak, mashed potatoes, and sweet tea later, and we relax, waiting for our food to come. "Say, I think I know this place."

"You've been here before?" James asks. "When?"

"More like I know the reputation. Thanks for not ordering me one of their gut-bomber burgers."

While we wait, I fill James in on my visit with Shayanne and about my work this week with Doc. In return, he tells me about the ranch, how the horses and cows are doing, and just general things. It's comfortable and easy, just like always.

The food comes, and for twenty minutes there's little more from our table than the satisfied sounds of two people feeding their hungry bodies with warm, comforting food that fills their stomachs and calms their minds. Afterward, James leads me down the sidewalk to a small bar.

"Drink?"

"Why not?" I agree, and we go inside, James of course holding the door for me as we do. It's no honky-tonk, but it's certainly not the normal type of place I go. Country music is playing from a jukebox in the corner, loud enough to dance to but not too loud to drown out close conversations.

We sink into a booth, side by side, and the waitress brings us a couple of beers without us even having to order. Sipping mine, I can feel James's gaze on me as he follows my mouth on the bottle, my throat working to swallow the cold liquid. The tension that's always buzzing just under the surface with us comes back quickly, thickening the air between us like lightning does just before it strikes.

James reaches forward with his thumb and sweeps it up and down my cheekbone, eyes locked on mine. "I'm sorry about the past few days."

"I thought cowboys never apologized? They just sang sad songs with a guitar?" I reply, smiling. "James . . . whatever it is, I'm not upset. I'm just glad I'm here with you right now."

He leans forward, and I'm ready for his kiss, but he bypasses my mouth, lips going to my ear to whisper huskily, "Let's dance, Soph. I want to hold you in my arms, and move with you. Maybe drive you half as crazy as you're driving me. Then . . . then maybe I can tell you what's on my mind."

If only he knew, I'm way more far gone than he is . . . drive me crazy? He has already done that in spades.

He's got me curious what is on his mind, but I also can't stop thinking about his muscled body on top of me, his thick cock buried inside me, and the way his eyes crinkle at the corners when he laughs and when he comes. I have a flash of dragging him home right now to make that happen.

Instead I nod, following him to the dance floor with the few other couples already swaying there. He leads me in a two-step, not something I'm particularly familiar with, but since we're pressed so tightly together, it's easy enough to just move with him.

James wraps our hands up to his chest as the song changes from a twangy, upbeat song to something slower, romantically melancholy, and he holds me tight as he buries his face in the top of my head. We stay that way for several songs, just swaying with the beat, pressed together so tightly I can feel his cock thickening between us.

All these questions, all this emotion inside me, but the truth is . . . whatever is happening between us, there is always a connection sparking. It's exciting, but there's a chance it'll burn me up. I'm willing to be burned this time, though; James could burn me to ash right now. I sigh happily, lost in the moment, but as the song stops, he whispers in my ear, "Let's get out of here."

He throws money on the bar for our couple of beers, tipping a hatless salute at the waitress as we leave. We walk back to the truck and pile in, the quiet tension building between us again. I trace circles on his thigh as he drives, paying more attention to his reactions than where we're going, so I'm surprised when I realize he's taken me back to Outlook Point. Stopping, he backs up this time, then jumps out to lower the tailgate and sit down on it.

I hop up beside him, feet swinging loose in the air. Something's happened in the past few minutes; there's an awkwardness that's not usually there between us, and I think maybe I've made some sort of mistake again. "James?"

He swallows and reaches over, taking my hand. "I know I said it earlier, Sophie. I think I need to apologize for bolting. I uh, well . . . I'm not sure how to say this. You know how at the beginning of the summer, we'd said, maybe not in so many words exactly, but basically that we could be casual while we're both here?"

My belly fills with ice, and I clench my fist in my lap. I knew it! Something must've tipped him off before I'd even realized. *Damn it, Sophie. There you go, getting feelings for a guy when he's not willing to do the same.* But . . . but I thought everything . . . fuck my life.

"James, I know we said that. And I apologize for whatever I did that scared you, but whatever I'm feeling, the fact is . . . I'm going to school in a few weeks, and you're going back to the rodeo. So it's fine. I'm a big girl. I can handle this right now, and whatever's to come. I promise."

James looks shocked and blinks before an ironic smile crosses his face. "What are you talking about, woman? I'm the one apologizing, not you. I'm sorry for getting spooked by my feelings. I—wait, what'd you say?"

We look at each other, both our jaws hanging open as it sinks in. For four days, we've been nervous because . . . because . . .

"Okay," I say before my guts fail me, "we say it on one . . ."

"Two . . ."

"Three. I've fallen for you."

"I'm in love with you," James says at the exact same time before his smile widens and he leans back, while I slap my hands over my mouth, the shock and question in my eyes as James starts to smirk. "You've fallen for me?"

Not moving my hands, I nod. Lowering my hands a little so I can speak, I ask what has to be the dumbest question in my life. "You're in love with me?"

He grins and nods. "That's why I ran away last weekend. It hit me that you were going back to school and there was gonna be some other guy or, hell, guys, chasing after you. And I don't want that. You're mine,

Sophie. And that was a scary, freak-out aha moment, and like an ass, I ran. I'm sorry."

I run my thumb over the back of his hand, joy melting the ice I'd had in my belly just a few seconds ago. "I thought maybe I'd unconsciously done something that frightened you. But I'll admit that I didn't fully realize it until I was talking to Shayanne. I had an aha moment then too."

We just look at each other in awe for a moment, before we both admit it, to ourselves and to each other. "I love you."

My brain immediately whirls, joyful jumping and laughing mixed with questions. The questions win, and I let go of his hand to look down on Great Falls, kicking my feet out as the uncertainty of the future sweeps over me. "What now?"

James laughs. He understands that there's a lot more than just two words in that question. "I have no fucking idea, Soph. I only know a few things for sure. One, I've got to ride finals in November to take care of my family. I've got contracts with sponsors expecting me to ride, and the better I ride, the bigger the check they cut. I can't shirk that responsibility to my family."

"I wouldn't want you to shirk anything because of me," I reply, and James smiles. "What?"

"You cut me off mid-rant," he chuckles. "Two, I'm so in love with you that I want to spend every waking minute with you, and sleeping ones too. And three, I need to make love to you right now."

As he says the last bit, he hops off the tailgate and moves in front of me, forcing my legs wider to accommodate his width.

Dipping down, he devours my mouth with a fiery kiss, and I can feel it. How could I have missed it before? This man loves me, and I love him right back.

Yeah, there's a million questions that we haven't gotten to. School, the rodeo, the ranch . . . for now, to hell with all of it. Now is the time for making love.

"Well then, Cowboy . . . how about you show your cowgirl what it feels like to fuck when you're in love?" I tease, pulling on his shirt. I hear a button pop, but I really don't care as the tigress inside me is fully unleashed. I kiss the warm skin of his chest, nibbling on his nipple before James chuckles and pushes me back.

"You give making love a dirty name," he growls, smiling. "If that's how you want it . . . yee-haw."

James reaches down, pulling off my boots before grabbing the waistband of my jeans. I'm glad I've already gotten them unbuttoned because he doesn't pause, pulling jeans and panties off in one huge inside-out *schwoomp* that makes my butt thump on the cool plastic of the bed liner. I reach for my tank top, but James doesn't care, kissing up the inside of my thighs and consuming my pussy.

"Holy fuck!" I yell breathlessly as his mouth and tongue slowly move over my wet folds, licking and sucking until I'm not sure if the stars I see are from the sky or from his tongue fluttering over my clit. I reach down, grabbing a fistful of his hair and grinding up into him, moaning deeply.

The only thing stopping me from coming in seconds is the icy chill from the edge of the tailgate, where it's still metal, digging into my ass. It's just enough to hold me back, and I wrap my legs around James's head, relishing the sensations he's creating inside me.

James lifts my hips and bites down lightly on my clit, making my eyes fly open and look down to see him staring at me, his mouth mumbling something that's absorbed by my pussy, turning the words into more ripples that flood my body, but I get the message: no coming . . . not until we do it together. "Yes, my love. But you'll have to be . . . oh God, you better be quick. Your tongue is amazing."

James chuckles and pulls back, setting my ass down as he reaches for his belt. "I know. And it's all for you."

James undoes his jeans. I can't see him, but I feel the wide head of his cock nestle against me, and I spread my legs wider. "All of me . . . all of you."

Reaching forward, James grabs the tailgate before driving into me in one thrust, our hips meeting in a sharp smack that sends ripples up my spine. James grunts like a bull, and I close my eyes, holding on as he takes me hard, pounding my body and sending hot pulses coursing through me. I squeeze him, wrapping my legs around his pumping hips as he buries his face in my chest, using his chin to push my tank top down enough to capture my left nipple and bite just enough to pull me back again.

"You better hope nobody comes to Outlook Point on a weeknight," he gasps as his hips speed up. "Because I'm not stopping until I come deep inside you. You're mine, Sophie. Only mine."

"Totally yours," I groan as I feel his cock swell. I'm trembling on the edge, riding my orgasm for as long as I can to draw it out for James, until he cries out, his bellow echoing over the valley as he comes. I'm right with him, pulling him in tight as I get swept away, my fingers digging into the cold metal of the tailgate as my pussy clenches around him and I hold him with my body, my heart hammering in my chest.

"God, I love you," James rasps when he can speak again, gathering me into his arms. "I promise you . . . we'll figure the rest out together."

"I love you too . . . and I know we will," I promise him, holding him close.

CHAPTER 22

JAMES

The next morning, I don't want to leave Sophie's warm bed, her hair scattered around her like a halo as she shifts about dreaming.

My lip curls up in a smile, and I wonder if she's dreaming about us. After the night we've just had, I couldn't imagine a dream better than what I'm waking up to.

I can't believe she's in love with me, too, that she's mine. I really do wish I could just stay here like this, not letting life and questions about the future intrude on this perfect moment, but I've got chores to do. Responsibilities to attend to.

It makes me think, my fingers twirling a lock of Sophie's hair. Both she and Mark have told me that I tend to think other folks are putting pressure on me, when it's really me putting pressure on myself.

But why? Why would I do that to myself? I'm supposed to be the wild one, the one who just does his own thing and doesn't worry about responsibilities or consequences.

Does some small part of me *want* to stay with my family on the ranch? Am I growing up, wanting to put down roots? I guess I always knew I would eventually, but sure as hell never figured it'd be now.

Then again, if this is the time, Sophie's the woman I'd want to do it with. It might take a miracle—she's still so "city" in so many ways.

But Pops being gone has changed things. I want to do right by him and Mama, take advantage of every minute. And am I really doing that on the circuit? The more I think about it, the more I'm really not sure.

I'd miss the thrill, of course . . . the energy and excitement, the unknown of what's gonna happen in the next eight seconds, the new horizons to see every day.

But maybe Pops was right and there's something to be said for a day's solid work and knowing you've taken care of your people the best way you can.

All I know as I carefully extract myself from Sophie's arms and get dressed is that I've got some hard thinking to do between now and finals. Once I'm ready, I plant a soft kiss on Sophie's forehead. "Bye, Soph. I'll call you later, okay?"

She mumbles in her sleep for a moment before one eye opens, and she smiles sleepily. "Bye, Cowboy. I love you."

She quickly snuggles under the covers, and I watch her, already snoring lightly again, for a moment before I whisper in the cool air, "I love you too."

Silently, I slip out into the dark predawn morning, heading home. It feels good, feels right, and for the first time, I go happily and willingly, not begrudgingly.

I'm barely through morning chores and out moving the herd to another pasture when I hear Mark's infamously loud whistle from up by the barn. He's quite good with it. He even won a prize at a county fair for being so damn loud, netting him $118 and a little trophy.

Curious, I pull my horse around and head toward him, vaguely wondering if Paul Tannen has decided to make another visit after my fight with Brody. Letting my horse go into the enclosed pasture behind the barn, I see Mark and Luke already waiting on me.

"What's up? By the way, the cows are fine in the west pasture."

Mark nods, like he expected nothing less. Then again, he shouldn't; I know what I'm doing. "Did some checking around in town. Asked some folks a few questions about Paul Tannen."

I meet Luke's eyes as he looks back, eagerness and trepidation mixed equally in his like I'm sure is visible in mine. "Well," I say impatiently when I see Luke isn't going to break the ice, "we're waiting . . . out with it."

"He's a gambler," Mark says after a moment. "Likes to run up to the Indian casinos almost every weekend, playing poker mostly. Word is he's flush right now, but he's known for having some high highs and low lows because he bids like he'll never lose. With him being up right now, he's looking to expand property—that's why he made the offer on our land. But . . ." He pauses, a sigh escaping as he looks skyward. Mark is never one for melodrama, so his reticence to spill makes me all the more edgy.

Also, Mark might be the strong, mostly silent type, but when he does open his mouth, he isn't exactly subtle.

"What happened?"

"Me asking questions, it got folks wanting to know why, so I was honest that he asked about buying us out," Mark replies. "Seems he owes some people money, and they're thinking they should be paid *before* he goes increasing his spread. I might've rustled up a little trouble for him. Unintentionally."

I wince, knowing this could get very bad very quickly. "Wow. A gambler? I never would've thought. I mean, it just seems unlike the man, you know? He always struck me as the type who's as tightfisted as they come."

Luke grunts his assent, looking over at Mark. "So, whatcha thinking?"

Mark sighs and pushes his hat back before nodding to himself. "He might not be the best type of man, but I do my best. And if I created problems for him, I owe it to him to let him know. I'm thinking we go over together, make it clear we aren't interested in ever selling, and apologize for any issues my questions might've triggered."

That's Mark, and one of the reasons he's the one that'll take this ranch into the next generation. He'll stand up for what's right, even if it hurts him. Luke nods, looking concerned, though. "Him and his boys aren't gonna like us showing up unannounced and spilling some family secrets. Might get ugly."

I'm already riled, anger left over from Brody's sucker punch, but I hold it back. "We can take care of anything they bring up. Paul Tannen brought this on himself; we're just protecting our property. And Mark is doing the right thing by letting him know there might be trouble headed his way."

Luke sighs, and Mark gives me a wary eye. "We are not going in there spoiling for a fight or looking to start an argument. We go in calm and controlled, all of us, or I'll go by myself."

I shake my head in disbelief. "You're not going over there alone! One wrong word, and Luke's going to be the one left running this place because you're going to end up in the hospital for six months."

"Then I guess you're going to stay calm?" Mark asks softly. "Even if Brody acts like a dumbass?"

He's asking, but it's not a question, not really. I nod, knowing he's right, just like he always is.

Luke spits in the dirt; he's picked up a habit of chewing sunflower seeds when he works in the barn. "Hey, what about Shayanne? Should we tell her along with Paul and Brody? She's young to be dealing with this kind of family drama."

"I don't know," Mark admits. "If she's there, she's there. We'll just ask to speak to Paul and Brody. If the rest of the family is there, we'll deal with it."

A thought hits me, and I smile a little, knowing I can actually contribute something besides muscle and good looks to this family for once. "Actually, Sophie might be able to help. She hung out with Shayanne last week. Maybe she can give her a call for a girls' night?"

Mark nods; the decision is made. Mark gives us both one more warning as he reseats his hat to head over to the mechanical barn to start his work for the day. "I think it goes without saying that there won't be a word about this at dinner with Mama."

"Right," Luke and I both agree. Going inside the house to grab a big drink of water and refill my canteen, I fetch my phone to call Sophie. It's about lunchtime; maybe I can catch her now. "Hey, Soph! How you doing, darlin'?"

Sophie chuckles lightly, sending a shiver through me that has nothing to do with the chill of the ice water trickling down my chest. "Oh, are we doing daytime calls and pet names now, Cowboy?"

I laugh. This woman gets me at every turn, calling me on my shit and making me grin more than a man has a right to. "Yes, honey-bunch," I reply sarcastically in a voice more suited for an old sitcom than anything else. "That's exactly what I'm doing, snookums."

Sophie laughs, making me smile even more. "If you're going to be a smart-ass, I won't tell you about this awesome dream I had this morning. I was all snug in bed, dreaming of this hot guy, and then poof, there he was in my room, kissing me and saying 'I love you' in between doing things I really can't describe around a bunch of innocent kittens and puppies. But when I woke up, he was gone. Must've just been a dream."

Glancing around to make sure no one's in hearing range, I grab my canteen and head out onto the porch, keeping my voice low, just in case. "It'd have been a dream if I could've stayed snuggled up with you all warm and soft, but the ranch calls. You understand, right?"

I think most girls would be pretty put out with their guy always slipping out of bed at stupid o'clock, but Sophie just takes it in stride like she does everything else. "Of course I do, James. Besides, what if

I have to roll out of bed at midnight to take care of someone's dog? Would you hold that against me? Work only gets done if you do it."

I grin, thinking Pops would've liked that saying quite a bit. "Well, depending on what we were doing right before that midnight call, I might be a little put out," I reply. "But thanks for understanding. Can I ask you a favor?"

"Sure. As long as it's not butt stuff. That's a nope."

I can hear the smirk in her voice, and I peek around to make sure I'm alone before I answer her. "Dammit, now all I'm gonna be thinking about all day is fucking that tight ass of yours while you wear my hat. I think you could handle it. Slow and easy while I rub your little clit . . . I'll make you love it, crave it even. You sure about that no?"

I can hear that her breathing has picked up from my words, her body likely already heated for me, but she doesn't answer. Instead, she shifts around, and I hear a door lock.

"I can hear you breathing harder, Soph," I continue, even as my cock throbs in my jeans and I think I might need to find my own little patch of privacy. "You're thinking about it, aren't you? Would I be the first to take your ass, claim you completely? You'd love it, I promise. I'd make your virgin ass come all over my cock."

A shuddering noise comes through the line before she finally speaks. "Fuck, James. You drive me crazy." Her voice is raspy, tight, and I know she's thinking about it. "Maybe," she finally says. "We'll have to do some work, some play, see what you can do . . . maybe."

Right now, that's more than enough, and more than I thought she'd give, considering we started out just teasing, and this wasn't at all where I thought this conversation was going. "Deal."

Luke pops out of the barn, giving me a questioning look and waving. "She gonna call Shayanne?"

Oh yeah, that was why I called. I'd damned near forgotten with thoughts of taking her that way. "So, Luke just reminded me, I have a favor to ask, if you don't mind?"

Sophie laughs shakily, but hums. "Getting me horny in the back of the office wasn't the favor?"

I grin, carefully avoiding how I think it'd be a lot better if she were horny down by the pond, or even right here in the middle of the yard. "No, as sexy as that conversation was and as much as I'll be thinking about it all day, this one involves Shayanne."

"Shayanne?" Sophie asks. "Nope. I don't share my man, I don't care how pretty the girl next door is."

I laugh, then give her a quick rundown of what Mark told us, editing it so that Sophie isn't quite let in on all of Paul Tannen's vices, and ask if she'd mind calling Shayanne for a girls' night in. "Think you can do that?"

"I think I'll have a full set of soaps to send out for Christmas gifts if I do, but hell yeah!" Sophie says. "But . . . what about you?"

"I promise, tomorrow night I'll be all yours to do whatever you want," I reply. "It's gonna kill me to not have you in my arms tonight, especially considering I'm expecting the Tannen meeting to go shitty, despite Mark's stoic nature. But I'll make it up to you."

~

By the end of dinner, Mark, Luke, and I are all feeling a bit shifty inside, I think. At least I am, for sure. You can never really tell with Mark, and Luke is so good at playing mellow that I'm not always sure if it's real or a front. He should have been a poker player instead of Paul Tannen; it's hard to know when Luke's bluffing you or not.

But I have enough butterflies for the three of us, so we're probably good. My goal is to not punch anyone. Should be easy enough, but I'm not sure, considering we're going into the proverbial lion's den to tell him he's fucked.

I can't picture any outcome where this goes well.

The short ride over is quiet; there isn't really all that much to say. Either what Mark says is accepted, or it isn't. Either someone starts some shit, or they don't. No matter what, though, while I won't be the first to throw a punch, I'll make damn sure that my brothers and I are the last ones standing if things go stupid.

We've been silent the entire ride as we all get our game faces on. Pulling up in the dirt driveway, I notice that the Tannen house is just a little . . . I'm not sure, maybe the word I'm looking for is . . . *dingier* than I last remember. It's not that things aren't trimmed and such, but the paint's looking old, the trim looks a little weathered, like maybe more than once Paul's stretched the budget on household maintenance in order to cover his gambling losses. It sort of makes me wonder just how he was able to afford that new truck of his, or how he could actually buy us out even if we were willing to sell.

By the time we stop, Brody is already on the front steps. We climb out as he walks toward the truck, his eyes already squinty and looking like he's ready to start something.

"You boys got some fucking nerve showing up here."

Mark, who decided not to wear a hat for this visit, still doesn't flinch as he looks Brody stone-cold even. "Not here on a social visit. Got something I need to tell your dad. You too. Paul around?"

Brody's eyes narrow further, like he's trying to visually read us and see what's going on. Finally, he gives in with a jerk of his head toward the house before walking back inside. It seems to be the only invitation we'll be getting, so we follow.

Inside, it's more of the same. Everything is practically spotless, just . . . older and more worn.

As we come into the front room, Paul's coming down the hallway, but he stops when he sees us, delight obvious on his face. "Ah, boys . . . I hope you have come to your senses. Ready to talk some figures?"

Mark shakes his head and stops just a few feet inside the room, far enough in for Luke and me to be in with him, but not so far we can't hightail it if we have to. "No, sir. Here on a related problem, but we're not interested in selling."

"I see. What seems to be the problem?" Paul replies, the congenial salesman replaced with truculent disdain and a little bit of menace. His boys hear it too. Bobby and Bruce have joined us now, fanning out beside their father. For some reason, it reminds me of elementary school, when the teacher tried to have us play dodgeball. Two teams lined up, staring at each other across the court . . . just waiting for that red ball to drop.

Mark and Paul are eyeballing each other, taking each other's measure. The tension in the room could be cut with a knife, everyone on edge and waiting for the first move.

Finally, Mark breaks the silence. "Well, you coming around, aggressively trying to buy us out so quick after Pops passed made me curious. We ain't close, so I wondered how a man like you, with a big spread of his own, a fancy new truck and such, could have the funds to get a loan for a property our size. So I asked around a bit . . ."

Paul interrupts, his face going a furious pink. "You mind your own goddamn business and keep your nose out of mine, boy. Seems your daddy didn't teach you the basics of being a good neighbor."

Mark stays calm, even as I see Luke's fist tighten at Paul's comment about Pops. "Our father taught us good fences make good neighbors, just like Robert Frost said. Now, this is a courtesy, and you'd best listen, sir. I asked around, and found out about your gambling activities. Seems you like some pretty high-stakes poker games up at the casino."

As Mark talks, I sense the agitation in Paul building, but my eyes never leave Brody, since he's the one on my watch. I notice the way his eyebrows shoot up in surprise when Mark mentions gambling, and the way his eyes ping-pong between Paul and Mark for a moment before he returns his look to me.

I can see there's confusion there. Maybe he didn't know about his daddy's gambling issue either? If not, this could get uglier than ever . . . and we may not be the ones fighting.

Mark continues, his voice still low and respectful. "Apparently, there's some 'poker buddies' of yours that seem to think they should be paid back for your debts before you go buying up more land. I didn't know anything about it; I wanted to just know what lit a fire under you so much for getting our property. If I fetch trouble down on your head about that, I apologize. But considering you have your own responsibilities to worry about, both here and in town, I think we can officially call any business you might be considering regarding our land to be finished."

Paul is blustering, sputtering and rambling angry nonsense. "Well, I never . . . in my own damn house. You disrespectful punk . . . ruined everything . . . I oughta . . ."

It seems he's more strung out about the real issue than us, and all three Tannen boys are looking at each other with questions in their eyes, obviously shocked at the extent of their dad's gambling, but still in defense mode as Paul rants.

Paul gets it together enough to stab a threatening finger in Mark's direction. "Get. Out. Get off my land, and do not ever step foot on it again."

He turns away, waving a hand in Brody's direction before storming down the hallway, an obvious "deal with this" gesture. Brody puffs up, handling his assignment and letting all his stirred-up anger drip from every word. "You heard him. Off and don't come back."

Mark nods once and we back up, sort of covering for each other as we head down the hallway to the door. Right before we walk out, Mark looks back, eye to eye with Brody. "Same goes for you too. Stay off our property; no more stupid shit."

Brody just glares icily at Mark, who seems to decide that's as much of an agreement as he'll get. Inside the truck, it's silent until we turn off Tannen's land onto the main dirt road. Luke speaks first, glancing into the rearview mirror as he does, probably making sure nobody has a shotgun pointed our direction. "Think they're gonna stay away, handle whatever money issues Paul's led them into?"

Mark grunts, speeding up a little. "Hope so. Done on our side unless they start something. Agreed?" He asks like it's a question, but really, we know it's an order and nod accordingly.

"I was watching Brody when you started talking about the gambling," I note. "He had no idea. Totally shocked."

Luke chimes in, agreeing. "Bobby and Bruce too."

Mark sighs and slows down as we approach our gate. "Not our problem. Let them handle their business, we'll handle ours, and hopefully, they'll never cross. The important thing is, he's not gonna try buying the ranch out from underneath us, and he's not gonna keep hounding Mama about selling. Done. Problem solved."

I nod, hoping he's right, and trusting that if anyone can protect the ranch, it's Mark. He's smart enough to watch for sneaky business tactics and rough enough that he could put a beatdown on someone if necessary. It's what makes him a great fit for being the boss.

I've got another issue to deal with, though. "Uh, guys? Mind if I ask you a question?"

"You're asking for permission now? Sophie's a good influence on you. What's on your mind, James?" Luke asks.

I turn to the side in the back seat and look toward town. "I'm going to have to fill Sophie in on what happened, and her and Shayanne are gonna realize that I pulled a fast one by encouraging their girls' night. Think Sophie will be mad? Hope Shayanne doesn't hold it against Sophie too."

Luke glances at Mark, who shrugs. Luke looks back at me, grinning. "Girls deal with their shit in their own weird ways. You assholes and my horses are complicated enough for me. I say you let them figure it out for themselves and stay out of it. And hope Sophie doesn't put you in the doghouse for using her to get little Shayanne out of the house while the big boys talk. Good luck, man." He says it like I'm already a dead man walking, leaving no doubt what he thinks will happen when Sophie and Shayanne hear about tonight's meeting.

I lean forward, reaching over and flicking his ear hard. "Thanks, asshole. Really helpful advice there."

CHAPTER 23

SOPHIE

Typing away at the computer by the front desk, I'm looking forward to getting off work. It's not that I didn't enjoy the day; I mean, I got to help a mama basset hound deliver six adorable puppies, but I'm looking forward to my night with Shayanne.

Wrapping up the last of my notes, I pop my head into Doc's office. "You need anything else? I'm about to head out if we're good for the day."

Doc grins, looking up from his own computer where he's handling paperwork. He's got an office manager, but he still checks everything since it's his name on the checks to the IRS. "You're in a sure-fired hurry, miss. Got a hot date with your rodeo man tonight?"

I laugh. Doc's great about my relationship with James. "Nope, not tonight. I'm actually having Shayanne Tannen over for a girls' night in. We're doing spa treatments and pampering ourselves. It'll be fun tonight, but my gorgeous manicure won't last ten minutes after I get to work tomorrow."

Doc nods thoughtfully, leaning back in his chair. "Shayanne? Nice girl. Such a shame about her mother, though. Shayanne was just a tot herself when she passed. But she seems to take good care of her dad and brothers. There's a tough cookie under that bubblegum shell."

"She's great, once you get her to take a breath in between bursts of talking. Did you know she's making these goat soaps? They're pretty amazing. I told her she should try opening up an online shop."

"I knew they had a goat herd, but didn't know Shayanne was making soaps. Selling them sounds like a good idea if she wants to. Might even see if the resort tourist shop would sell them?"

"Oh my gosh, that's a brilliant idea! I'll tell her that tonight!"

Doc laughs, nodding. "Hey, I know I've done this several times, but you won't blame me when you get my age. Mind if an old man gives you some advice on something besides veterinary medicine?"

"Sure, what is it?"

"Shayanne is a sweet soul, and like I said, she's a tough country kid, but she's sheltered in a way most young 'uns aren't these days. She's been the caretaker of their family for a lot of years, and doesn't have a whole lot of outside interactions beyond an occasional trip into town. It's just . . . I'm glad you're being friendly with her because I think she could use a friend. Maybe broaden her horizons a little bit to the possibilities beyond their thousand acres."

"I'll keep that in mind, Doc. I think I'm just as excited as she is to hang out tonight. I've made some friends"—I smile as Doc raises one bushy eyebrow at my characterization of James as a friend, but I continue—"but having a girlfriend around to do girly stuff is something I've missed. I think maybe we're good for each other."

He grins and gives me a nod. "Well then, you'd better skedaddle. And bring in one of her fancy soaps for me to try if you don't mind. See you tomorrow!"

Before he's even got his screensaver unlocked, I'm off like a flash to set up and make my house presentable for company. I'm definitely no slob, but if we're going to be spending the night doing various beauty treatments in my tiny bathroom, I want it sparkling. And I've seen Shayanne's version of clean—the woman could do surgery on her countertops.

Seemingly minutes later, the house is ready, and I am, too, and just in time because I hear a truck pulling up out front. I run to open the door, thrilled to see Shayanne again. "Hey, Shay!"

She hops out of her truck and runs up, giggling madly with a bag over her shoulder and her eyes lit up like twin diamonds. "Thank you for inviting me! Are you ready?"

"Absolutely!" I promise her, caught up in her enthusiasm. "Pizza is on its way, plus extra cheesy breadsticks. I've got cardboardeaux for me and grape juice for you chilling in the fridge, and all my nail polishes lined up for you to pick from. And if you get bored with swapping stories and treatments, I've got all my favorite rom-coms on Netflix ready to go! Let's get this girls' night in started!"

I do a little booty shake, arms raised up high, celebrating our plans, and Shayanne laughs until I grab her arms and jerk her around, forcing her to dance with me in the front yard. "Come on, I know all the horseback riding you do must've loosened those hips. Don't make me give you lessons here in the front yard—show me what you've got!"

Shayanne blushes but does a halfway decent hip roll. I'm sure she can do better, especially since she sasses back, "Good enough for the price of admission?"

"It's a start," I tease, leading her inside. "Now, first things first—you're ditching those cowgirl boots and soaking your feet. I've already got that ready right here in the living room for both of us."

In between treatments, which start with salt and baking-soda foot baths that leave our skin soft and totally smell-free, we talk about our day. "So, yeah, if you're looking for a puppy, give them a call," I tell Shayanne, who's been gushing over the pictures of the basset pups I helped with today. "Although . . . is a basset hound the best for a ranch?"

"Maybe not, but who cares?" Shayanne giggles. "I'd just baby this little pup and teach it to watch the goats. They can't run as fast as the cattle and don't get as riled up."

"And they're great kissers," I say, making her laugh. "What? Those big, slobbery lips and sad eyes? How could you not want to just smooch the hell out of one?"

"Doggy breath, that's how! You know, Daddy says . . . oops."

"Oh, hell no you didn't!" I mock protest, standing up and duck walking across the room. The foot soaks gave way to toenail polish, and I currently have little foam spacers in between each toe, making me very off balance. "Now you've done it, and we haven't even gotten through the pizza yet. I'm smacking you, and you're gonna let me."

Shayanne looks at me nervously, half turning away, but I lean over with a grin and smack her ass. "There, now don't let it happen again, or else I'm gonna think you like it. Hear me?"

Shayanne laughs along, saluting me. "Aye-aye, Captain. Won't let it happen again, sir. I mean, ma'am."

I try to keep my faux-stern look, but we both dissolve into giggles. "So . . ." she says, grinning, "how are things on the romantic front? You look a lot more at peace than the last time we talked."

I shrug, tossing back the last of my wine. "You were right. I didn't realize until you started interrogating me, but you were right."

"About what?"

"That I've fallen in love with him," I reply, fishing for a slice of bacon and bell-pepper pizza. "That what started out as summertime fun has turned serious."

Shayanne nods wisely, grabbing a breadstick and chewing it slowly. "Well, it was so obvious considering the way you were talking about him. So, now what?"

"Well, we talked last night. It was . . . changing. We both said I love you."

Shayanne squeals, dropping her breadstick and jumping to her feet. *"Whaaaaat?"* she says before dancing around the room happily. "Oh my gosh, Sophie and James sitting in a tree, K-I-S-S-I-N-G. First comes love, then comes marriage, then comes Sophie with a baby carriage . . ."

"Sit down, you goof! And don't *ever* do that again." I laugh, unable to be angry at all. She's just too cute.

Shayanne stops abruptly, turning to me questioningly. "Wait, what about school? What about the rodeo?"

It's my turn to be unsure as I play with a piece of bacon on my pizza for a minute before answering, "I don't know. We haven't gotten further than saying I love you, and then, well . . . you know."

"I don't, but I can make some guesses," Shayanne says lightly. "Go on."

"I know James is feeling some pressure to stay here this year more than ever, but honestly, I think it's more him putting pressure on himself than his mom or brothers. He loves the rodeo; he lights up when he talks about it. I don't want him to give it up on a whim and be unhappy. If rodeo makes him happy, he should do that. And school starts for me in a few weeks. I've got to go; I want to be a vet someday. I just don't know how that works out."

Shayanne shrugs, sitting back down next to me. "But if you love each other, you'll make it work. If there's one thing James Bennett is known for, it's going all-in. Good idea or bad, once he's agreed, he goes whole hog. He's legendary around here for some of his stunts in his younger days, but he always follows through, even with running away to join the rodeo. He'll move heaven and earth if he has to." She nods like it's just that easy.

I smile, because she's right—that sounds just like James. "Enough on me. How about you? Any guys on your radar . . . a townie maybe?"

Shayanne snorts and shakes her head. "No way. Definitely not a townie, and honestly, I rarely leave the ranch, so I don't know how I'd actually even meet a man. I'm doomed to a life forever alone, caring for my bachelor brothers, the spinster sister."

She feigns a melodramatic faint, plopping back on the couch. I laugh and slap her leg with a breadstick. "I doubt it's that dire, Drama Mama! You've just been watching *The Bold and the Beautiful* too much. Oh, speaking of leaving the ranch . . ." Shayanne gives me a cautious look, but I continue, "I know you weren't so sure about selling your soaps online, but Doc had a great idea. You could sell them at the shop up at the Mountain Spirit resort. Easy delivery if they need restocking, close to home, and the resort is just an email away—no website needed."

Shayanne nods, her eyes lighting up. "Actually, that is a great idea. Especially since my soaps are locally known from the farmer's market when Brody sells them. It'd be a way for people to buy them all the time. I like it! Tell Doc thank you for the brilliance."

"Will do," I tell her. We're wrapping up the messy spa treatments, sitting down to watch a movie and eat a second round of pizza when a loud truck pulls up outside.

Shayanne looks at me, smirking. "You expecting James tonight? Or is your cowboy that needy for your sweet lovin'?"

"Stop, silly," I say with a shake of my head, heading to the door, but whoever is here is already pounding a fist on the outside. *Boom boom boom, boom boom boom.* Startled and a little frightened, I peek out the peephole and see Brody, every inch as tall and wide as I remember him from the Fourth of July festival. He's just as mad tonight, although he looks sober at least. "What the—?"

I crack the door, leaving the chain closed. "Yes?"

"Shayanne here? She's coming home now," Brody grumbles. It's not a question, more of a command, and it irks me that he thinks he can just boss her around.

"Hang on one second. Let me talk to her." I close the door, ready to give Shayanne shit about her overbearing brother, and turn around to see her already slipping her shoes on and grabbing her bag.

My shoulders slump a little, but I square up, keeping my voice low and supportive. "You don't have to go just because he says so."

She smiles ruefully; I think she understands the thoughts in my head. "Yeah, I kinda do. He's a good guy, a good brother, so if he came all the way to town to get me, it's for a good reason. I'll call you?"

I nod, wrapping my arms around my waist, uncertain about this whole thing. But Shayanne's calm, if a little regretful that our evening's been cut short. I open the door and see Brody looking frantic, worry written all over his face for a split second before he morphs it back to anger.

"Shayanne, get in the truck. We need to talk on the way home. Bobby can drive your truck home."

I see another guy getting out of Brody's big truck and already heading for Shayanne's. Presumably that's Bobby. He's not quite as big as Brody, but still big enough, with that sort of farm-boy build that can heave hay bales for a couple of hours without getting tired.

"What's going on?" Shayanne says, adjusting her bag. "I basically just got here."

Brody gives me a hard look as he answers Shayanne. "We'll discuss it on the way home. But you," he says, pointing a menacing finger at me, "you're with James Bennett, yeah? Tell them something for me. Tell them thank you and to stay the fuck away from us."

Confused, I nod before turning my eyes to Shayanne, mouthing, "Call me."

She nods, worry written all over her face. I'm still not sure I should let her leave with him, especially when he's so mad about something that I'm not even sure he should be driving, but she's an adult and knows him better than I do.

It's a small peace when I see Brody turn to Shayanne, the anger dripping off him as a sense of weariness takes over, definitely calmer but more morose.

It's quiet, but I think I hear him say something about finances.

I realize that maybe whatever was happening tonight with James's meeting with the Tannens was probably to shut down their purchase offer again, and now Brody is asking about their finances.

I bite at my bottom lip, worrying about Shayanne and her family, and James and his family. James said when he asked me to get Shayanne out of the house that they had to go talk to Paul Tannen . . . and I'd say things didn't go well.

Which puts me in a bind. Because the Bennetts feel more and more like my stand-in family, and Shayanne is my best friend in town.

Frankly, I don't want to play the role of Benvolio in this little redo of *Romeo and Juliet*.

CHAPTER 24

JAMES

The frogs croak, and the crickets chirp as I sit on the edge of Pops's pond, my feet dangling from the dock as I reflect on the day. Sophie called, asking about Brody coming over to basically drag Shayanne home, but I told her it was fine. Brody might want to tear my head off, but I could never picture him doing more than saying boo to Shayanne. When Sophie asked, I was totally honest and explained our visit and that they had some family stuff to go over.

"Well, I guess Doc might want to make visits to the Tannens' a solo thing for a while," Sophie said, sighing. "Thanks for being honest with me, though. Um, do you want me to come over?"

That simple question touched me more than I could have said, but I had to refuse. "It's late, darlin', and while nothing would feel better than holding you through the night, I think it'd be best if we stuck to the original plan. See you tomorrow after work?"

"Okay . . . tomorrow. I love you."

"I love you too," I replied, and it felt so natural to say it. It almost makes up for having to drink alone by the pond, my head whirling with thoughts.

Tonight could've gone very differently. Would Mark and Luke have been okay without me here? Three on four isn't great odds, but two on four's worse.

Would I even *want* them to be okay without me? I've started to enjoy the fact that when Mark comes out of the office, he gives me a look of gratitude when he sees that I've already gotten a heap of work done. I know Luke feels the same way—it's the only way he's been able to keep his breeding lines going this year. Sure, I don't have any glamour in what I do around the ranch, but for the first time in my life, I don't really mind it that much.

I toss a rock across the pond, watching the moonlit circles waver where the rock pings along the surface. Finally, I take a deep breath and look up at the moon. "Pops, can I talk to you for a second?"

There's no answer, of course, but in my head, I can hear him clear as day: *Sure thing, hellion.*

It makes me smile. No one has called me hellion in years, but he always did when I was a kid. "Pops, I'm at a crossroads, and I don't know what to do. I've always dreamed of the rodeo, doing the circuit, and I have loved every minute of the freedom, the excitement. But without you, it feels like I should be here. I think it's time to come home."

I don't want you feeling a duty to the land just because I've checked out. Is that your only reason, because I've moved on?

I pause, before admitting something I'm not sure I was ready to admit even last week. "It's more than that, though. I think I'm ready to be the man you wanted me to be, helping Mark take care of the ranch and looking out for Mama. And that's scary. Being in one place terrifies the fuck out of me, and I don't know if I can do it. But I want to."

Go on, boy. You always were the one to counter Mark. He says one word when he needs five, you say ten when one's needed.

I take a swig of beer, needing the liquid courage even as the old adage from Pops makes me smile. "There's a girl, Pops. And she's great, crazy enough to challenge me, but she's got her head on straight. She's got a plan, though, and I'm pretty sure it doesn't include me, definitely doesn't include staying anywhere near the ranch. She's way too good for me, but I want her anyway. I love her, Pops."

Sounds like you've got something more important than a ranch, James. Land comes and goes, cattle comes and goes . . . but a good woman is forever.

I duck my head for a moment, all the thoughts that have been swirling coming together in one certainty: I love Sophie. Whatever it takes, I need to be with her. If I have to follow her, I'll do it.

But still, if there's a way to be with Sophie and take care of my family, I have to try. I don't know how that's possible yet, but there has to be a way.

Resolution settles into my heart, my mind made up. I'm jumping ship, diving into the deep end of responsible adulthood. Pops didn't raise a scaredy-cat, so if figuring this out with Sophie and my family is what I need to do, then that's that. I've been running wild with desti-nation: undetermined for so long. I've moved week to week with the rodeo, always knowing that it was *my* thing, never having to compare with or compete against my brothers, my father, or my family name. But it's time to man up, take charge of my future, and create the life I want. With Sophie and on the ranch with my family if possible.

I thump my chest over my heart, looking up. "Thanks, Pops. Love you."

Love you, too, James. Always have, always will.

With a weight lifted off my shoulders, I toss back the rest of my beer and head back toward the house. I don't get far before I realize that Mama is sitting on the back porch swing, sipping a glass of tea and looking at the stars.

Mounting the steps, I lean against the railing, smiling. "Isn't it past your bedtime, young lady?"

Mama laughs at me, and pats the seat beside her. "That it is. But there seemed to be a lot going on this evening, and I knew you boys were gonna need a little something."

She offers me a glass, and I see another abandoned empty one on the table. I raise an eyebrow, silently questioning, and she answers quietly, "Mark's. He's fine. Just feels bad that he stirred up a hornet's nest for someone. He's got a heart of gold underneath that cold exterior, you know."

I do know that, but it's hard to remember sometimes when the tinman act rarely cracks. I sit down, and she pours me a glass out of the pitcher. I take a big gulp of the sweet tea, but as it hits my stomach, I start sputtering. "Damn, Mama . . . that's not tea!"

She swats at me, still smiling, though. "Language, James. And it is too tea. Just with a little kick from the bourbon."

She says so much in a few words, it takes me a moment to figure out which part to reply to. I decide to start with the unspoken part of her statement. "So, Mark tell you about Paul Tannen?"

Mama sips her tea again, waving a hand at me. "Pshaw, boy, I knew you bunch were going over there en masse tonight, figured it was to warn them off trying to buy again. You three aren't exactly subtle, you know. Now, I didn't know about Paul's gambling until Mark just told me. I hope he gets it together; he's got folks depending on him . . ." She trails off, shaking her head. "What is it with you men and wanting to play the odds?"

I shrug, knowing that in my own way, I gamble just as much as Paul Tannen. What else do you call it when you climb on the back of a bull? "The boys didn't know about Paul either. Now it's all out in the open, though. Seems Brody is taking it seriously. Sophie said he came and got Shayanne, was asking about their finances before he even got her in the truck."

Mama clucks her tongue, rocking the swing lightly. "Shame it's on the kids to take care of it, but at least they know now and can be on the lookout for any problems. Speaking of Sophie, I haven't seen her in a bit. You been going into town more?"

I nod, relieved to be able to talk it over with Mama. "Yeah, we had a bit of a . . . thing a week or so ago, but Mark kicked my ass and sorted my head out. We had a great date yesterday, made up for my running scared."

Mama laughs, and I guess it's the bourbon tea that's got her a little more loose-lipped. "James, I know about makeup sex. Your Pops and I would sometimes argue over stupid stuff, just so we'd have something to make up over."

I shiver, laughing a little uncomfortably. "Things I don't need to know, Mama. As far as I'm concerned, you and Pops had sex exactly two times to have Mark and Luke. I'm a product of miraculous conception."

"Okay, if that's what you want to believe," she says, her eyes twinkling. "Your father was a good man, in every sense of the word." I cringe, and she laughs. "Fine, fine . . . what happened with Sophie?"

I smile, scratching at my lip nervously because this is major, and I want Mama to like Sophie. I know she's been fine with her at dinner, but this is different, decidedly more serious than a dinner guest. Finally, I reach over and take Mama's hand. "I love her, Mama. I know it now— she's the one. And I'm ready to stay here on the ranch, help handle things here and not ride bulls anymore, but I need to be with her. Wherever she's going, I'm going. I'll find a ranch-hand job near her school if I can. If not, I'll do whatever it takes to support us so I can be with her."

Mama smiles, her tone teasing as she squeezes my fingers back. "I knew it. I told you months ago. Men can be such morons, even the ones I raised. Best-laid plans . . . 'Just for the summer, Mama.' As if."

She's mocking what I told her shortly after I met Sophie, and I remember her muttering "best-laid plans" under her breath. It makes me smile, and wonder just a little. "You didn't know back then. Hell, I'd just met her then!"

"Uh-huh," Mama says dismissively. "Whatever you need to tell yourself, son. That woman had you on a string from the word *go*. Glad you finally realized it. She's a good one. I definitely approve."

She leans over, bumping my shoulder with hers, and the breath I'd been holding releases in relief. "Thanks, Mama."

"And you know you're always welcome here. This is your home, no matter if you're riding rodeo or chasing after Sophie. This is home."

I nod, putting an arm around her shoulders and hugging her tightly. "I know, Mama. And I'm ready to be here, help on the ranch. And hopefully someday really soon I'll be able to, but I need her. She's got all these plans, and I'm just hoping she can pencil me in somewhere."

Mama looks at me like I'm crazy. "James, that girl is just as spun as you are. Don't you think she's got the same thoughts you have? That she's going to have to figure out how to balance being a vet student with you riding rodeo? Have you even filled her in on your ideas for settling down? Have you asked her to stay?"

I shake my head, confused again. "I can't ask her that. She wants to be a vet, and I want her to have what she wants."

Mama sighs, like I've taken leave of my senses. "Well, there's more than one vet school in the country, son."

I look at her, nodding but unsure. "I know, but she's already been accepted in the program she wants."

Mama nods, still dragging me along to her goal. "My point is, you don't get to decide what the future looks like. It's something you two decide together. Your father never would have come out here to set up a ranch if I'd said I needed to stay where we were. You're leaving out a rather important detail here, though, aren't you, Romeo?"

I grin at the nickname, nodding.

She raises an eyebrow, continuing, "What about rodeo? You say you're ready to not ride anymore, stay here or wherever she is, but you're giving up something you love. And you're already committed to finals in November. You earned that spot. Are you sure you want to give that up?"

I sigh, leaning forward and downing the rest of my spiked tea. "I am committed. But I can train anywhere, maybe fly out to the fall circuits instead of driving. Then head to Vegas a bit early and make it my farewell ride. And then . . . come home . . . or to Sophie, wherever she is."

Mama pats my back, just like she used to when I had lots of questions and not enough answers as a younger man. "Sounds like you've got some serious conversations to have with her. I know it feels like a lot, but I'm sure you two can work it out. Love always finds a way. In fact, did I ever tell you about the time your Pops came to see me . . ."

As she launches into a story about their early dating days, I'm at peace for the first time in a long time. Maybe Pops was right all those years ago.

This is the life . . . working your land, providing for your family, loving your woman the way he loved Mama, and swinging on the back porch at night, surrounded by stretches of dark sky and stars.

This is it. I'm back where I started physically, but in such a different place mentally.

I just hope Sophie wants to live this type of life too . . . with me.

CHAPTER 25

SOPHIE

Sweat stings my eye. I'm in the middle of administering a vaccine to a particularly ornery nanny goat when my phone buzzes in my back pocket. I'm out in the back of Doc's office, in the small area he has for farm animals whose owners bring them in instead of us doing house calls. After a little love to the feisty creature, I release the gate to the pen, letting her back out to hop around free so she can work off her anger with me.

Smiling at her antics, I apologize. "Sorry, the shot's for your own good!"

The goat bleats at me, and I step back and pull my phone out to see a message from Shayanne.

Can you talk?

Of course! I text back. The goat I'm treating doesn't mind!

A moment later, my phone rings. I watch the goat while I jump straight in, foregoing a greeting. "Are you okay?"

Shayanne giggles, like I haven't been worrying about her for the past twenty-four hours. "So, you're seeing other goats behind my back, huh?"

"You're not the only people with goats around here," I remind her, relieved a little. "Are you okay?"

"Of course I'm okay, silly. Sorry if Brody scared you. It was a rough night here, I'll admit. Did James tell you what happened?"

"Yeah, he told me about it late last night when we talked after you left," I reply, wiping my forehead again. "I'm sorry it was hard. But you're okay, and your family is okay?"

Shayanne sighs, and I know she's not being completely honest, but she's doing her best to tell me what she feels comfortable with. "Yeah, Brody's got it under control. We stayed up all night going over the books and the bank statements. Apparently, Daddy's been using a separate account to float his gambling wins and losses, so it doesn't affect the ranch books exactly. But it definitely affects us overall."

Shayanne sounds resigned. "Brody and him got into it. I don't know if you noticed, but Brody is a little bossy."

I snort. That's one way to put it. "Yeah, I noticed."

Shayanne laughs a little, brightening some. "Well, he gets it from Daddy, so at least he comes by it honestly. Anyway, he told Daddy to pay his debts and then strongly suggested that if he's gonna gamble, he consider just who he's playing with and that any further windfalls be put toward paying off our ranch. I think that's a good idea, so hopefully Daddy'll listen."

Brody Tannen, you just jumped up about a thousand points in my book. "Brody is really looking out for your family, isn't he? I guess I've only seen him mad, so maybe my perception is skewed."

Shayanne sounds a little shy suddenly and a bit apologetic. "I think we were all a little skewed. Daddy was telling us stuff about the Bennetts . . . I didn't pay it much mind, but he was good at getting my brothers riled up. If the Bennetts were as bad as Daddy says, I don't think Mark would've told him about ruffling feathers. Those debts . . . they're not with nice people. But we'll handle it."

"I know you will. And you're right, I don't think Mark had bad intentions. That man definitely has a hard exterior, and although I'm not sure there's a gooey caramel center like some romance-book hero, he's at least got a sense of morals and a good heart. By the way, you totally just said *Daddy says*, and I'm smacking you when I see you."

Shayanne laughs, and I'm glad to have lightened her day, even if only for a moment. Doc pops his head outside, calling my name before he sees I'm on the phone. He mouths, "Sorry," and ducks back inside.

"Hey, if you don't mind, duty calls . . . that's D-U-T-Y this time, although I guess I don't know if it's D-O-O-D-Y yet. Gotta see what Doc needs."

"I understand. Definitely no poop in my day, thank goodness. But I need to make dinner. I think I'll go with Daddy's favorite meat loaf and Brody's favorite cheesy potatoes. Kinda smooth it over with happy, full tummies for both of them."

I laugh. It seems country women have been doing kitchen diplomacy for centuries. "Hey, I'm glad you're okay, honey. If you need anything, call me . . . anytime. Okay?"

We say our goodbyes, and I'm so relieved. It seems like Brody is a good guy after all, just one who is vehement about protecting his family. I can understand that.

Jake would do anything for me, and vice versa. Actually, more than once he has. Reminding myself that I need to give him a call sometime soon, I head inside, searching for Doc. All I have to do is follow the squealing sounds. Bacon is back with her owner, and she's none too happy that Doc is disturbing her sleep.

"Hey, Doc. Can I help?"

He sits back, looking very frustrated with the cute little piggy he's dealing with. "Yes please. I remembered that you and Ms. Bacon got along fabulously, so I thought maybe you could grab her without getting her so riled up. She's not feeling very well apparently."

"Of course." I walk over to where she's lying on the tile, pet her head, and coo, "Who's my good little porker? That's right, you are. Come here, Princess Bacon."

As the pig calms, I gather her up with her blanket easily, and head toward an exam room. After a quick exam and question-and-answer session, we quickly deduce that Bacon isn't feeling well because her owner is sprinkling shredded cheese on her food every day. The irony doesn't escape me, considering what Shayanne's going to feed her family later.

"She doesn't need that much cheese. A nibble here and there, a few times a month is fine," Doc tells Bacon's visibly relieved owner. "But pigs need to eat pig food and veggies. Let me print you out a list."

The owner squabbles a bit, trying to tell Doc that the pig food is just so boring. "How can you expect my baby to be happy with pig pellets and celery?"

Doc grins. "It's pig food for a pig. It's designed to give her the nutrients she needs. And she doesn't know any better! If you want to treat her, do it with veggies. A healthy diet will keep her healthy, or you can just come see me every time she gets the shits from whatever crap you've been feeding her." By the end of his rant, he's obviously fed up with Bacon's owner.

I bite my lip to contain my giggle, focusing my attention on Bacon as I pet her, feeling her belly for any distention. So, *that's* why Doc wasn't so mad at me about how I handled James after Briarbelle's foal was born. He's not terrible, but he's definitely not the best at bedside customer service either when someone's endangering their animal.

As Doc walks out to get the list of approved pig foods, I love on Bacon some more, chatting with her owner, who looks pouty. "If he wasn't the only doctor in the county who handles pigs, I'd—"

"He's a bit gruff, but he's right," I say soothingly. "It's not a treat if it makes her sick. She seems to be feeling better now, though. Probably should stick with just the pig feed for a few days, no treats, so it's gentler on her stomach. Then slowly, after a few days, you can add her Cheerios back in moderation, a few days after that, a single treat. Don't worry, Bacon'll still be happy, maybe more playful, and her poop's going to smell a lot better."

"Really?"

I nod, scratching Bacon's belly. "Totally."

After Bacon is happily headed back home with her owner, all apologies for not treating her right, Doc looks at me with an odd expression. I'm lost for a second, checking my zipper and my nose, thinking something must be wrong. "Doc?"

He laughs, shaking his head. "You're fine, girl. I'm just thinking . . . I don't know what I'm gonna do around here without you. This summer has shown me that I need to slow down, get some help around here. Just too bad it can't be you since you're going back to school."

My heart soars at the compliment from a veterinarian that I respect so much, but at the same time, my stomach drops because he's right. I'm leaving. August is just around the corner. I've already seen the high school football team out on the field starting their drills as I drive home from Doc's office.

I try to squash the sadness that threatens to overwhelm me at the thought of leaving, pasting a smile on my face. "Thank you so much, Doc. That's quite the compliment from someone like you. I really have learned so much. I hope my practice is basically . . . this . . . one day."

I gesture around the room, conveying that he's pretty much got my dream gig. Doc smiles, looking around the exam room fondly, but I can tell he's really seeing beyond it, to all his years caring for animals. "Yeah . . . so, Miss Sophie, I'm not randomly buttering you up. I have a proposition for you. Say no if you want to, of course, but I'll admit that I'm hoping you'll say yes."

Intrigued, I raise my eyebrows questioningly. "You've definitely got my attention."

Doc grins, shaking his head. "Once upon a time, I was a young buck going to vet school. I went to State, which is just south of here. Not long of a drive, even. Damn fine program; taught me a lot even if it's not quite as famous as some of the other ones around here. Anyway, I've still got a few friends up there, buddies I check in with about unusual things. Hell, one of them even has me come in to give a speech every year to his newbies. I get all dandied up in my best cowboy boots and practice my grizzled accent just to put the real country-doc act on them."

I'm nodding along, wondering where the point is in this story as he continues, "So, I called up a buddy, told him about this exceptional intern I've had this summer. I told him how she can basically run the clinic, did a red-bag delivery on her own without breaking a sweat, charm any animal—beast or man. And I told him that I was gonna be real sorry to see her go back to school in the fall."

I blush at the praise, but inside I'm basking in it. "Doc, I just—"

He keeps going—I think he's worked himself up to the point the only way he'll get this out is if it comes out in one long blurb. "So, I asked him if there was any way we could pull some strings, get you a spot in their program. And I'll leave the long of it out . . . but anyway . . . there's a spot at State for you if you want it. You can go to school here, work for me as much as you want, flexible schedule of course because I remember what vet school was like, probably even stay in your little house if you like it. I think there might be a cowboy that'd be happy to have you around, too, if I'm not mistaken."

I'm speechless, my jaw hanging wide open as my mind races. I could transfer, go to school here, and work with Doc? I could be with James! My heart jumps in joy before I remember that he's leaving for the rodeo, and it plummets again.

But even if he's gone, I could go to school and work. I could see Shayanne and the Bennetts, even be closer to Jake. And when James isn't on tour . . . well, he does call this place home. It'd be a fuller life for sure. I've always tried to do things on my own, not be a burden to my brother, but maybe I don't have to stand on my own two feet in isolation just to prove that I can. I can make my way and still be surrounded by friends and family, maybe even find that work-life balance Jake is always talking about.

"Can I really do that? Just up and change plans that way?" I muse to myself, but Doc hears me and answers.

"It's still vet school, just in a different place. I'd say with a better support system too. And that's not just me being selfish."

I nod. Doc doesn't include that it's an opportunity to learn a lifetime of experience, to work side by side with Doc and maybe, in a few years . . . Trusting my gut, I know the answer.

A grin breaks across my face, and I grab him in a wild hug. "Yes! Oh my gosh, that's awesome! It's . . . *yes!*"

Doc laughs, trying to jump for joy a bit with me. He's spry for his age, but jumping is a little much for him. "Oof, you're gonna break me, woman!"

I laugh, letting go and stepping back. "Thank you so much! And I promise I'll bust my butt, make dean's list every semester."

"Of course you will," Doc says, slightly calmer. "And you'll need a pay raise when you do. To top the one you're going to be getting right off the bat, of course."

I grin at the irony. "Well, considering this is an unpaid internship, I think that's completely fair. What are you thinking?"

"I'll double your pay."

"Doc, two times zero is still zero," I reply, laughing. It doesn't matter what he's going to pay me per hour—getting to stay here and learn is invaluable, and getting to see James is priceless.

Doc sees it, and smirks. "Two times zero is zero? Must be that new math to me, because from what I see, adding you to this practice is a lot more than one and one being two."

CHAPTER 26

JAMES

I promised Sophie we'd do something fun after I picked her up from work, but all I can think about is getting her up to Outlook Point. It's kinda become "our place" and seems like the best place to talk.

And there's so much I want to talk to her about. I have to get her to see that we can make this work, that we can have the future I know we both want. I'll do whatever I need to in order for that to happen. Sure, I've got November . . . but after that, life's open for me. And that means after November, I'm all hers, no matter where that takes us.

I take a big breath as I walk to the door of Doc's office, giving myself a pep talk. "Alright, man. Time to ride. You've got this."

Doc is waiting inside as I enter, a big shit-eating grin on his face. "Well now, howdy there, James Bennett."

"Hello, Doc." I don't know what's up with him, but I can't hang around for too much chatter with him today. I'm the one with a plan for once, but patience isn't exactly one of my virtues, so I'm ready to get this show on the road. Or *not* on the road, as the case may be.

But that's probably too much to even hope for, so maybe on the road is right. Straight to wherever Sophie's school is. My mind is running away from me again, too excited to stay focused.

Doc says something else, but I shake my head. "Sorry, Doc. Woolgathering. You know how it gets at the end of the day."

I tap my head, and he chuckles. "You might want to get used to it, James. Tends to happen a lot more when you get to be my age. By the way, I believe Sophie is ready. Said she was gonna change shirts real quick."

As he talks, I hear the side door open, and Sophie walks in. I know she's been working all day, caring for the animals and getting dirty, but right now, you'd never know it. She looks fresh, her hair falling down in waves from the ponytail I know she's worn all day, face bare except for that strawberry lip gloss I love to taste on her, and in tight jeans that are worn at the knees from work but painted over her hips and thighs like they were made just for her curves.

I've seen women at rodeos who are wearing their finest not look this good. How could I have even considered not spending every day with this woman? She's everything I could ever wish for, everything I could ever want, just . . . everything.

My face breaks into a smile, and I have to take a moment to catch my breath before speaking. "Sophie, you look gorgeous."

She smiles back, obviously thrilled at the compliment but giving me shit nonetheless. "Well, I smell like perfume on a pig, but I guess it'll have to do. If I'm too animal-y, we'll just say it's you because I know you've been on a horse all day. Deal?"

"Wrong," I tease. "I've been with the cows all day," I say as I stride up to her. I bend down to cover her mouth in a hot kiss, wrapping my arms around her back as I tilt her slightly.

Our lips move against each other, begging for more, and as she opens to invite me deeper, there's a sound behind us. "Ahem . . . this ain't Animal Planet, you two."

Shit . . . I forgot about Doc. Setting Sophie back down from where I'd pulled her up to her toes to reach me, I wipe at my bottom lip, grinning sheepishly. "Uh, sorry about that. Kinda forgot you were here."

He laughs, scratching at the back of his neck. "I figured. I was young and in love once too. I would've just left you two alone, but you're standing in front of the door I need to go out." We move to the side, and he walks out, laughing as he grabs his hat. "See you Monday, Sophie. I'll call if anything interesting happens. You two remember . . . behave yourselves. Or at least don't get caught misbehaving."

He gives Sophie a big wink as he leaves, and for a moment I wonder what that's all about, but then my mind is back on more important matters. The woman I love, who's standing in front of me with sparkling eyes, a beautiful smile on her lips, and a shine to her heart that shows through in every inch of her body.

I take Sophie by the hand, leading her out the door and waiting for her to lock up before putting her in the truck beside me. Her face is glowing with excitement. "James, guess what? I have the best news ever!"

I interrupt her with a finger to her lips, interested but needing to get this off my chest first. "Wait. I have something to say too. Can you give me a few minutes?"

Since talking it over with Mama last night, I know this is what I have to do. And I need to do it properly, to lay the right foundation for us. Whatever she wants to say, whatever news she wants to share, probably about her fancy vet school, can wait until I say my piece.

Hopefully.

She nods, and it's quiet as I drive. Even with the silence, it's comfortable. Our hands are on each other's thighs, like always, and she's mindlessly drawing lines and shapes, seemingly at random but driving me wild nonetheless.

I pull up to Outlook Point and help her into the truck bed and down onto the blanket I've spread out. Sophie points at the view and then to her mouth, so I nod, grinning at her goofiness. She wants to talk about the view, that's fine. I just want to say what's on my mind before she gives her news.

"The view is so different during the day," she says quietly, snuggling into my arms. "Even with the sun going down, you can see all of town and way out to the mountains on the other side. It's gorgeous. Now I'm not sure which I like better, the daytime view or the nighttime one with all the stars that make you feel so small and like a part of something grander all at the same time."

I smile, stroking her hair softly. "My favorite is at night with the stars reflecting back in your eyes as I watch you come apart for me."

She blushes instantly, and it's adorable. Turning to me, she chuckles, scratching at my arm sexily. "Soooo, are you going to say what you wanted to say, or was that just a ruse to get me to shut up before you seduce me?"

There's a worried note to her voice, and I want to put her at ease right away because I think the rest of what I say might scare the shit out of her. I smile and kiss her temple before opening my heart for the first time. "Sophie, I realized something . . . well, I mean, I already knew, but I love you."

She cups my face in her hand, interrupting me with a soft kiss on my cheek. "I love you, too, James. Buuuut . . . ?" I look at her in confusion, and she grins sadly. "In my personal experience, that sentence goes 'I love you, but . . . '"

I shake my head as understanding dawns, and I stroke her cheek, looking her directly in the eye, my face serious. "No *but*s, not anymore. All day I've been trying to find the words for what's been brewing in my mind. And it comes down to two simple things. I love you, *and* I've never felt like this before. You've changed me, made me happier than I have ever been, made me face a summer that could've been really shitty with Pops being gone and turned it brighter than I could've ever dreamed."

She starts to speak, but I cut her off. "Hang on, I've been practicing this. Trust me, the damn cows are sick of hearing me babble this over and over, trying to find just the right way to say it."

She nods, a beautiful smile on her face. "Okay, go on. No more interruptions until you say you're done."

I nod and hug her with one arm. "So, this summer has been awesome and eye-opening for me, in more than one way. I realize that my family needs me, the ranch needs me. So, after Vegas, I'm retiring. I'm done competing."

Sophie gasps, her words pouring out as soon as I nod that it's okay. "Oh my God, are you sure? That's so huge! But you love riding, James."

I nod, agreeing. "I do, but that was a kid's dream, and I've lived it for a lot of years. I have a man's dream right here . . . with my family and, hopefully, with you."

I pause for a second, and I can see a tear in the corner of Sophie's eye. Hoping it's a happy tear, I plunge headfirst into the rest of what is on my heart. "So, I'm growing up and settling down, and I want to settle down . . . with you. Now, this isn't a proposal. I'm damn crazy, but that'd be a little fast even for me. But what I'm asking is if you can see us working somehow? I know you'll be at school, but I can move there, too, or go back and forth. Whatever it takes, whatever you need because I need you."

I stop, running out of words but feeling like it's not enough to show what's in my heart, to make her choose me like I've chosen her.

Sophie grins. "My turn now?"

I take a big breath, bracing for . . . something, but I nod.

Sophie smiles, seeing my own nervousness, and strokes my cheek. "First off, I love you, too, James. *And* if you feel like you're ready to leave behind riding bulls in favor of working with your family, I support that. I support you if you want to keep riding as well. I daresay your Pops would be damn proud of you, too, either way. I never got to meet him, but even I know that. As for moving with me for school, that's my news. Doc seems to have taken quite a shine to me, and he worked a bit of magic, so I'm going to school at State. I'm staying here . . . for school, for Doc. And for you. *Us.*"

I'm stunned into silence, mouth hanging open in shock. Sophie laughs and lifts my jaw closed. "Say something," she teases lightly. "Just to make sure your brain hasn't short-circuited."

I blink, then hug her tightly. "This is better than I could've dreamed. Holy shit, Soph. We're doing this? For real doing this?"

She nods, laughing and grinning like crazy. "Yep, Cowboy. Seems our summer fling just got a wee bit more long-term." She holds her hands up about an inch apart before widening them as far as she can. "Well, it's more like this big."

"I think you're off on your measurements there, darlin'," I say with a laugh. "This is forever, Soph."

I throw my arms wide and swing side to side, encompassing the entire panorama of the view in front of us. I hop off the tailgate, grabbing her hand and pulling her with me to spin her around and around. We laugh and spin until we're dizzy, hanging on to each other for balance before I pick her up.

Her legs go around my waist, and I attack her mouth, needing to taste her, sweet strawberry and, underneath, something that's just Sophie.

Our tongues tangle and fight for control, neither of us giving in until I catch her bottom lip in my teeth, nipping at her just enough to get her attention.

She moans, throwing her head back a bit and grinding her pussy against me. I carry her toward the truck, my body on fire. "Fuck, woman. Get in the truck. I'm taking you home and fucking you bowlegged."

She shakes her head, pushing away from the door. "No, I can't wait. Set me down."

I shift her up even higher, not letting her go, growling lightly. "Nope, this is forever, Soph. I'm fucking you in a bed like a proper fucking gentleman."

Sophie laughs and scratches at the back of my neck. "Right now, I don't want a proper gentleman. I want you, Cowboy, fucking me in the bed of your truck, under the sunset in our special place. Then later, in bed."

She winks, and while the blood rushes to my cock, she takes advantage and wiggles her way free. Prancing away, she runs around to the back of my truck, throwing off clothes as she goes. "Come on, Cowboy. Show me what you've got!"

I grin for a split second before giving up and racing for the back of the truck. "Damn it, Soph. You spoil my game every time. I'm trying to be all polite and treat you right, and you go and surprise me."

In the split second it takes me to follow her to the truck bed, she's naked . . . and gorgeous. Lying back on her elbows, legs scissoring in need, the golden sunlight catches little sparks in her hair, lighting her up like an angel. But the devil is in her eyes as she dares me to follow through on her plan.

Sophie licks her lip where I bit her earlier. "How about it, Cowboy? You wanna ride?"

I'm climbing up into the truck already, reaching for my shirt. "Fuck yes."

I pull my shirt over my head, ignoring the sound of a popped seam on my T-shirt in my eagerness to get to Sophie. She giggles, jerking her head to the side just in time to avoid the flying shirt before grabbing my belt. "Mine!" she says happily, tugging on my buckle. "All mine!"

"All yours," I repeat, leaning down to kiss her softly. "All yours."

Sophie melts under the slow tenderness of my kiss, wrapping her legs around me as our kiss deepens, our souls meshing while I run my hands over her curves, relishing this woman who has given herself to me.

I kiss down her throat to her breasts, nipping and tasting the softly tanned skin until she's moaning, wiggling underneath me in need. "James . . ."

"Mine," I tease, letting my tongue hang out before slowly circling her nipple with just the point of my tongue. Sophie gasps, arching her back to offer me more, and I can't resist. Sucking her nipple into my mouth, I nuzzle and feast on her stiff nub, guided by her reactions. Tugging lightly, I let go to kiss over to her other side, repeating my loving until she grabs my hair and pulls me in, groaning for more while at the same time pushing my head down, knowing where this is leading.

"Patience, darlin'," I joke as I kiss down her belly. "I'm going to take care of you . . . such good care of you."

Sophie's breath catches as she lifts her hips, giving me total trust and control in one simple gesture. It almost makes me stop in awe of this woman and how she surprises me.

Kissing below her waist, I let my breath tickle over her pussy, watching her lips quiver and clench from the air dancing over them. "Mmm . . . even your breath feels good," Sophie murmurs, running her fingers through my hair before I bring a hand up to cup her mound, massaging lightly. "Oh fuck . . . that's amazing."

I murmur promises, letting my words and lips tease her folds. "Every day, I'll give you all I am, Sophie. Always." I slip two fingers inside her pussy, and she gasps, her eyes wide. I slide them in and out, gathering her wetness and tracing it over her clit in slow circles to tease her.

A deep moan comes from Sophie's chest as she begs for more. "Mmm, Cowboy . . . I like this a lot," she groans, and I move closer to suck and nibble on her tender flesh, pressing my fingers in deep.

I hum happily, making her hips buck as she fucks herself on my fingers. I lick her mound, finding every fold that she likes stroked, driving her wild as I flick across her needy clit. I consume her with my hungry mouth and lips while pumping my fingers in and out, giving her more.

Sophie is mindless, her cries coming with every panting breath as she chases her orgasm, but I'm not nearly ready for her to come just yet. I place my other hand on her hip, stilling her movement, and Sophie freezes, looking down at me. "Fuck, James . . . it feels so good. I love it."

"I love *you*," I whisper before stroking my tongue over her clit again. She tries to lift against my hand, but I hold her steady, licking faster, nibbling and sucking on her hard button until she's whimpering, begging for release.

I fasten my lips over her clit, flicking it with the tip of my tongue as I hum, knowing it'll send her over the edge. Sophie cries out, arching her back as she comes, her pussy tightening around my fingers. I stroke them deep inside her as I lick, drawing it out for her and letting her feel the amazing pleasure of her release. Fresh, tangy, amazingly just like strawberries, she coats my mouth, and I take it all, my cock throbbing just from the taste and scent of my woman as she comes.

My woman. The phrase alone has me ready to come, and as Sophie relaxes back down to the truck bed, writhing as she recovers from her orgasm, I know I have to have her now. Reaching down, I undo my pants, stripping as quickly as I can while Sophie wiggles, giggling happily. "Want a hand?"

I shake my head, getting to my knees between her legs. "No," I reply as I push her knees up to look at her perfect pussy. "What I want is for you to rub your yummy little clit as much as you want while I fuck you. You're gonna come again . . . cream all over my cock this time."

"That I can do," Sophie chuckles as I grab her hand, kissing her fingertips and then pressing her hand to her mound. I watch for a second, slipping my own hand up and down my throbbing shaft.

"Fuck, Soph. Show me how you touch yourself. That's so damn sexy." Not able to wait a second longer, I pull her knees even wider and line up my cock head with her entrance.

If I live another thousand years, I'll never forget the look of love and desire mixed in Sophie's eyes as I drag my cock through her folds, the moment of anticipation so sweet.

I press inside with a groan as I feel her grip me tightly, a breathy sigh breaking through her lips as I settle in balls deep, giving her a moment to adjust to my thickness.

It feels like an eternity passes in an instant, but it's heaven either way. Looking into Sophie's eyes, I lean forward, kissing her lips softly as I feel her begin to slide her hips up and down, begging me to move. "James . . . please . . ."

I moan as I feel her knuckles rubbing against my stomach as she starts to stroke her clit. "Mmm, that's making you squeeze my cock. I wish you knew how good this feels." I try to hold back, enjoying the sight and feeling of her pleasuring herself, using me. But I can't wait anymore, and I pull back and stroke inside slowly again, both of us groaning as I bottom out with force.

I speed up, watching Sophie's fingers as I pump in and out of her tight pussy, both of us frantically chasing our pleasure. Sophie pulls her knees up so I can go even faster, my balls slapping on her ass as I pound her tight hole, making her whimper. "Yes . . . yes . . . please, James . . . that's it."

It's just right, the tender emotions underneath the rough fucking as we rise together harder, faster. My hips are pistoning as her fingers blur across her clit, and I can feel her clenching and pulsing around my cock as she gets closer and closer. "Oh fuck, James. I'm gonna come!"

I grunt, thrusting in and out as hard as I can, and Sophie's eyes roll up as she cries out, her pussy damn near choking me as I stroke one last time. Her orgasm sends me over the edge, and I cry out, too, exploding deep within her, pumping her full with all I have. It feels like I come for hours, my muscles clenched in a never-ending moment of pleasure. Sophie holds on to me tightly, her legs wrapped around my waist as she rides it out until everything unknots and I collapse into her arms, both of us sweating and gasping.

I meet her lips in a soft kiss, stroking her hair as I look down in the near twilight. "You okay?" I ask.

Sophie smiles, tears glittering in the corner of her eyes. "That was . . . we're doing that again. As soon as we get home."

I smile and gather her in my arms. "For now, though, I just want to hold you, feel you in my arms and know that I love you."

Sophie reaches around, holding me close as our hearts slow. My cock softens and slips out of her, both of us frowning when it does. "Shower when we get back, and round two?"

Sophie nods, smiling softly. "James?"

"Yeah?"

"Promise me one more thing."

"What's that?" I ask, knowing I would promise Sophie anything.

"Promise me that you're going to ride your ass off in November . . . and that no matter where the future takes us, we'll be together?"

"I promise," I whisper without hesitation, kissing her lips softly. "Now . . . you've got eight seconds to get in the truck before I start driving back home. What do you say?"

Sophie grins and reaches down, grabbing my ass. "I say it'll take you more than eight seconds to find your damn keys the way you got out of those jeans. They could be at the bottom of the valley for all we know."

Sophie laughs again, and we get dressed. On the drive back down, she leans into me, playing with the new hole along the side of my shirt before looking up at me at a stoplight. "James . . . there's just one thing."

I turn my head, raising an eyebrow in question. "What's that?"

"I haven't told my brother that I'm switching schools for a wild cowboy yet. I think he's going to have a few choice words to say about that."

She keeps laughing, and I wrap my arm around her. "Maybe instead of telling him I'm wild, you tell him that you've *mostly* tamed me? Surely that'll help."

I grin, thinking that whatever brother Jake has to say on the topic, Sophie is gonna do whatever the hell she wants. Lucky for me, she wants me.

CHAPTER 27

SOPHIE

After we get home and a round two in the shower, James leaves me at home to call Jake while he runs to grab us some takeout. I could see in his eyes that he understood I needed to be alone for a few minutes for this, and he promised to bring back the biggest burger he could find before giving me a kiss goodbye.

I joked about it before, and I really am going to do what I want because this feels right, but he's my big brother, and he raised me. I want him to tell me I'm making the right choice. I dial, taking a breath for courage while it rings.

When Jake picks up, he sounds happy. Then again, most days since meeting Roxy he's sounded happy. Guess I understand that now. "Hey, baby sister! What's up in hicktown?"

I laugh. "It's not hicktown, I'm barely outside the city limits!"

He laughs back, and I hear a rustle as he leans back. "Alright, what's up in the outer limits of Great Falls then?"

There's not a lot I can say, so I just jump in with both feet. "Um, a lot actually. That's why I'm calling. You see, it's been a great summer here, a *really* great summer, and . . ."

Jake's voice switches from his brotherly teasing to his more parental seriousness, and I can hear the concern in his voice. "Spit it out, Sophie. What's going on?"

"Okay, so here's the thing. I really like working with Doc—that's the vet I've been working with here. And he likes me, too, thinks I've done great work, and he offered me a job. And secured me a spot at State for vet school. I can go to school and work . . . here."

Jake hums but sounds relieved. "Okay, but still vet school, right? You're not ditching school to clean up animal shit, are you?"

I laugh, shaking my head. "No, definitely still vet school. Although vets do have to clean up plenty of shit regardless. Sort of goes with the territory."

"Alright, aaaand?" Jake asks, still serious but not as worried, it sounds like. "There's obviously more because that's major but not something you'd be freaking out about, and I can feel you shaking through the phone."

Okay, that's it. My brother's either a secret FBI profiler or a psychic, because my foot hasn't stopped tapping since I sat down. "There's a guy."

Jake chuckles. "The rodeo clown?"

"He's not a clown," I protest. "He's a bull rider. If anyone's a clown around here, it's you. But yeah, him. I love him, Jake. He's the one."

I hear his sharp inhale, and when he speaks, his voice is low and serious. "Are you sure? I always knew you'd meet someone, and I'm happy for you, but I can't say I like that it's some wild bull-riding rodeo star that I haven't even met. Uh, so how's that going to work? You staying for school and a job while he goes off and rides . . . bulls?"

I hear the doubt in his voice, and I rush to reassure him. "No, he's retiring. Not for me—well not *entirely* for me. His family needs him, and he's ready to come home, settle down too. I told him that if he wants to keep riding . . . we'd find a way. If you and Roxy can juggle your careers while raising little ones, I can juggle school, work, and him being back and forth on the circuit."

Jake doesn't sound convinced just yet. "So, you're switching schools . . . for a great job opportunity and guy you love? And he's retiring to come home . . . for his family and for you? Is that what you're telling me?"

I nod, then realize he can't see me. "Yeah, that's what I'm saying."

"Does he treat you right? I mean, it sounds like you have your mind made up, but put mine at ease here."

Somewhere in the background, I hear Roxy yelling. "Are you talking about that hot cowboy I found on the internet?"

I grin and Jake groans. "Hang on, let me put you on speakerphone. I'm not playing pass the message."

There's a click, and then I hear Roxy. "What are we talking about here? Are you riding off into the sunset with your hot cowboy, Sophie?"

I laugh. That's Roxy. She might be a mother, she might be ten years older than me . . . but she still gives exactly zero fucks and will say what she means. "Uh, kind of, but not exactly."

Roxy claps. "It's like a chick-flick western movie . . . the sassy vet and the sexy rodeo star!"

Jake groans. "Do not call him sexy."

"Whatever, he is. I looked him up online, and let me just say, Sophie . . . well done, ma'am. Well done. I could've been a Bennett Babe myself. When do we meet him?"

I grin at her antics; her enthusiasm about virtually everything is one of the things I love most about her. "Well, school starts in a few weeks, so I'm going to be swamped, but if James is riding in November as his farewell retirement ride, I'm damn sure going to Vegas with him. What if you guys meet us there?"

Roxy screams, and I can only imagine her fist pumping. "*Vegas?* For the rodeo? Hell yes, we're *so* doing that. Jake, I'm gonna get you some cowboy boots and a hat. I'm gonna dress you up like a walking, talking cowboy fantasy come to life! Now, Sophie . . . you're sure about him, right?"

"He treats me right, and he's a good man. I'm as sure about him as anything I've ever been sure about in my life. Jake . . . we okay?"

Jake sighs dramatically, and I can see it in my head. He knows I'm doing this and there's not a damn thing he can do about it except be happy for me. "Yeah, kid. You grew up a long time ago, and definitely don't need my permission to switch up your five-year plan. God knows, I understand getting sideswiped by love in the strangest of ways."

I grin, thinking back to the craziness when Jake and Roxy first started dating.

"But, Sophie, Vegas sounds like a plan. Send me the dates, and we'll see you there."

I smile, thinking that went far better than I'd expected.

"Thanks, Jake. Thanks, Roxy. I love you guys."

"You deserve it, baby sister. All I've ever wanted is for you to be happy. If he makes you happy, that's good enough for me," Jake replies.

I can't help but smile. "Thank you again, Jake. He really does. He makes me so happy my face hurts from smiling all the damn time."

Jake clears his throat, like he's a little choked up. "That's good to hear, kiddo. Start school, stay in hicktown, but keep in touch. I expect to hear from you on a regular basis no matter *how* busy you get."

"Yes, sir!" I mock salute at the phone. I hear James's truck pulling up in the drive, so I should probably wrap this up. "I feel like there's more to say, but I gotta go, Jake. James is back, and besides, it sounds like Roxy has a bit of wardrobe planning to discuss with you."

I can hear the grin in his voice as he answers, "Boots and hat? What the hell have you done to me, baby sister? It's a good thing I love you. Bye, Sophie." And with a click . . . it's done.

Big brother's approval received and plans to meet soon. I feel like my heart is glowing in my chest. Definitely not the plan I had, but I don't think I could've dreamed up something this amazing.

"Is the coast clear, or is Jake on his way to come kick my ass?" James asks, coming in.

I laugh, waving him in. "No, he's good with it. Said as long as you make me happy, then he's happy."

James pulls me into his arms, holding me tightly. "And what would make you happy right now, Soph?"

I tap my chin, acting like I'm thinking, but I already know the answer. "How about if you feed me and then fuck me all night long, Cowboy?"

James grins, kissing the tip of my nose before letting go. "Woman, you're way too damn easy. I'd happily do that every day for the rest of my life. You need plates, or are the bags good enough?"

"What, you think just because you're not at home you get to eat like a heathen?" I tease. "Oh hell no, Cowboy, I'm gonna have Mama teach me everything needed to run a proper country household."

"Yes, ma'am," James says with a smirk. He gets plates, and we eat dinner together . . . cozy, comfortable, but there's an element of heat underlying everything, and it's not from the delicious food. It's him, it's me; when we're together, I just can't help but want him. Now, always, forever.

I virtually wolf down my burger whole before taking mercy on him. "Alright, that should do for some sustenance . . . for round one. You ready to ride, Cowboy?"

James looks at me for a split second and then stuffs the rest of his french fries in his mouth in one huge bite before grabbing me.

"Now for dessert," he growls before kissing me passionately. I clutch at him, but he takes my hands and forces them above me, his powerful grip making it useless to resist. Like I'd want to anyway. "Question is . . . slow and tender or quick and hot?"

"Quick and hot," I whimper. Slow and tender we'll have hours, days, and years for . . . right now my body says it needs to be stuffed full, ridden hard, and put to bed wet.

James nods, fumbling at the bathrobe I put on after our shower until he gets the belt untied, exposing my skin to his rough touch. I love the way his calluses rasp on my back and down to cup my ass as he grinds against me, our lips melting in a searing kiss that robs the breath from my body even as it stokes the fires inside me.

"Get those pants off, James," I whimper as his tongue finds my ear. "I need you."

James pulls back, just enough to undo his jeans and pull his T-shirt off. I hop onto the kitchen island as he pulls his cock out, already hard and ready for me.

"Is this what you want?" James mock teases me, dragging the tip of his cock up the inside of my thigh. "You want this in your tight little pussy?"

"Fuck yes," I gasp, spreading my legs wider. "I want you to fuck me and make me scream your name so loud the neighbors hear me."

"We can't have that," James says, grabbing the terry-cloth belt of my robe and holding it up to my mouth. "Bite down, don't let go, and I swear I'll make you come so hard you pass out."

"So, you want me to be your little filly, huh?" I tease before biting the cloth. "Do it, Cowboy."

James grabs my wrists again, thrusting forward hard with his cock until he's all the way inside. I gasp around the cloth. I'm glad he's got me so turned on, and that we've already fucked twice tonight . . . God, he's so fucking big.

He doesn't stop, pulling back and thrusting again, savagely hammering my hips with his cock as his lips kiss and nibble on my throat and neck. I'm moaning; it's so damn hot and good to feel him on this edge of control, pounding me but holding back just enough to make sure I'm feeling good too. His hands let go of my wrists, and I clutch at his forearms, swept away by his strength as he fucks me harder and harder.

I'm growling, moaning his name, but the belt muffles my noises just enough. James isn't quiet, though, grunting and growling as he ruts against me, his cock pumping in and out almost in a blur.

I don't know how we last, but we do. It must be the three orgasms I've already had, but sweat breaks out on our skin as James fucks me with all his might, my whole body shaking as he pounds me again and again. I clutch at him, so overwhelmed that I'm not able to even wrap my legs around him but needing him closer. I scratch his forearms, and James loses it, holding me down and fucking me wildly, his eyes wide and animalistic. I love it—I'm the only woman who can do this to him, and he's all mine.

I feel him swell, and I squeeze him the best I can, begging him to take us the rest of the way. My pussy clenches over and over, my body's trembling with exhaustion and overload, and James knows it. With a final primal scream of conquest, he slams deep inside me, coming hard. I scream, too, biting down hard on the belt in my mouth as black stars shoot across my eyes. It's intense, so intense of an orgasm that my heart feels like it's stopping in my chest, but James has me, I'm . . .

"Hey."

I smile and reach up a weak hand to cup his face tenderly. "I think you fucked me unconscious. But no bragging."

James exhales, laughing softly. "I wasn't sure you were okay there for a second. You good?"

I pull him up into my arms, holding him tight. "Yes. Just hold me, carry me to bed . . . and in the morning, I'm making pancakes."

"With syrup?" he asks, and I can feel his cock twitch even as it softens inside me to slip out. I chuckle, knowing exactly what he's thinking about. "What?"

"With syrup," I promise. "Even, right?"

James gathers me in his arms, burying his face in the crook of my neck. "Even. I love you."

CHAPTER 28

JAMES

It's been a few weeks of bliss. I should be on my way out to the ranch, but I already told everyone I'd be in a little late because it's a very special day. Mark and Luke are okay with it; things are looking good as we prep for the fall sale. We're in a slow period, which is good for my training.

But today, at least right now, isn't about training or ranches. It's about Sophie, and as I stir the eggs to get them scrambled just right, I hear the shower shut off. "Hey, darlin', food'll be on in a few minutes!"

"Sounds good to me," Sophie calls back. I was tempted to join her in the shower, but she is on a schedule. "So, what should I wear?"

"White shirt, skirt, and pigtails for your first-day photos!" I tease, making her laugh.

"I meant what should I wear for class, not what I should wear for your wet dreams," Sophie says. "Fuck it, jeans and a T-shirt it is."

I'm about to protest, but Sophie comes out, and my words die on my lips. She's tied the shirt at her waist, but it doesn't matter. It's a rodeo T-shirt with my name on it, and I don't think I've ever seen anyone wear it so well. "Where'd you get that rag?"

"Oh, Roxy bought it and sent it to me. Said she found it at some garage sale. Told me the guy's a total loser, but I think he's kinda cute," she says with a wink.

I nod, unable to contain a smile as I spoon the eggs onto her plate and fetch the toast from the toaster. "Well, I'd say he's one handsome man. Bet he's got a total babe for a girlfriend."

"Oh, he doesn't deserve her in the least; she's way too hot for him," Sophie teases, smiling as I sit down. "You know I'd change if you really want."

I shake my head, taking her hand. "Darlin', you wear whatever you want. Just be careful—you might have some jealous classmates."

"Oh, I figure as soon as they find out I'm dating a famous rodeo star, the claws are going to come out hard and vicious," Sophie says without a care. "I've dealt with that before. Roxy taught me how to deal with the haters."

"Perhaps, but it'd be nice to have some friends," I point out, before shaking my head. "On second thought, tell everyone you're taken, especially the guys, so they know to leave you alone. You're mine."

Sophie laughs around her mouthful of toast and egg, swallowing with a gulp before daintily kissing my knuckles. This girl. "As if anyone could compare to you, Cowboy."

I laugh right along. "Come on, let's get you ready for your first day."

After a yummy breakfast, we both head out. I give her a sweet kiss and a smack on the ass before helping her into her newly purchased truck. It's old enough that it shows some character and history as a work truck, with a scratched-up bedliner and a few dings along one side. But I had a grumpy mechanic in town give it a once-over, and he said it'll go another hundred thousand miles if we take good care of it.

That was good enough for Sophie, who said it was perfect for driving around to ranches for work and getting to school in relative comfort. I agree, and besides, it lets Doc have his brown beast of a truck back.

I bang the hood twice, and she winks at me, moving her fingers in a walking motion. I see her mouth, "Even?" and laugh. I turn, jokingly rubbing my ass in my work jeans as I slowly make my way to my own truck, giving her the show she loves. As she pulls out, she honks the horn and gives me a thumbs-up. I laugh and blow her a kiss.

Driving out to the ranch, I think about the last few weeks and how great everything has been. Sophie and I have settled into a bit of a routine, spending almost every night together at her house. We'd decided to extend the rental agreement on it since it was so convenient for school, Doc's office, and the ranch.

It means getting up a little earlier, but Mark and Luke have been good about it. I think Luke's been happy to have the bunkhouse to himself again.

Anything that lets me spend as much time as possible with Sophie works for me, so early morning drives out to the ranch have just become my new normal. Like a regular Joe commuting to work, only my work happens to be on the family ranch.

Turning in the gate, I head straight to the barn to get busy, but I'm stopped by Luke, who's feeding breakfast to the horses. "How was she?" he asks, looking up. "Excited or nervous or both?"

I grin; Luke looks like he's a little excited himself. "She was good, but probably both. We'll hear all about her first day tonight, when she comes out for her celebration dinner."

Luke smiles, tossing a little hay in my direction. "Damn, James. I still don't know how you wrangled that one. She's way too good for a plug-ugly fucker like you."

I punch his shoulder and toss the hay toward the horses. "I know, asshole. You don't have to keep reminding me. And for damn sure, don't remind her. I try to keep her busy so she doesn't realize what a degenerate I am."

Luke laughs, raising one eyebrow. "I can imagine how you keep her busy. And I don't think you're as much a degenerate as you once were.

Think maybe you're finally growing up quite nicely. Taking after your big brother."

He preens a bit, so I have to torment him back. "Yep, Mark's a hell of an example to live up to."

Luke snorts, threatening me with the still half-full bucket of horse feed. "Little shit . . . I could still take you, you know?" He dances around a bit, putting his fists up and circling them around jokingly.

"Like hell you could," I joke. "Remember, while you've been sitting around the bunkhouse getting lazy, I've been training and riding."

I pop into a rough fighter stance, and it's on . . . brother style, meaning we mostly just swat at each other, ruffling feathers, and a few open-handed slaps to the shoulders and stomachs. I have been training, but Luke's no slouch, and my hand thumps off iron-hard stomach more than once.

It's nothing to really hurt each other, just burning off steam and connecting in some mixed-up macho way that no man really understands; we all just do it because it works.

It's only been a few seconds of tussling when Mark's voice booms and grabs our attention. "My money's on Luke."

I throw my hands up in the air, turning and glaring at Mark as Luke takes the opportunity to kick me in the ass. "What the hell, man?"

Mark leans against a post, smirking as I rub my ass. "Luke's got more experience, wise in his old age. He fights strategically so he doesn't tire himself out, unlike you who is just bouncing around like a damn rabbit wasting energy. And Luke doesn't get distracted enough to get kicked in the ass."

I bounce a little more, bobbing and weaving just to prove how fast I am. "Damn right I'm fast. Fast, strong, and agile. Just what I need for those bulls!"

Luke puffs up, stepping past me to confront Mark. "Hey, you calling me old, brother? You're older than me, old man."

Luke glances back, and I meet his eyes, no further communication needed as it's suddenly me and him against Mark.

Two against one, just like the old days. Mark laughs, more jovial than I've heard him in months, and it's on like Donkey Kong.

We move in a coordinated effort, one that we've likely done dozens of times before, but it's not long before Mark has bested us both. He's done this hundreds of times himself, and knows how to not get cornered or surrounded.

So, it's the same result as it's been for at least the past twelve years, a stalemate that has all three of us laughing by the end. Plopping onto a bale of hay, I continue my trash talk. "One of these days, Mark, you're going to find yourself on your ass with the two of us standing above you."

Mark grins, wiping his forehead. "Actually, I'm sure that's true. But the important thing to remember is," he says as he reseats his baseball cap, looking at both Luke and me to make sure we're paying attention, "the important thing to remember is that it wasn't today."

He gives us a middle-finger salute, laughing as he struts out proud as a peacock while Luke and I are still catching our breaths.

I look over at Luke, and he's grinning too. It feels good, like old times, and I realize how much we needed that. "You know, we should chase him down to the damn pond and make him jump in like we used to."

"Yeah . . . but later," Luke says with a laugh. "How about Saturday? That way he can't complain we're just slacking off."

With a grunt, I rise to my feet, dusting off my butt. "Sounds good. Well, work won't get done if we don't do it. See you later?"

Luke nods and heads back over to the horses. "Yep, dinner."

Luke gets one last swat in as I walk by, knocking my hat off my head, but in a slick move I couldn't repeat if I tried, I manage to catch it and play it off like I'd done it intentionally.

"Oooh, check those skills. Hand-eye coordination at its finest. It's like I'm famous athlete or something."

"About as famous as my left testicle," Luke jokes, giving me a middle-finger salute just like Mark's. I head out feeling lighter, brighter, more settled here on the ranch than I'd ever thought possible.

After a hard day's work, I head to the house even though I haven't heard the dinner bell yet. I want to clean up a bit for Sophie's celebration dinner before she gets here, but when I get close to the house, I see her truck is already here, neatly parked next to mine.

I stop in the kitchen doorway, taking in the scene in front of me. Mama has out dishes of flour, an egg concoction, and chicken spread across the counter, and both her and Sophie have on aprons.

"Now, what you have to do is make sure you get your egg wash all over, or else your flour's gonna have holes in it," Mama explains. "You said you've done that before, right?"

"I did fish, and it was a tempura batter, but yeah, kind of," Sophie says. Mama glances at me and smiles, but Sophie's concentrating, so it's a total surprise when I swoop in and grab her in a hug from behind, picking her up and spinning her away from the counter so as not to disturb Mama's setup. I'm no fool; I know better than to do that.

Sophie whoops loudly, swatting at my hands around her waist. "James, what are you doing? Put me down."

"Fine, but it'll cost you," I joke. "And no asking Mama for help."

"Deal, deal! Now, set me down, or else you're never going to have dinner ready!" she laughs. I set her down, turning her once more so that she's facing me, and kiss her lightly, respectful that my Mama is standing right there. I wipe a smudge of flour off her nose and then grin.

Sophie hugs me again before stepping back. "And hello to you too. Is that what it costs? A kiss. Cheap."

"Well, a kiss and something else. *Maybe* we'll see about that later."

I draw out the word *maybe* to make her remember her earlier promise to consider a bit of booty play. We've done a lot of fun and crazy

things in the last few weeks, including christening every piece of furniture and every room in the house, along with her new truck, but we
haven't breeched that barrier. I might be having just as much fun teasing
her about it, though, because every time we joke about it, she blushes
so prettily. It's definitely on the short list of things to do.

I see the moment she realizes my meaning, sparks lighting in her
eyes. "Sure. Even?"

I chuckle gruffly and shake my head. "Hell no, woman. Never
mind."

Mama is looking at us, amusement written all over her face. I give
her my most dazzling smile, but she's not having it. "Nope, that slick
charm ain't working on me. You'd best get out of here so Sophie and I
can make dinner."

I pause, glancing at the counter again. "What are you two making?"

Mama grins at me, knowing I already know the answer and that
it's a major one. "I'm teaching Sophie how to make my famous fried
chicken. Now get out of here before my oil gets too hot."

I nod my head, stopping to give Sophie a quick kiss on the forehead
and then moving over to do the same to Mama, whispering in her ear,
"Thank you."

I'm almost out of the kitchen when I hear Mama call my name, and
I turn back to have her cross over to give me a hug of her own. "James,
you did well with this one. Lord knows I didn't think you ever would,
much less be the first of your brothers to find someone. But sometimes
fate has its own plan for us."

I nod, looking at Sophie and seeing the shine of tears in her eyes.
"Indeed it does, Mama."

Mama turns back to the chicken, and I mouth to Sophie, "I love
you."

She blows me an air kiss that I fake capture and stick in my back
pocket with a pat.

Making sure Mama's not looking, I wiggle my butt at her a bit, too, grinning like a fool. She giggles and waves me out, getting back to work.

Dinner is better than I ever could have dreamed. The only thing missing is Pops, but something tells me he's sitting in that vacant chair, listening in as Sophie tells us all about her first day of vet school.

"Wasn't much, actually, mostly the paperwork side of things, but I did get to catch Doc's speech," she says with a laugh. "He pretended like he didn't know me at all, and you should have seen that getup. Looked like an old Gary Cooper movie or something. All he was missing was a bandanna around his neck."

We ooh and aah over the fried chicken, proclaiming it the best batch ever. "I'm going to have to work harder tomorrow for training, I just can't help myself," I say as I reach for my third piece. I give Sophie a cartoonish lovestruck look. "Must be because it has a little extra touch of love in it."

Mark grunts, rolling his eyes. "Man, is all your game that cheesy? Sophie, what the hell do you see in this little shit?"

He's totally kidding, and she laughs, but answers seemingly honestly, "Maybe I like a little cheese? Keeps things playful and fun. It's a lot better than a stick up the ass. Maybe you should try it sometime?"

We all bust up at that idea. The thought of Mark being silly and goofy is so foreign. I think he was born serious and never considered being any other way. Mark wags a finger at Sophie, mock gruffly. "I'm gonna take a hard pass on being like this jackass over here. But as long as you like him, no returns allowed. You broke him, you keep him."

"Oh my God, did you just make a joke?" Luke asks, smacking his chest like he's having a heart attack. "Bucket list . . . complete!"

"He did," I confirm. "Mark has made a joke. I didn't think it was possible. Still, Luke, you need a bigger bucket list."

Dinner continues, joking and fun, comfortable camaraderie at every turn. Sophie is just as much a part of the family as we are, and with every comment it seems more and more like our little circle is complete again.

At least, it is for me. After helping Mark and Luke clear the table, Mama chases me and Sophie out, telling Luke it's his day to help clean up. "But, Mama—" he starts.

"When you get yourself a woman worthy of learning my chicken recipe, you can get excused once in a while too," Mama says. "Now fetch a dish towel!"

Sophie and I laugh as we walk out into the darkness, hand in hand. "So, your work went well?" she asks quietly. "You all were so interested in what I did today, I felt like I never got a chance to ask."

"It did . . . and before you ask, I'm ready for the fall circuit too," I reply. "The training area Mark helped me set up in the mechanical barn is getting good use. I was able to do three sets of six one-armed chins today."

"Thought those forearms were looking a little extra muscly," Sophie jokes, patting my arm. "Remind me to come out and ogle you getting all sweaty."

"Anytime you want . . . I'd love for you to work out with me. I won't hold you to the one-armed chins, though," I tease. "Also, remember I'm in Springfield this weekend, but I'll be gone and back before you know it. Give you a good chunk of study time while I'm gone at least."

Sophie smiles. "I know, I already set up a study group for Saturday but told them we had to be done by six so I could watch my man kick ass. I'll be cheering louder than anybody . . . in our living room."

Sophie laughs softly as we reach the pond and sit down on the soft grass. It's starting to get a little cooler at night, and I know before too long the grass will start to yellow as fall takes hold. "You know, I never expected this," I say softly as I hold Sophie close. "That first day . . ."

"Oh, you were hot even when you pissed me off," Sophie chuckles. "This pond, though, there are a lot of good memories here."

"Yeah, that first time . . . should have known you were special right then."

Sophie hums, kissing my fingertips. "It took me a while too. We're obviously both hardheaded. So, did you decide?"

I nod, kissing her neck. "Called my sponsors today. Finals is my last ride. Some were disappointed, but they understood. I don't need the thrill anymore, not when you're in my life. You're all the thrill I'll ever need."

"Well, I can't promise to be as adrenaline inducing as a bucking bull, but I promise to keep you on your toes at every turn, Cowboy."

"You always do, Soph. And I love it."

I lay her back, leaning over on an elbow to take in the whole picture that is Sophie . . . her beauty and her soul, shining in her eyes even in the moonlight. I'm lost in her, unprepared when she presses against my shoulder, flipping our position as she straddles me, a big grin of delight across her face.

I laugh. "Every damn time, woman." But before she can make a move in her position of power, I reach behind her neck, pulling her down to me. I kiss her quietly at first, just enjoying the touch of her lips on mine, with her sweet strawberry flavor and the press of her tiny hands as she fists my shirt, desperate for more.

But I hold back, keeping it slow and steady, stoking the fire we always have between us. She's already writhing against me, breathless when she sits up and locks eyes with me. "I love you, James."

I smile back, stroking her thighs idly. "I love you, too, Soph." I pull her back down and whisper in her ear, "Now . . . about that *maybe*."

EPILOGUE

JAMES

'

I'm in my Vegas hotel room, dressed in my best jeans and button-down, hat pulled down low as I take some deep breaths and jump up and down to burn the nerves out a bit.

This is a big moment, one that could change my life. Check that, *will* change my life. Giving myself a pep talk, I head down the hallway. "You've got this, Bennett. No doubts. Be solid and sure. Anticipate, adapt, anchor in."

One last shudder, and I take the first step . . . and knock on the door to Jake and Roxy's suite. Jake opens up almost immediately, a smile on his face. "Thought I might be seeing you again soon. Come on in, Cowboy."

Okay, I can live with Sophie calling me Cowboy, but Jake doing it is going to take a little adjusting to. I mean, Sophie looks like a country girl most of the time now, with hair that's rich and shiny with highlights not because of chemical treatments, but the natural effect of good living and plenty of sun. Her skin glows with health of hard work and being outdoors.

Not that Jake's some city-boy pushover. He's fit and trim, with eyes remarkably like his sister's and a man's grip when we shake hands. It's just weird getting used to talking with a man whose suit looks like it might cost more than his sister's truck.

"Thanks, Jake. You enjoying Vegas?"

Before he can answer, I hear Roxy holler from the bedroom, "Hey, Cowboy!" She's a cute little firecracker who'd hugged the hell out of me the first time she saw me, and when she repeats the nickname, I decide with a smile that I'd better just get used to hearing it from the whole family.

"Yeah, it's been interesting, that's for sure." We'd met for dinner the last two nights as I introduced Sophie around to all my rodeo friends and family, and so far, Jake seems okay with me.

He's a little guarded still, definitely sizing me up. Roxy, though, seems to think I'm the best thing since sliced bread, and I've been hoping her opinion will rub off on her husband because I need Jake to like me. He's been everything to Sophie, and she's my everything, so we need to get along.

He directs me to the couch as he heads over to the wet bar. "Drink? You look like you could use one."

I shake my head, holding up a hand. "No, thank you. I ride tonight, so no alcohol."

He shrugs, sitting down and sipping an amber liquid from a crystal glass as Roxy comes in and sits beside him. "So, what's up? Seems like you have a million things you should be doing to get ready for tonight, but here you are, just after noon, dressed to the nines."

I swallow the nerves in my chest, taking a deep breath. Roxy seems to catch on and starts grinning, but keeps her mouth shut as I get started. "I know it's fast, and you just met me. But I want to ask for your blessing. I'd like to ask Sophie to marry me."

He sets his drink down on the table between us, his eyes never leaving mine. Sitting back, still not saying a word, he eyes me for a long time before he speaks. "Let me ask you a few things. You love her?"

"Of course," I reply with a strong nod. "More than anything. I never thought it could be like this . . . yeah, I love her."

"And what about school?" Jake asks, his voice still even and hard. "You'll make sure she finishes?"

I shake my head. That's not my style. "I won't *make* her finish, but I'll support her doing whatever it is she wants to do. Her education is her own. I don't believe in forcing her into anything. Not like I could, anyway."

He smirks, so I think I got that answer right, tricky bastard. I'm reminded of Sophie's stories about Jake . . . he's damn near genius-level smart and protective as hell of his little sister.

"And rodeo? You're really okay with tonight being your last ride?"

"It's my last *competition*. I love riding, and I'm good at it, so I won't say I'll never hop on the back of another bull just for the hell of it to see if I can ride him. But no matter what happens tonight, there's something better waiting for me at home . . . Sophie. My family needs us, so that's where we'll be, not on the road three-quarters of the year. I have loved this life, living on the circuit and flying by the seat of my pants, sometimes literally. But it's time to make a new life."

He nods once more, silent for a few long seconds, both of us eyeing each other.

Finally, Roxy can't take it anymore and laughs. "For fuck's sake, Jake. Tell Sophie's sexy cowboy yes, so he can get back to whatever cowboy shit he needs to do for tonight. Quit torturing the man. I think it'd be damn fine for him to go out on a high note of winning the finals just for his new bride-to-be."

I laugh—that was exactly my plan. Win, lose, or flying off the back of a bull with my ass in the air, I'm hoping I have the best prize tonight, and that's Sophie.

Jake shrugs, sighing in defeat. "Seems you've got Roxy's approval." He pauses, then stands up and sticks out his hand. "And you have mine. Treat her like your life depends on it. Because it does."

Jake breaks into a smile and pulls me in for a bro-hug with a firm pat on the back. "Welcome to the family. Fair warning, we have some pretty crazy traditions in our crowd. Hope you're as wild as Sophie says."

I have no idea what that means, but he gave his blessing to let me marry Sophie, so I'll do whatever crazy shit he can come up with if it means Sophie walks down the aisle to meet me.

"Thanks, Jake."

With a relieved sigh, I'm off to do "cowboy shit" to get ready for tonight.

SOPHIE

James has been training so hard for months. He's done practice rides on every quality bull within a day's driving distance of the ranch and has flown out and back damn near every weekend for the fall circuit.

Every weeknight, I'd study at the kitchen table while he did abdominal workouts in the living room. Luckily, it's a small house, and he's been my favorite distraction. I've turned into quite the Peeping Tom, staring at him as he works up a sweat, wanting to lick the ridges of his six-pack . . . and sometimes even getting to do it. The only time I get real work done is when he does his balancing trick, standing barefoot on a medicine ball with his eyes closed for an hour every night before actually meditating.

He says it's not a trick, but when I tried, I would've busted my ass if he hadn't caught me. But he makes it look easy, lifting one foot or the other, sometimes intentionally getting off balance to improve his reaction speed and balance corrections without falling off. He says it's similar to riding on a bull, minus the adrenaline buzz.

But I know he's nervous, wanting to go out on a high note and without injury. He says his head's in the right place. I never knew how much of bull riding is mental.

I knew it was physically a beating, but James has been mentally going over every detail of all the potential rides. He's been reviewing every tape he can find on the different bulls he might draw this week and talking strategies with fellow rodeo buddies. I guess I'd just thought he got on, grabbed hold of the rope, and fought for the best result. But there's so much more to it than I thought. It's been fun to learn about it from James these last few months.

It's finally time for the main event, and I'm jittery as hell. Jake and Roxy sit beside me on one side, Mama and the guys on the other. They'd flown out to see James's last ride too. Luke calls it "the end of an era," and while there's been a mischievous tone as he says he could "cash in on his last name with the buckle bunnies," I can tell it's all in jest.

He could use a little break, though, Vegas style. Mark, too, but they're both here for their brother first, social life second.

"And now, ladies and gentlemen, let's put our hands together for the preliminary scoring rounds!" the announcer says. The crowd cheers wildly, and the action begins, rider after rider trying for their magical eight-second mark for scoring.

I find that as soon as the gate opens, I hold my breath, and I can't let it go till the rider is safe. This is intense, powerful, raw. It's sexy as fuck, and I understand why there are buckle bunnies now . . . seeing a rider atop a beast, challenging and winning the battle for dominance, not to mention the hip thrusting. Yeah, I'm thinking I could save a horse and ride a certain cowboy.

When James is up for his ride in the final round, my throat's already raw. He scored on his first ride, an eighty-nine that stood up for the next five rounds, but now I'm nearly exhausted. Mark leans over and holds his program out.

"If James can hold on, he's sure to get a good score considering the bull he's on. He does that, he wins big. Maybe even *really* big."

I smile, patting Mark on the knee. "I don't care. I just want him to get off the bull in one piece. That's all I need."

Mark grins, leaning back. "You do know what he does for a living, right?"

I shiver a bit, nodding. "I know what he did for a living and is doing one more time. But this isn't like watching tapes at home when he's sitting beside me safe and sound, explaining stuff to me. Makes me glad he's wearing that protective vest and helmet. This is . . . wild."

I gesture all around to the screaming fans, television cameras, and huge animals. Mark grins, unruffled by the madness surrounding us. "Yes, yes he is. Wild."

I see James climbing into the chute, and I grab Mama's hand. She's squeezing me as tight as I'm squeezing her. The bull is shuffling about, already agitated. It looks bigger than my truck, but that can't be true. Either way, it's still scary.

I can't see his face because of his face mask, but James gives a brusque nod, and the gate flies open. It's magnificent. It's terrifying.

Time crawls by in slow motion but is also somehow flying by faster than a blink. Not that I do—my eyes are wide as James works to stay on the bull. Each ripple of the bull's flanks sears itself into my brain as it kicks, spinning and fighting to send James flying. James hangs on, though, his left hand up over his head and his heels spurring the bull on for more. *I can take what you've got, big boy. Give me some more!* he says with every dig, a deadly dance full of jerky elegance and grace.

My heart's in my throat as I observe the tango between beast and rider, the tenths of seconds creeping by until I feel ready to scream for someone to check the fucking clock—something must be broken.

The buzzer sounds, and time speeds up in a flash. James releases his grip, hopping off and running for the fence while the clowns do their jobs, and the bull quiets down while James mounts the fence. He's already celebrating, and the crowd is going crazy. I hear the announcer overhead. "Folks, Mr. James Bennett from Great Falls! What a show! Let's see those results . . ."

I take my eyes off James for a split second to look at the board. When **96.5** pops up, the crowd roars again. I have no idea what's going on, but I know in the nineties is awesome, so I cheer too.

"Holy shit!" Luke yells, clapping me on the shoulder. "Talk about going out in style!"

"Why?" I ask, and Luke points to the big electronic scoreboard, where James's name is flashing, along with the note **WORLD RECORD SCORE (TIED)**. My jaw drops, and I can't even hear the announcer as the crowd goes apeshit. James glances at the board and pumps his fist again, ripping off his helmet and thrusting it aloft.

"Nobody's gonna beat that. James is the champ," Mark says in excited wonder. He stands up, his mask of chill slipping for the first time I've ever seen as he thrusts his hands in the air. *"Fuck yeah, James! That's my fucking brother!"*

Even Mama is cheering, too excited to slap Mark for his bad language, or maybe it just doesn't matter. We leave our VIP seats, heading back to the staging area, where there's a woman interviewing James.

I can't even form words, looking at James's wide smile. It's obvious how happy he is with his ride, and I'm thrilled for him. He really wanted to go out on a high note, and now he's scored even higher than he'd hoped. We stand off to the side, and I see James's eyes light up when he notices me. He gives me a little nod and, with a hand, waves me closer.

I do as asked, able to hear the reporter, a woman in a hat who I know more from her Saturdays covering college football. "So, retiring in your prime? We thought you had a few more years of riding in you. What led you to make that decision, James?"

James shrugs and reaches out, pulling me into the shot and putting an arm around my shoulders. "Well, I thought I'd be riding for a few more years, too, but the best-laid plans sometimes get sidetracked by fate. First, though, my Pops passed away this spring. So I'd like to dedicate this ride, this record, to him . . . John Bennett."

I look at Mama, and tears are slipping down her face, but she's smiling. The reporter nods, about to ask another question, but James interrupts, "Excuse me, one other thing. You wanted to know why? Well, here's why."

James steps to the side a bit, pulling me into the center of the shot and leaving me laughing in confusion. "What are you doing, Cowboy? This is your moment. Shine."

"I am," James says, dropping to a knee and reaching into his shirt. He fishes around, and I see that under his collar, he's got a chain around his neck, and attached to it . . .

I gasp as the ring comes into view, the diamond not huge, but beautiful, sparkling, and pure. *Oh my God, is he doing what I think he's doing on live television?*

Oh my God.

"I thought about doing this at home," James says as the reporter sticks the microphone by his cheek to catch his words, "by the pond or at the point, but it seems fitting that as one stage of my life ends here tonight, another starts. That's how life goes, always a new opportunity in every day. And I want to spend the rest of my life chasing crazy with you every chance we get. Sophie, will you do me the honor of being my wife?"

I know the reporter and cameraman are both looking at me—I suspect the entire arena is watching as everything seems to have gone completely silent—but I can't answer. I'm too busy bawling big, fat tears as he takes the chain off and unsnaps the link, holding the ring up for me.

I know I'm grinning like a loon through the tears, and the words jump out before I can think to stop them. "Did you have that in your shirt the whole time you were riding?"

James nods, smirking. "Every time, woman. I asked you a question. Think you might stick to the topic at hand?"

I laugh, swiping tears from my cheeks. "Of course, Cowboy. Yes, I'll marry you, James."

He slips the ring on my finger, then stands and picks me up all at once. Our kiss is greeted by an enormous roar from the crowd, and suddenly Luke and Mark are here, too, pounding their brother on his back while Jake hugs me tight. I peek and see Roxy hugging Mama, too; good thing they're both huggers, I guess. While there's still a dogpile of loving celebration happening, James picks me up high, depositing me on his shoulders like I'm the one who just won the title and heading for the exit.

"Wait . . . there are still more riders!" a rodeo official says, running up. "You can't just leave! You gotta collect your prize check and the bounty on the world-record ride too!"

James starts to argue that he's leaving with his fiancée, but I squirm until he lets me down. "What, darlin'?"

"You're always going to be my Cowboy," I tell him quietly, looking up at him. "And I'm going to have you for the rest of my life. But this night . . . go back. Give the fans one last salute, one last chance to cheer you and chant your name. Don't worry; I'm not going anywhere."

He kisses me fiercely and turns back, following the rodeo man, who looks massively relieved. Mama comes over, hugging me. "I always knew you were the woman for him. You're giving him a new life."

"No, Mama . . . we're giving it to each other," I reply, hugging her back. "Come on, let's go watch your baby boy take a victory lap."

Mama laughs, "I think he's already got the prize he wants. You."

And I guess she's right. Maybe I am his prize, because James is definitely mine. Maybe a little tamer than he used to be, but still wild . . . just for me.

ABOUT THE AUTHOR

Wall Street Journal and *USA Today* bestselling author Lauren Landish welcomes you into a world of rock-hard abs and chiseled smiles. Her sexy, contemporary romances—including her wildly successful Irresistible Bachelor Series—have garnered a legion of praise from her readers. When Lauren isn't plotting ways to introduce readers to their next sexy-as-hell book boyfriend, she's deep in her writing cave and furiously tapping away on her keyboard, writing scenes that would make even a hardened sailor blush. Lauren lives in North Carolina with her boyfriend and fur baby. For all the updates and news on her upcoming books (not to mention a whole lotta hunks), visit her website at www.LaurenLandish.com or follow her on Twitter (@LaurenLandish) and Facebook (@Lauren.Landish).